CHERUB

THE SLEEPWALKER

ALSO BY ROBERT MUCHAMORE

THE RECRUIT

THE DEALER

MAXIMUM SECURITY

THE KILLING

DIVINE MADNESS

MAN VS. BEAST

THE FALL

MAD DOGS

CHERUB

MISSION 9
THE SLEEPWALKER

ROBERT MUCHAMORE

Simon Pulse
New York   London   Toronto   Sydney   New Delhi

This book is a work of fiction. Any references to historical events, real people, or real places are used fictitiously. Other names, characters, places, and events are products of the author's imagination, and any resemblance to actual events or places or persons, living or dead, is entirely coincidental.

SIMON PULSE
An imprint of Simon & Schuster Children's Publishing Division
1230 Avenue of the Americas, New York, NY 10020
First Simon Pulse hardcover edition October 2015
Copyright © 2014 by Robert Muchamore
Originally published in Great Britain in 2014 by Hodder Children's Books
Jacket illustration copyright © 2015 by Sammy Yuen Jr.
All rights reserved, including the right of reproduction in whole or in part in any form.
SIMON PULSE and colophon are registered trademarks of Simon & Schuster, Inc.
For information about special discounts for bulk purchases, please contact
Simon & Schuster Special Sales at 1-866-506-1949 or business@simonandschuster.com.
The Simon & Schuster Speakers Bureau can bring authors to your live event. For
more information or to book an event contact the Simon & Schuster Speakers
Bureau at 1-866-248-3049 or visit our website at www.simonspeakers.com.
Designed by Karina Granda
The text of this book was set in Apollo MT.
Manufactured in the United States of America
2 4 6 8 10 9 7 5 3 1
Library of Congress Control Number 2015936201
ISBN 978-1-4814-5663-0 (hc)
ISBN 978-1-4814-5664-7 (pbk)
ISBN 978-1-4814-5665-4 (eBook)

CHERUB

THE SLEEPWALKER

WHAT IS CHERUB?

CHERUB is a branch of British Intelligence. Its agents are aged between 10 and 17 years. Cherubs are mainly orphans who have been taken out of care homes and trained to work undercover. They live on CHERUB campus, a secret facility hidden in the English countryside.

WHAT USE ARE KIDS?

Quite a lot. Nobody realizes kids do undercover missions, which means they can get away with all kinds of stuff that adults can't.

WHO ARE THEY?

About three hundred children live on CHERUB campus. JAMES ADAMS is our fifteen-year-old hero. He's a well-respected CHERUB agent with several successful missions under his belt. Australian-born DANA SMITH is James's girlfriend. His other close friends include BRUCE NORRIS and KYLE BLUEMAN.

James's sister, LAUREN ADAMS, is twelve and already regarded as an outstanding CHERUB agent. Her best friends are BETHANY PARKER and GREG "RAT" RATHBONE.

STAFF

With its large grounds, specialist training facilities, and combined role as a boarding school and intelligence operation, CHERUB actually has more staff than pupils. They range from cooks and gardeners to teachers, training instructors, nurses, psychiatrists, and mission specialists. CHERUB is run by its chairwoman, Zara Asker.

AND THE T-SHIRTS?

Cherubs are ranked according to the color of the T-shirts they wear on campus. ORANGE is for visitors. RED is for kids who live on CHERUB campus but are too young to qualify as agents (the minimum age is ten). BLUE is for kids undergoing CHERUB's tough 100-day basic training regime. A GRAY T-shirt means you're qualified for missions. NAVY is a reward for outstanding performance on a single mission. Lauren and James wear the BLACK T-shirt, the ultimate recognition for outstanding achievement over a number of missions. When you retire, you get the WHITE T-shirt, which is also worn by some staff.

CHAPTER 1

BACK

Bethany Parker had been away on a mission for eight months, which was long enough for plenty to change on CHERUB campus. There was a line of freshly planted saplings along the path that led to the main entrance, new floor tiles in the main building, and an enormous satellite dish in the gravel outside the mission preparation building.

But it was the other cherubs that really made Bethany feel like she'd missed out: Girls had different hairstyles and cute boys had succumbed to acne; there were qualified agents she'd never even seen and new red shirts who seemed impossibly tiny.

As she stepped out of the elevator on the ground floor,

Bethany spotted the handler Meryl Spencer. The athletically built Kenyan broke into a warm smile.

"Nice tan, Bethany. We've been hearing good things about you."

Bethany was slightly embarrassed by the compliment. "Thanks, miss . . . I'm looking for Lauren, have you seen her around?"

"She's probably over by the vehicle shop. There's supposed to be some kind of race or something. I expect your brother, Jake, will be up there too."

Bethany felt guilty as she realized she'd prioritized finding her best friend over her kid brother. After jogging down a short corridor, she stepped through the back doors of the campus's main building and ran down the path between the all-weather tennis courts. Her combat trousers and boots felt clumsy after eight months in parts of Brazil and the United States, where she'd rarely worn anything heavier than shorts and sandals.

The sun was dropping below the horizon as she crossed the deserted playing fields. Orange light pierced the trees and made her squint, but being back on campus felt good. The cool evening air was a change from the humidity, and she deliberately ran through the muddiest part of a goalmouth because she felt more at home with a bit of CHERUB campus stuck to her brand-new boots: after a struggle she'd discovered that her old pair didn't fit.

"Lauren," Bethany shouted as she came over the brow of a slight hill. Down below, a crowd of thirty kids were gathered in the parking lot. They mostly faced toward a squat workshop with aluminium sides. The three sets of hangar-style doors along the front were open. Inside were brightly lit workstations covered with tools, and four cars in various states of disassembly.

All vehicles in the CHERUB fleet got upgraded in this workshop: stiffer suspension, satellite tracking, performance-tuned engine, plus tinted glass and subtly altered controls to make life easier for underaged drivers. To ensure the highest standards of reliability, routine servicing and repair work was also done on campus, along with occasional special jobs, such as fitting a car with a hidden compartment or installing listening devices.

Quite a few people turned to see who was shouting. Lauren Adams gasped as she recognized her best friend. She backed out of the crowd and charged up the hill to give Bethany a hug.

"My god," Lauren screamed happily as the two girls pulled each other tight. "I didn't even know you were back. Why didn't you text me?"

Bethany smiled and made a little squealing sound. "I wanted it to be a surprise."

"When did you get back from Brazil?"

Bethany looked at her watch. "Our jet landed at the RAF base down the road five hours ago, but I had to go straight into an emergency debriefing with Maureen Evans, and then I had to see the chairwoman."

Lauren looked at her friend's navy CHERUB T-shirt. "Promotion, too. Well done!"

"Zara told me I deserved black," Bethany said. "But you only get that for outstanding performance on *more* than one mission, no matter how long you're away."

Lauren nodded sympathetically, though she was secretly pleased that she still outranked her friend. "So how was the mission?"

"Hard work, but we took care of business in the end. How about you, are you still suspended?"

Lauren shrugged. "I spent a few days doing security tests on RAF bases, and I helped a pair of new agents settle into a mission over in Northern Ireland, but I'm still banned from going on any big missions of my own for another month."

"I brought you back a present, but I thought I'd save it for your birthday next week," Bethany said before stopping to give a curious look at a small girl dashing up the hill toward them.

"This is Coral," Lauren explained as the six-year-old sidled up to her. "When I got punished I had to go and help out in the junior block. You know, putting the little red shirts to bed and reading them stories and stuff? But I enjoyed it, so I still go over there to help out, and I get enough learning credits out of it that I don't have to do stupid dance or drama classes anymore."

"Cool." Bethany smiled. "Though I've never understood what you've got against drama classes."

Lauren tutted as Coral slid her hand in Lauren's trouser pocket and shyly nuzzled her leg.

"Drama's *so* moronic," Lauren moaned. "Remember that time Mrs. Dickerson had us waving our arms around pretending to be trees for a whole hour?"

Bethany laughed as she imitated the teacher's voice. *"Breathe deeeeeeep and feel your body move with the wind rushing through your branches."*

"I wouldn't mind so much, but you can't breathe deep," Lauren said. "That drama studio has no windows and it always stinks of feet."

The two girls laughed harder than the joke deserved, because it felt good being back together.

"Coral, this is my friend Bethany," Lauren said as she pulled the little girl out from behind her legs. "Stop acting daft and say hello."

Bethany squatted down and gave the tiny girl a smile.

"Coral's only been on campus a few days," Lauren explained. "Her big brother's already rumbling with the other red shirts, but Coral's a bit overwhelmed, so I'm keeping an eye until she settles in."

"Hello, Bethany," Coral said as she reached out to shake hands.

Bethany noticed chips of Lauren's black nail polish on Coral's fingernails as she took her little hand. "Aren't you formal!" she said. "Nice to meet you, Coral."

Coral seemed less shy after the introductions. Lauren and Bethany each took one of her hands and stretched the youngster between them as they walked downhill toward the gathering in front of the vehicle workshop.

"So what's going on in the garage?" Bethany asked.

"It's mainly about boys flexing their egos and getting grease on their overalls," Lauren said. "You can cut the testosterone down there with a knife."

"I see," Bethany said, though she clearly didn't.

"They retired a couple of the old golf carts the staff use for getting around campus," Lauren continued. "But instead of scrapping them, Terry Campbell has been helping some of the boys convert them into racing carts by fitting motorbike engines. You know what James is like about anything even *slightly* to do with motorbikes? I've hardly seen him since we got back from summer hostel."

"And my brother's involved too?"

Lauren nodded. "Jake's part of James's crew."

With Coral still holding their hands, Lauren and Bethany eased between the crowd and stepped through the open front of the garage. There were two golf carts, each surrounded by boys in blue overalls.

The carts were dented and rusty after more than a decade of plying the paths around campus, but instead of being allowed to die with dignity, they'd had their batteries and electric motors stripped out and replaced by the engine and transmission from a motorbike, and a selection of dubious accessories stuck on the outside. James's team had added four sets of wing mirrors, gold paint, and go-faster stripes.

"What a heap of crap," Bethany said, making sure everyone heard as she stepped up to James Adams's stocky legs, which poked from beneath the jacked-up cart.

"Hey, sis," Bethany's eleven-year-old brother, Jake, said as he turned away from a tool chest. "Did you bring me a prezzie?"

"I've got three loads of dirty laundry you can have if you like," Bethany said before giving him a brief hug. Like most siblings, Jake and Bethany loved each other deep down, but in their case, you needed a submarine with a powerful searchlight to get there.

James slid out from under the cart and spoke to his

three teammates as he sat up. "I put a clamp and half a roll of sticky tape over the seals, so we shouldn't have any more problems with oil pressure."

"I'm back, James," Bethany said, grinning and holding her arms out exuberantly. "Are you pleased to see me?"

James shook his head with contempt as he lifted up the cart and kicked away the jacks before lowering it to the ground. He was shocked at how different Bethany looked. She'd grown eight centimeters, she had much nicer boobs, and the tan made her look older than thirteen. If she'd been a couple of years older, she was the kind of girl he'd probably try getting off with.

"You've certainly changed," James said as he looked around and saw that the other two members of his crew—thirteen-year-olds Rat and Andy—practically had their tongues hanging out.

"Bethany, listen to this baby when we fire her up," Rat said eagerly as he lunged toward the cockpit and reached in to press the starter button.

"I'm nearest," Andy said as the two boys leaned into the golf cart from opposite sides and almost cracked skulls.

Andy reached the button first, and there was a clattering sound, followed by a huge plume of foul-smelling exhaust and finally a roaring noise that made the metal walls of the workshop shudder.

"Mr. Campbell showed us how to tune the exhaust to make it as noisy as possible," Andy shouted as he studied Bethany's reaction.

"Pretty cool, eh, sis?" Jake yelled.

The noise made Coral squeeze her hands over her

ears as Lauren and Bethany looked at each other and shook their heads. Lauren leaned across, shouting into her best friend's ear, "I *think* we're supposed to be impressed by this."

Bethany shook her head and laughed. "They're so manly! How can we possibly resist them?"

CHAPTER 2

BARGAIN

Karen had to collect six coupons in the newspaper. Once she had the full set, she went online and battled with an overloaded airline website for the bargain of the century, snaffling four flights for a long weekend of Christmas shopping in New York with her son, daughter, and mother-in-law.

The offer was only valid on certain flights on certain days of the week. She ended up only being able to book flights in September, and even then she had to pay a supplement to get the earlier flight back so that the kids would only miss one day of school (the headmaster gave her a withering look, as if the loss of a single Monday would destroy her children's career prospects).

But Karen liked the idea of taking her kids to New York, and she bit like a Rottweiler whenever a bargain came her way. Despite check-in queues, the godawful in-flight food, and monster snarl-ups passing through immigration when they arrived at JFK, it had been a good weekend.

They'd been up the Empire State Building; they'd stayed in a swanky hotel and melted a pair of credit cards at an outlet mall ten miles out of the city. Karen's mother-in-law spoiled the kids rotten, and the two youngsters had loved every junk-fueled, sleep-deprived minute.

Angus was eleven and Megan, nine. They had the right-hand pair of seats out of the four in the jet's center aisle, with their mum next door and grandma fast asleep at the opposite end. They were two hours out of New York, and the crew had dimmed the cabin lights and turned up the heat to try and get the passengers to rest, but Angus was under the spell of a new Game Boy game, and Megan had found a film to watch on the little seat-back screen in front of her. Their mum would have preferred them to catch up on sleep, but air travel always gave her a thumping headache, and she wasn't going to fuss as long as they kept quiet.

Megan's film was a romantic comedy about a biker who falls in love with a doctor he meets after crashing his motorbike. The biker shaves his beard, buys a suit, and gets a straight job, which leads to all kinds of situations which were hilarious, if you asked Megan, or boring romantic crap, if you asked Angus. He'd watched the first five minutes before flipping open his Game Boy.

But as the film neared its climax—when the biker

throws a punch at a wedding and runs away in shame before discovering that the doctor loves him for who he *really* is, not who he's pretending to be, Megan's headset kept going on the blink and she was only getting sound out of one ear. She reached under the armrest and swiped Angus's headphones from his lap.

"Hey," Angus snapped as he reached across and grabbed the plastic headband. "What are you playing at?"

"Mine are busted," Megan said. "You're not using 'em."

"But I might use them later."

"You can have them back then, you jerk," Megan said as she pointed frantically at the little LCD seat-back screen. "My film's almost finished and I can't miss the end."

Karen opened her eyes and looked crossly at her children. "Pack it in, you two. Angus, give her the headphones."

"But then I'm screwed for the whole rest of the flight! I know what she's like. She says it's for a minute, but I'll never get them back."

Karen grabbed her own headphones and waved them in the air. They were still wrapped in cellophane. "Angus, if you need headphones later, you can have these," she said. "Now, can it. You're both acting like spoiled brats."

Karen was partly cross with the kids, but also with her mother-in-law, who let them eat junk food and get away with murder. It always led to them acting hyper.

Megan couldn't resist a triumphant smile as she snatched her brother's headphones. But as she gave the cord a tug, the two-pronged jack at the end snagged the underside of Angus's Game Boy, and it slid off his lap and hit the carpet between his legs.

"Careful, you slag," Angus snarled.

Karen's eyes opened wide. "Angus, how many times have I told you not to call your sister that? It's a very unpleasant thing to call a girl."

Megan tutted. "He's so dumb. He doesn't even know what it means."

Angus laughed. "It means you like letting boys feel you up."

Before Angus knew it, Karen had grabbed her son by his newly purchased New York Yankees shirt and squeezed his arm. "Grounded," she said firmly. "I will *not* tolerate you speaking like that, Angus. . . . Two weeks, no pocket money and no rugby club, either."

"What!" Angus gasped. "That's bogus. I just got into the first team."

Megan scrunched down so that she could keep watching her film below her mother's outstretched arm. Karen let go of Angus when she saw the filthy look she was getting from the woman sitting across the aisle. She felt like a bad mother for losing her temper, for clawing Angus, and for having a son who spoke noisily about his little sister getting felt up.

Angus scowled defiantly at his mum. "Dad paid over a hundred quid for new boots and kit. You can't stop me going to rugby."

"Watch me," Karen said as she gave him a look that made it clear she meant business. "If I'd used that language when I was your age, your granddad would have put me over his knee."

Angus thought it was probably best not to push his mum any further, and he reached between his legs and picked up the Game Boy. He'd paused the game when he started fighting with Megan, but the pause had been knocked off when the Game Boy hit the floor and now the *game over* screen flashed on the tiny display.

"Now look what you've done," Angus said as he dug his sister in the ribs.

"For god's sake, you two," Karen shouted as she pulled off her seat belt and jumped out of her seat. "Can't you leave each other in peace for five minutes? Megan, you come across this side, and I'll sit between you."

"But it's the end," Megan protested. "There's like two minutes to go."

"Now," Karen steamed as she popped the buckle of her daughter's seat belt and hoisted her to her feet.

As Megan stepped up on to her seat cushion, Karen realized that they'd woken up the couple in the seats in front, and there were "bad parent" stares coming at her from all directions. Megan straddled the armrest and dropped into her mum's seat, then began a desperate attempt to reconnect her headphones and find the right channel on the LCD screen.

Angus undid his seat belt and stepped into the aisle.

"And where do you think you're going?" Karen asked.

Angus rolled his eyes, as if his mum was the stupidest person on the planet. "There are so many places to go on an aeroplane, aren't there?" he said. "Where do you think? I need a piss."

Angus was bitter at being grounded. The only way to get back at his mum was to maximize her embarrassment, so he made sure that the word *piss* came out loud enough for everyone to hear.

The eleven-year-old had kicked off his sneakers, but aeroplane toilets aren't the cleanest places on earth and Angus didn't fancy planting his socks in someone else's urine, so he reached under the footrest and grabbed his Nikes.

As he wriggled his sock into his right shoe, there was a deafening bang. The floor shuddered, and there was a grinding sound as the jet rolled violently to one side. Angus's hip slammed painfully into the seat across the aisle. Within a second his feet were off the ground, and his head bashed into a tray table before he began a help-less slide across the laps of three passengers toward the windows.

Just before Angus smashed headfirst into the side of the aircraft, a man's hands reached up from the middle seat and saved him. One hand caught around the waistband of his tracksuit bottoms while the other thumped into his chest, pinning his body against the seat backs. The blow knocked the wind out of him, but it was less painful than going headfirst into the aircraft window would have been.

The hands were all that kept Angus from crashing into the luggage bins and light fixtures as the aircraft continued to roll. People screamed as they realized the aircraft was flying upside down. Angus's legs dangled as plastic cups, spectacles, meal trays, and iPods rained on the plastic ceiling. The long hair of a woman in the row behind hung over her head, and a steward who'd been walking along the aisle slammed into the roof.

But there was some relief as the roll continued and the jet came full circle. Although the aircraft continued to shudder, some sense of normality returned as people realized that they were back the right way up and apparently staying there.

"Everybody get in your seats and fasten your belts," a steward shouted tersely as he stepped over the debris in the aisle and rushed to help his stricken colleague.

The interior of the jet became oddly calm as people, not knowing what to expect, cast their eyes upward, as if awaiting instructions from god.

Too stunned to speak, Angus found himself being manhandled by the three adults he was lying across. He was soon standing in the aisle, facing the embarrassing reality of tracksuit bottoms down to his knees.

But people had other things on their minds, and even Megan was too shocked to smirk as her mother tugged Angus back to his seat.

"Sit down and pull your belt on tight, sweetheart. Are you okay?"

Angus's chest hurt where he'd been pinned against the seat backs, but it wasn't bad, and he gave his mum a reassuring nod, before turning to thank the stocky man who'd saved him from a nasty bump on the head.

"What happened?" Megan asked.

Her grandmother reached across and put a hand on the girl's knee. "It was probably just turbulence, sweetie."

"But there was that big bang," Angus said anxiously, searching for the Game Boy he'd left resting on his seat.

A calm female voice came over the intercom. "Ladies and gentlemen, I'm Maxine O'Connor, your copilot. We appear to have suffered a mechanical failure, and my colleagues and I are currently trying to establish the exact cause. In the meantime, please stay in your seats with your seat belts tightly fastened and keep the aisles clear to enable the crew to access any injured or distressed passengers. Also, we appear to have some injuries, so if there is a doctor or other medical practitioner onboard, we would appreciate it if you could make yourself known to the cabin crew at this time."

CHAPTER 9

CLOTHES

Lauren wanted a chance for a good talk with Bethany, so she was pleased when Coral found a couple of playmates and started chasing around the parking lot.

The two teams of four boys were wheeling the golf carts out of the workshop into the open air. Several had taken off their overalls, and Bethany was surprised by James's look. While she'd been away, he'd let his hair get longer, he wore a silver stud in one ear, a black short-sleeved shirt, ripped Diesel jeans, and a pair of skate-boarder shoes with fat red laces.

"What happened to football shirts and trackies?" Bethany asked, clearly—but reluctantly—impressed by the transformation.

"He's still going out with Dana," Lauren explained. "She kept teasing him for how he dressed like a slob, and he's gotten totally vain. You see how he leaves the top two buttons of his shirt undone? He's been working his chest in the gym and wants everyone to know it."

"That's sick," Bethany laughed.

"A bit camp if you ask me." Lauren smirked.

"Definitely a big improvement, though," Bethany said. "So what about you and Rat?"

Bethany had more experience with boys than Lauren, who recoiled half a step with embarrassment. "We're still good mates, you know?"

"Who cares about that?" Bethany tutted. "I want to hear about tangled tongues and fingers roaming inside forbidden garments."

"Every now and then we end up doing something," Lauren said, feeling more and more awkward. "Like, if there's a birthday party and there's a lot of snogging going on."

A yell came out of the workshop, and everyone went quiet and turned toward Terry Campbell. His long white beard and cable-knit jumper made him look like a man who spent his weekends tinkering with steam engines, but he was arguably the smartest man on campus.

As director of CHERUB's technical department, Terry handled tasks from fixing the espresso machine in the staff lounge to preparing specialized equipment for missions and writing the software that integrated the hundreds of CCTV cameras and sensors that protected the campus from intruders.

Terry was passionate about encouraging bright youngsters

to become engineers, and in his spare time he ran projects with groups of CHERUB agents. Over the years he'd helped teams of youngsters make everything from motorized gliders to solar-powered drinks coolers.

"Listen up," Terry said, addressing the whole crowd. "I've done some weight and power calculations, and these carts could easily top a hundred kilometers an hour. Racing at that sort of speed in golf carts isn't exactly safe, so instead of racing wheel-to-wheel, we're going to do a time trial and see who can make the quickest run from this parking lot here, across campus to the lot behind the dojo and then back again via the main building."

A disappointed groan rippled through the crowd.

Lauren mumbled to Bethany, "That's so lame. I only turned up in the hope of seeing fireballs and carnage."

It took almost twenty minutes for Terry to spread sentries along the improvised circuit to make sure that nobody got mowed down by one of the souped-up golf carts. As the race drew near, more kids and staff had come out to the garage, and groups stood at various points around the circuit.

Wearing a crash helmet and flameproof overalls, Rat shook hands with fourteen-year-old Stuart Russell, who was driving the rival cart.

"I *hate* Stuart," Bethany said. "Why are his front teeth so big? He looks like he's been gnawing at a tree trunk."

Lauren grinned. "Shakeel's captain of the other team, but I guess we've got to support James, Jake, and Rat."

"They're our boys." Bethany nodded, before taking a deep breath and bellowing with all her might: "Come on, *Teeeeeeam* Rat."

Rat climbed into his cart. Andy helped him do up the three-point safety harness as Bethany's chant set off a round of jeering in the crowd. It was hard to judge, but James's team seemed slightly more popular.

"Win and I'll flash you my tits!" Bethany shouted.

Lauren laughed. She'd forgotten how outrageous Bethany could be when she got carried away. From behind, a girl called Tiffany—who used to be a friend until Bethany dropped her iPod in the bath—shouted, "Who'd want to see your flabby bod, Bethany Parker?"

Within a second Bethany had stormed over to Tiffany and was right in her former friend's face. "Do you want a smack in the gob?"

Tiffany put her hands on her hips. "Try it. See where it gets you."

So Bethany did, and the crowd's attention turned away from the imminent race toward the two thirteen-year-old girls rolling in the gravel. Both were skilled martial artists, but that didn't stop it from turning into an old-fashioned cat fight, with the pair grappling each other, churning up the tiny stones, yanking hair, and clawing with long nails.

"Dirty cow," Bethany screamed.

"You can talk you boy-crazed slapper," Tiffany screamed back.

Jake grinned at James. "I love watching girls fight. They're *so* funny."

After thirty seconds, Bethany's recent lack of fitness and combat training began to show. She gasped for air as Tiffany pressed her knees on Bethany's shoulders and avenged the opening punch in the mouth.

Lauren realized that her friend was about to get hammered. She charged in and grabbed Tiffany around the waist. Meanwhile, Terry Campbell had plowed into the crowd with his two team captains behind him.

"Pack it in you two," Terry shouted as Lauren dragged Tiffany away.

James and Shakeel grabbed Bethany as she stood up, but she tried to charge at Tiffany.

"Lemme go." Bethany snorted. "I'm gonna rip her eyeballs out."

Tiffany didn't regard her opponent's best friend as a neutral, and she flailed about trying to kick and elbow Lauren until a couple of older girls grabbed hold and told her to calm down.

"Stop being so bloody stupid," Terry Campbell shouted as Bethany and Tiffany shot evil glances at each other through the fading sunlight. "Any more of this nonsense, and I'll report both of you to the chairwoman."

Tiffany wagged her finger. "You're lucky your pal saved you. Five more seconds and I would have busted your jaw."

James still had his hands gripping tightly under Bethany's armpits, and he pulled her back as she reared forward and snarled, "Hardly surprising, Tiffany. Your big butt weighs more than my whole body."

"Stop it," James ordered. He let Bethany go, but as he did so he gave her a sideways shove to emphasize that he was stronger than her and that she wouldn't get far if she made another lunge for Tiffany.

"Dammit," Bethany said angrily as she combed her fingers through her dark hair, showering the ground with bits of gravel. "I can't believe she pinned me. I'm so weak; I've got to get back in training."

"She's not worth getting punishment laps over," Lauren said soothingly as she rested her hand on Bethany's back. "And you didn't do that badly. That first punch: she's bleeding out the corner of her giant trap."

"I owe you one," Bethany grunted. "I'd have lost half my front teeth if you hadn't pulled her off."

By this time most of the crowd had turned back toward the race. Terry Campbell looked up at the sky to check the light before taking a stopwatch from the pocket of his overalls. Bruce pressed the button to start up the motorcycle engine, and within ten seconds the air was filled with blue haze.

"Another blow for the environment." Lauren coughed.

Terry lowered his hand to indicate that he'd started the stopwatch, and Rat floored the accelerator pedal. James smiled proudly as a few chants of "Go, Rat" came out of the crowd. Everyone seemed impressed as a cart that had spent a decade hanging around campus at fifteen kilometers per hour blasted uphill with its back wheels chucking up dust and gravel.

"We're running the engine on the highest octane, superunleaded," James explained to the girls as Jake and Andy joined them. "We've altered the fuel injection so that it puts a very rich fuel mixture into the cylinder to increase power, and we even downloaded a hack for the engine management chip, so that you can rev it much harder and—"

Lauren interrupted. "Like I *really* care about your stupid engine, geek boy. We're just here hoping we get to see something blow up."

James realized he sounded a bit of a loser as Terry counted out a full minute before releasing Stuart's cart onto the circuit. Shak's team had stripped the roof from their cart, and James was worried because it looked more stable as it powered up the hill.

"Ready to lose, my man?" Shak beamed as he gave James the finger.

Despite being a year younger, Shak was taller than James and had a similar chunky build. "I'm so glad we took the top off. And finding that set of fresh tires at the scrapyard should give us way more traction."

"But our computer hack gives us at *least* twenty extra horsepower," James bragged.

Shak shook his head exuberantly. "It's not how much power you've got, baby. It's how much power your wheels can get down on the road."

Bethany and Lauren looked at each other and deliberately broke into loud yawns as the drone of the high-powered carts receded into the distance.

"I think I preferred it when James was only obsessed with girls," Lauren said.

"I've got a joke about that," Shak said happily. "Who wants to hear it?"

"Nobody," Jake said firmly. "You and your bloody jokes . . ."

"Why are motorbikes better than women?" Shak asked, ignoring the protests.

Lauren tutted. "Because you don't need permission every time you want to ride on your motorbike."

Shak was disappointed. "You've heard it."

"You told it at the dinner table last night," Jake pointed out. "It wasn't funny then, either."

"Where's Dana, anyway, James?" Shak asked. "Didn't your bird want to see your dinky little cart getting crushed, along with your ego?"

James shrugged. "She's reading some book. She said she's happy for me to be involved in this project as long as she doesn't have to hear anything about it and I don't come near her until I've washed off the smell of petrol."

"Sensible girl." Lauren nodded. "Although I question her taste in boys . . ."

"It's one of the coolest things about Dana," James said. "She likes her own space, and she doesn't mind if I go off and do my own stuff."

"I thought she was going to that racing place on work experience with you," Andy said.

James nodded. "Yeah, if she gets the other place."

"What work experience?" Bethany asked.

Lauren pointed at James. "All the fifteen- and sixteen-year-olds are doing two weeks' work experience. Mr. Campbell set James up with some university mate of his who runs a motorcycle racing team."

Jake shook his head. "He's so lucky. Most kids end up working in a clothing shop or something like that."

"James is always lucky," Shak noted. "He's got more jam than Sainsbury's."

Everyone's ears pricked up as it became clear that the distant drone of two motorbike engines had become the distant drone of one. The crowd went quiet, and the rival crew members traded nervous glances, wondering who'd broken down.

James felt his phone vibrating in his pocket. He slid it open and heard his girlfriend's voice.

"Is the flaming golf cart on the road toward the main building anything to do with you?" Dana asked, clearly amused by the idea that James's pride and joy was going up in smoke.

"Flaming?" James gasped. "Can you see the driver? Is he okay? Can you tell if it's Stuart or Rat?"

James was worried by the news of flames. He'd reattached a faulty fuel line before Rat set off. If he hadn't done it properly, it could easily break off and cause a fire when leaking fuel touched the hot engine casing.

Lauren got pushed aside as the two teams of nervous boys gathered around the phone at James's ear.

"It's some way from where I'm standing," Dana said. "The driver looks okay and a couple of the staff are running up there with fire extinguishers."

James was desperate to know whether it was his cart. "Can't you run up there to get a proper look?"

"I'm upstairs in my room," Dana explained. "I'd have to put some trousers on and wait for the elevator. Mind you, there is one thing. The first cart that went by had a roof, and this one looks like it doesn't."

James broke into a huge smile. "A cart with a roof went by before this one?"

As soon as James said this, Andy and Jake started to grin.

"Definitely," Dana said.

"Why didn't you say that in the first place?" James groaned. "My cart has a roof; Shak's team cut theirs off."

Shak didn't stick around to hear James and his teammates gloat. He raced off to check on his stricken cart, with his two younger assistants behind him.

"You've got to feel sorry for Shak's team, though, haven't you?" James said, before breaking into laughter and giving Jake a high five. "Not!"

By the time James's team had finished hugging one another and jumping up and down, Rat was driving up the hill to complete his circuit of campus. He'd seen the fiery demise of his rival and drove cautiously, not bothering to take any risks.

But while James and his crew were ecstatic, the crowd was clearly underwhelmed as it drifted away. They'd spent over an hour waiting around. There'd been no proper race, and they would have gotten a better view of the fire if they'd stayed in their rooms in the main building.

"Boring," Lauren complained as they headed for home.

Bethany shrugged. "Remember a few years back when Arif built that powerboat? The rudder jammed and it went around in circles until it sank?"

Lauren nodded. "Now *that* was worth getting off your arse to watch."

CHAPTER 4

DADDY

For a minute it seemed like things had gone back to normal on the jet. People were shocked, a few reached into the aisle or around their feet to recover cell phones. Up near the galley between economy and business classes, an Asian doctor crouched over the steward who'd hit the ceiling and cricked her neck.

But as air rushed noisily past the fuselage, the passengers were unsettled by intermittent shudders ripping through the airframe. The pilots couldn't devote their time to staring out the side of the aircraft, so the stewards passed through the plane asking passengers in the window seats to look outside for anything unusual. Angus watched as his grandmother touched a stewardess, who stopped walking and turned back.

"Is there going to be another announcement soon?" she asked.

The stewardess was as frightened as everyone else, but did her best to hold it in. "The pilots are trying to work out what caused the bang and made the aircraft roll. We'll let you know as soon as we're sure what's going on."

At the opposite end of the strip of four seats, Angus scoured the carpet trying to see where his Game Boy had ended up, while the need to pee grew worse. Karen had reached into the seats on either side and held Megan and Angus's hands.

She clutched them a little tighter as another groan ripped through the aircraft. The lightweight cabin fittings flexed to such a degree that several overhead lockers popped open, and luggage thumped dangerously into the aisle.

An American at a window seat jumped up and shouted to the stewardess, "Ma'am, I think something just broke away."

"Did you see what it looked like?" the stewardess asked urgently as she dashed down the aisle toward him. "Are you *completely* sure?"

"Pretty sure." The man nodded. "We're moving so fast, but it definitely looked like something. More of a glint in the sunlight than anything else."

"I think I saw something too," a woman in the row behind added. "Like he said. It was rectangular. A strip of metal or something."

The stewardess nodded. "I'll run up to the cockpit and tell the captain." Then she raised her voice. "Can everyone at a window seat please keep lookout and report if you see anything unusual."

Angus felt a touch of relief as the words *listen to announcements* disappeared off his LCD screen. Maybe the pilots had decided that everything was okay. He slid his hand out of his mother's grasp and flipped the channel until it came to the screen that showed flight information.

The red trail behind the little aircraft on the screen had doubled back on itself, and the nose pointed back toward North America.

"We've turned around," Angus noted.

Megan hurriedly flipped her own screen to the aircraft information channel. As she got there, the woman sitting in front of her spoke with alarm.

"We're losing height: four thousand meters."

Angus looked at their position over the North Atlantic. He saw how far they'd flown in the two hours since leaving New York, and he reckoned that they were at least an hour away from dry land, even if there was an airport right on the coast.

Everyone went silent as an upbeat voice came over the intercom. "Hi, this is Maxine, your copilot. We're still trying to understand precisely what occurred to the aircraft, but I can confirm that we are having some difficulty controlling the plane due to a partial failure of the hydraulic system. We *have* now successfully adjusted our course for the nearest airport and expect to be making a landing in Newfoundland as a precautionary measure in approximately eighty-five minutes. To help you relax, we've taken the entertainment system out of emergency mode. However, we would ask that all passengers please remain seated for the remainder of this flight."

The copilot didn't sound rattled. Once again Karen reached into the laps of her two children, but this time her hands rested gently rather than clutching tight.

"I'm *absolutely* busting," Angus said.

Megan looked across and managed a smile. "What is it about boys? You have to go every two minutes."

Karen seemed more concerned. "Well, if you're really desperate, I'll have to ask the stewardess next time she comes by."

Angus looked at his screen and saw that the plane had dropped another five hundred meters. "We're still going lower," he noted.

His grandmother leaned forward in her seat. "Pilots change altitude all the time to avoid pockets of turbulence," she explained. "I was flying over Australia years back when we visited your auntie Marian. It got so bad that your grandfather's false teeth flew out."

Karen had heard this story before, but the kids hadn't and they thought it was hilarious.

"False teeth are so gross," Angus said. "Remember that time we stayed in the hotel and they were on the table beside Granddad's bed?"

Megan shuddered. "*Don't* remind me."

Angus felt better now he knew where they were going, and as if to prove his grandmother right, he saw the numbers on the display. "We're back up to four thousand," he said.

"Holy shit," a big scouser in a Fred Perry shirt shouted. "Stewardess!"

Angus looked down the aisle and saw the man standing up from his window seat a dozen rows behind. Several others jumped out of seats in the rows around him. There was too much commotion to understand any individual, but the news rippled through the plane.

"What did he say?"

"Who?"

"Back there. Something about a crack."

"Huge crack in the wing?"

"*Jesus*, you've got to be kidding."

"There's a crack over the wing."

"Is that what's going on down there?"

The news hit Angus like an anvil dropped on a cartoon bunny. His mum's wedding ring dug into his wrist, but he didn't complain. The stewardess sprinted up to the cockpit as Angus noticed that they were losing height again.

"Ladies and gentlemen, this is Maxine your copilot," came across the intercom, but this time she'd lost her cool. "I'm sorry to say we've received reports of a serious flaw in the airframe. Although we have some degree of control, we are currently finding it impossible to maintain height. We are in touch with engineers at our base in London, and we're doing all we can, but I must now ask you to listen carefully to the cabin crew, who will instruct you on the safe use of your life jackets."

"We're going to die," Megan blurted. It was a phrase the nine-year-old used when she dropped milk on a new carpet or scratched one of her dad's CDs, but for once it didn't seem over the top.

Angus watched the numbers on his seat-back screen drop below two thousand meters as a male steward began a public announcement.

"At this time we would like to ask all passengers to remove their life vest from the pouches beneath their seats and place them over their heads, in anticipation of a landing on water. Do not, I repeat *do not*, inflate the life vest until you have left the aircraft. Keep your laps clear and listen for an announcement from the cockpit. You must be ready to adopt the brace position as soon as you are told to do so. The cabin crew will now be taking to their seats and will not be able to provide passengers with further assistance."

"You can't land on the sea," Angus said frantically. "I saw it on the Discovery channel. They put life vests on aeroplanes, but nobody in history has ever used one successfully."

While the rest of his family pulled on their life vests, Angus went down the seat-back pocket and grabbed the kiddies' pack he'd been handed when he boarded the plane. He unzipped the plastic case and took out a tiny spiral-bound notepad and a cheap Biro.

"Angus, put your vest on," his mother ordered.

He didn't think there was any point, but he didn't want to argue with his mum, so he snatched the yellow vest from beneath his seat and pulled it over his head. It had a horrible plastic smell.

When Angus's head popped through, he saw that the height displayed on the LCD was rapidly closing on a thousand meters. Through the gap in the seats he saw that the couple sitting in front had decided to go out in a bout of snogging, and the adult nature of this made Angus feel young. He was never going to have a girl-friend, or get all hairy like his dad, or have a wife, or own a car. All that was left was a few minutes sitting in this seat, sweating and busting for a pee.

He rested the pad on his knee and gripped the Biro in his shaking fist. He thought about writing how scared he was, but he knew his dad would be sad when he read it and didn't want to make him feel worse. So he wrote about what was going on and finished by telling his dad that he loved him.

"What are you doing?" Megan asked as she watched her brother tear the small sheet from the notepad and slide it inside a plastic bag.

"I've written a message for Dad," Angus explained. "I'm knotting it in plastic so the paper doesn't get soggy and make the ink run when we hit that water."

Angus watched as his sister started looking around for her kiddies' pack. "I want to do one," she said.

"Here," Angus said as he passed the pen and pad over his mother's lap. It felt like the right time to be nice to your little sister.

"What did you write?" Megan asked.

"Draw him a picture," Angus suggested. "He'll like that."

"We're not going to die," their mother said warmly. "We've got jackets and life rafts. Someone will be on their way to rescue us already."

Megan wrote *New York* and started drawing a sky-scraper as her grandmother searched for another bag to knot it inside. Angus looked up at the flight information on his screen and where the height had been he saw the word *ERROR*.

The sound of the aircraft deepened as it closed on the water.

"Brace, brace, brace," came over the PA.

Angus pressed the top of his head against the seat in front of him, and Megan screamed in protest.

"I need to finish drawing," she shouted, as her mother bundled her forward.

There was a noise a hundred times louder than anything Angus had ever heard as they hit the ocean. He could feel the hairs in his ears dance. For some reason he thought about the fact that he needed to pee, and he hoped it was one of those dreams where you think a lot about peeing and wake up and have to run to the bathroom.

Angus's seat belt tore into his stomach as his head hit the seat in front of him with such force that the plastic buckled. The man in the row behind was obese, and his giant gut prevented him from leaning far enough forward to brace properly. The bones in the man's face shattered as it slammed into the back of Angus's seat at more than three hundred kilometers an hour. Angus's seat back crumpled under the fat man's weight, crushing his body until his ribs shattered.

Warm blood spilled up Angus's throat as his airway flooded. All the cabin lights went out and he felt absurd relief as he glimpsed his Game Boy under the seat. He couldn't breathe, and he could hear people screaming, but only in one ear because the other was full of blood.

Then the plane seemed to cartwheel. His feet were

over his head, and his mum made a peculiar kind of grunting noise. There was a flash of sunlight—perhaps the fuselage had snapped in half. Angus tried to work it out, but his head was numb, and his own blood had clogged his eyes. His lids were stuck fast, and he could see all kinds of crazy lights and patterns in his mind.

They were the last things he ever saw.

CHAPTER 5

KNOWLEDGE

Monday mornings on CHERUB campus always had a dull edge. Kids carried the weight of the week ahead on slouched shoulders and had bags under their eyes from lax weekend bedtimes. Cherubs could sit up for an entire season of Xbox ice hockey or an all-night party if they wanted, but got no sympathy from the staff if they were too tired to handle Monday morning.

It was still getting light outside. A fierce wind blew, and an occasional shower of red berries from a nearby tree pelted the windows of the campus dining hall. James sat in his usual spot. Dana and the twins, Callum and Connor, were also there, and all of them kept at least one eyeball on the plasma TV hanging from a wall five meters away.

Usually the screens had the sound way down, so you could only hear if you sat close by, but it got turned up if something interesting happened, and on this September morning the reporters were having a field day. One half of the split-screen showed a dark-skinned correspondent interviewing an FBI spokesman, while the other displayed a helicopter shot of a piece of fuselage bearing the Anglo-Irish Airlines logo bobbing on the choppy sea.

". . . and you can confirm that there are no survivors from the three hundred and thirty-four passengers and eleven crew members on board?" the reporter asked.

The FBI spokesman had an odd voice, like he'd been sucking helium out of a balloon. "The official search-and-rescue operation has been halted. Coast Guard and naval vessels are concentrating their efforts on recovering as much floating debris as possible in order to conduct a thorough investigation."

The reporter nodded earnestly. "Earlier information suggested that the crew heard an explosion aboard the aircraft approximately ten minutes before the airliner ditched into the Atlantic. Is there any indication at this stage that this was caused by a bomb?"

"I can confirm that an explosion was heard, but no terrorist group has claimed responsibility. Presently the FBI is working closely with the Federal Aviation Administration and the British authorities to determine the cause of the crash."

"And with tomorrow being the sixth anniversary of the attacks on the World Trade Center, the finger of suspicion must surely be pointing at Al-Qaeda or another militant Islamic group?"

The spokesman cleared his throat and repeated himself firmly. "At this stage we're ruling nothing in and nothing out."

James turned away from the screen and looked across the table at Dana. "Gotta be terrorists," he said. "The timing's just too perfect."

Dana nodded as she stirred honey into a bowl of porridge. "I don't mind flying, but when you're all strapped in and you look at how many people are crammed between you and the nearest exit, my stomach always does a somersault."

Callum—who'd got his ear pierced the same day as James—nodded in agreement, but his identical twin shrugged.

"We're all gonna die of something," Connor said. "I'd rather go quick in a plane than let something like cancer get me."

Shakeel was coming toward the table with a tray of food and a smile on his chubby face.

"Morning," James said. "You look pretty cheerful for someone whose golf cart turned into a flaming wreck."

Shak shrugged as he sat down. "I wasn't taking it as serious as you, and you know how luck has a way of evening out? I passed Meryl Spencer as she was pinning our assignments for work experience on the notice board."

Dana's eyebrows shot up—which was a rare occurrence for someone who acted disinterested as a matter of principle. "What did you get?"

"Angel Graphics," Shak said happily. "It's run by an ex-cherub. They do computer graphics and design, mostly. 3-D animation for adverts, kids' TV and stuff like that."

"Sounds good," Dana said. "Did you see what everyone else got?"

"You got Copthorne Racing."

James broke into a big grin. "Cool, we'll be together."

Shak made a little grunt. "Do you think, Mr. Adams?"

James stalled with a forkload of scrambled egg halfway between his plate and his mouth, but then carried on because he knew Shak was more upset about the golf-cart race than he was letting on, and a successful wind-up would help him earn back some points.

"You're full of it," James sneered.

Shak grinned. "Go see for yourself. It's pinned on the board outside Meryl's office."

James didn't want to get sucked into a wind-up, but Dana had nothing to lose by enquiring further. "So who's with me if James isn't?"

"Clare Lowell," Shak said as he hooked an entire rasher of bacon onto the end of his fork and squeezed it into his mouth.

"I thought you were Muslim," Connor said.

Shak grinned. "Some days I'm more Muslim than others."

"So," James said, still concerned that Shak was winding him up. "*If* I didn't get work experience at Copthorne Racing, where am I going?"

"Oh, that's the beautiful part."

Dana was starting to enjoy watching James suffer, and she smiled. "What did he get?"

"Deluxe Chicken," Shak said. "You know that crummy place in the parking lot outside the leisure center?"

"Yeah, right," James said, shaking his head.

Shak reached across the table and put his hand out to shake. "Five pounds says I'm not lying."

Shak was serious and James's *I don't believe you* expression wilted. "You're really serious?"

Shak wiggled his fingers, inviting a handshake on the bet. "Five pounds, James."

"But I spoke to Terry Campbell about this," James moaned. "He knows how much I like motorbikes and he's an old mate of Jay Copthorne. He all but promised that I'd get it."

"All *but* promised," Connor emphasized. "And who knows, maybe you'll learn to love the polyester shirt and those orange-and-brown–striped baseball caps. . . ."

"It's chicktacular," Callum added, deepening his voice to sound like a man in a TV commercial. "Feed the whole family for under a tenner with our summer sizzlers."

"That's not even a Deluxe Chicken advert," James said bitterly. "They're so crap they couldn't afford TV ads."

"You guys still haven't heard the best bit." Shak beamed. "Guess who James's little work-experience companion is going to be?"

James was starting to get angry. "How should I sodding know? Bugs Bunny?"

"Think of someone you used to have a very close relationship with," Shak teased. "And by close, I mean hands down the back of her jeans."

Dana laughed. "Not Kerry."

"Bingo bongo," Shak whooped.

James shot out of his seat. "Meryl's got to be having a laugh. She knows how awkward it's been since we broke up."

"Since you dumped her, you mean," Callum said. "Kerry might be going out with Bruce now, but she still hates your guts."

James shook his head. "That's a *bit* strong; I don't think she hates my guts."

Dana and Shak spoke in unison. "Yes, she does, James."

"Totally." Connor nodded. "I wouldn't be at all surprised if there was a little James doll with pins in it in her room."

"It must be a mistake," James said disbelievingly. "If it's Kerry in Deluxe bloody Chicken, I'll refuse to do it."

Connor shook his head. "Work experience is part of the campus curriculum. It isn't optional, and if you ditch it, Meryl will dish out *serious* punishment laps."

James grabbed his tray off the table. He threw it onto the conveyor belt that led into the washing-up room before storming off toward the elevator. When he got up to the sixth floor, he checked the printout pinned on the cork notice board. Just as Shak promised, his name was next to Deluxe Chicken, and Kerry's was on the next line down.

"Tits," he spluttered, before turning around and pounding on the frosted glass in Meryl's office door. But the light was out inside, and rattling the handle confirmed that it was locked. It was too early for Meryl to be coaching, and she hadn't been in the dining room, so James figured that she was most likely to be in the staff lounge on the first floor.

As he steamed back down the corridor toward the elevator, Rat and Andy emerged from a bedroom.

"Morning, James," Rat said cheerfully.

"All right?" James asked halfheartedly. "How's it going?"

He thought the pair were happy because of their victory in the golf-cart race the night before, but once he'd gone past, they started making loud clucking noises and flapping their arms like wings.

"Can I have fries with that?" Rat shouted, before diving back into his room with Andy right behind him.

They stood behind the locked door, howling with laughter. James wanted to have a go back, but the elevator was waiting and he had to catch up with Meryl before the first lesson.

Cherubs weren't allowed into the staff lounge and James had to stand outside the door and wait for a member of staff to enter, then ask if they could see if Meryl was inside. It was a couple of minutes before anyone came by, and Meryl took her sweet time coming out, which only made James angrier.

As well as being a handler who looked after the everyday needs of thirty-five cherubs, Meryl doubled up as an athletics coach. She came out of the lounge wearing a Nike waterproof and she had a whistle around her neck.

"What's up, James?" Meryl asked. She was usually pretty cheerful, but today she seemed distant, as if she wanted to be anywhere other than standing in a corridor, listening to a moaning teenager.

"My work experience," James said indignantly. "What happened to Copthorne Racing? I spoke to Terry Campbell about it and everything."

Meryl nodded sympathetically. "I know you had your heart set on that job, but Jay Copthorne called up and said that he's always had boys in previous years, and he's keen to encourage more girls to go into engineering."

"But how come I ended up with Deluxe Chicken? I mean, what made you think I'd want to do *that*?"

Meryl shrugged. "Twenty-six cherubs will be doing two weeks' work experience at some point over the next couple of months. I got together with the other handlers, and we looked at your application forms. We gave everyone we could their first choice, but inevitably not everyone could have it, and we had to assign them to the less desirable slots like Deluxe Chicken and the bowling alley."

"But it's so dumb," James spluttered. "I mean, I'm not even sixteen but I've already got top grade A-levels in math and advanced math. It's hardly likely that I'm gonna spend my life frying chicken and wiping down tables, is it?"

"Maybe you won't," Meryl said. "But work experience is about going out into the world and finding what real jobs are like. We use all our connections to get as many interesting job placements as possible, and I'd love to send everyone off to some fantastic jobs. Unfortunately, that's not how it worked out this year."

"But it's gonna be so crap," James moaned.

"How can you even know if you'll like something until you've actually tried it?"

"Because it's with Kerry, and we don't get on these days. What if I can persuade someone to swap jobs with me?"

"Absolutely not," Meryl said firmly. "It took ages to sort all the placements out. If you're allowed to swap or dodge out, everyone will start asking. And I know you and Kerry have a few problems, but you regularly hang out with the same group of friends. It's two weeks in Deluxe Chicken; it's not like we're abandoning the pair of you on a desert island."

James was annoyed about not getting the job at Copthorne Racing, but Meryl was a fair person. She'd done her best for everyone, and like Shak said, luck had a way of evening out.

"I guess I'm the chicken boy, then," he sighed.

"So what's your first lesson this morning?" Meryl asked.

James shrugged. "Spanish, which is okay except that Lauren's in the same class and she runs rings around me."

"I guess your day can only get better." Meryl smiled. "Can I get back to my coffee, if that's everything?"

As Meryl said this, she pushed open the door of the staff lounge. James glanced at the adults sitting inside and was surprised to see the gray head of CHERUB's former chairman by a bay window.

"Is that Dr. McAfferty back there?" James asked. "I haven't seen him for a very long time. He was a big help when I first came to campus, and I wouldn't mind saying hello if he's around later."

Meryl's lips thinned as she let the door close, and stepped back into the corridor. She leaned toward James and checked who was around before speaking quietly.

"Zara Asker had to drive out to Mac's house early this morning. His wife, daughter-in-law, and two of his grandchildren were on the aircraft that crashed into the Atlantic last night."

James felt like he'd been hit by a steamroller. "Bloody

hell," he croaked as he realized why Meryl had been acting so odd. "He must be in a right state."

Meryl nodded. "Mac has six children, but none of them live near campus. He broke down completely when he heard the news. Zara brought him back here because there was no way he could be left on his own."

"I can't believe it."

"Nobody can," Meryl said. "Mac's not fit to drive, so we've arranged for him to be taken down to his son's house in London. Everyone on campus will hear about this eventually, but we're keeping it quiet until Mac is off campus. We don't want things to be any more awkward for him than they are already—and some of the little red shirts aren't exactly masters of tact."

"Don't worry, I won't tell anyone," James said as he shook his head numbly. "Poor bloody Mac."

CHAPTER 6

PUNCH

Fahim Bin Hassam sat on the edge of his bed pulling a long gray school sock up his chubby leg. The eleven-year-old lived in a newly built six-bedroom house which overlooked Hampstead Heath, six kilometers from the center of London.

His room was large, with a computer, an LCD TV and Nirvana posters on the wall. CDs and PlayStation games were scattered across the floor, and a trail of damp footprints led from the en suite bathroom to a luxurious salmon-pink towel and a designer bathrobe balled up on the oak floor. His mum would complain if she saw the mess, but Fahim expected the cleaning lady to get there first.

He found a pair of gray shorts and a short-sleeved beige shirt in his wardrobe, then picked a preknotted brown-and-yellow tie off the floor. It was the uniform of Warrender Prep, a fee-paying school with a proud record of preparing students for entry into the finest English upper schools. However, if the one o'clock showdown between Fahim, his mother, and his headmaster went badly, this might be the last time he ever wore it.

After buckling a digital watch to his wrist, Fahim exited through a set of double doors on to a thickly carpeted balcony that overlooked his home's grand entrance. There was polished marble below and a miniature dome above.

His feet enjoyed the bouncy flooring as he moved down a curving staircase to the ground floor. At the bottom, a blue-smocked housekeeper polished the marble tiles on her hands and knees. They had a machine, but Fahim's dad hated the noise.

"Good morning, Fahim," the woman said in a dense Scottish accent.

He'd preferred her young Polish predecessor, who his dad had sacked after catching her on the phone to her boyfriend in Warsaw.

"I left a skid mark down the side of my toilet," Fahim said, grinning cheekily. "Enjoy!"

The woman tutted, but she didn't blame Fahim for his attitude. He'd picked it up from his father, who expected her to work overtime for no pay, despite the fact that he lived in a three-million-pound house and had two BMWs and a Bentley in the garage.

Fahim was tempted to glide into the kitchen on his socks, but he was in trouble at school, so it wasn't a good time to go around the house looking cheerful.

"Mum," Fahim yelled when he stepped into the kitchen and found it empty. "Mum, I'm starving."

The room was more than ten meters long, with swanky black cabinets and granite worktops. Fahim opened the door of a giant Sub-Zero fridge-freezer that cost as much as most families spend on their car.

He was pleased to find a pack of the Waitrose microwavable pancakes that he liked, and he spread them out on a plate. After zapping them for thirty seconds, he squirted on chocolate sauce and added a handful of overripe strawberries.

He sat at the breakfast bar and grabbed a remote for the screen mounted on the wall. As usual, his dad had switched the TV to the Al Jazeera news channel. Fahim had intended to flip around, looking for a cartoon, but he was intrigued by the images of the downed airliner. As he turned up the sound, he recoiled at the words scrolling across the bottom of the screen:

BRITISH GOVERNMENT SPOKESMAN SAYS THAT PROXIMITY OF ATTACK TO 6TH ANNIVERSARY OF 9/11 MAKES INVOLVEMENT OF TERRORISTS "HIGHLY PROBABLE."

There were no other Arab boys at Warrender Prep, and no matter how much Fahim explained that the *Bin* part of his name simply meant *son of* and was no different to a British boy with a name like John*son* or Steven*son*, his schoolmates couldn't resist calling him Bin Laden. They made jokes about his lunch box being packed with explosives and refused to sit next to him on school trips, in case he blew himself up. The plane crash would make this situation even worse.

After placing the pancake plate in the dishwasher, Fahim moved into the annex where his father worked. This part of the house was fitted out like a commercial office, with carpet tiles, strip lighting, and two offices: one for his dad and another for his uncle Asif.

As he closed on the office, Fahim heard his parents, Hassam and Yasmin, arguing.

"How can you possibly be sure?" Hassam shouted.

"I do your bookkeeping and spreadsheets," his mother replied coldly. "There are invoices from Anglo-Irish Airlines on our system."

"I run a container-shipping business," Hassam said, pounding on his desk as his son listened from the corridor outside. "We have invoices from a hundred companies every day."

"They will investigate—" Yasmin started, but her husband cut her off.

"This doesn't concern you," he insisted. "My business is in order, while our son runs wild. You spoil him. Why don't you deal with that while I worry about *my* business?"

"You know how they investigate," Yasmin said. "They recover every piece of debris. They lay it all out in a hangar and practically rebuild the aircraft."

"But nothing can be traced back to us," Hassam shouted. "I'm busy, let me work."

"This disgusts me. Over three hundred people are dead."

"Leave my office and let me work, woman."

"You're not the man I married," Yasmin said bitterly. "*You* disgust me."

Fahim backed down the corridor as his father roared with anger. He couldn't believe what he was hearing. After all the teasing he'd faced because he was Arab, the idea that his parents had something to do with a crashed airliner felt like a sick joke.

"Let go of my hands," Yasmin cried before sobbing with pain. Fahim couldn't see, but he knew his father was bending her fingers back, like he always did.

"Bitch," Hassam yelled as he cracked his wife hard across the face. She crashed backward onto a leather couch and sobbed noisily.

Fahim felt sick as he backed up toward the kitchen. He wished he was big enough to defend his mum, but all he could do was scurry upstairs to his room.

"What the devil's got into you?" the cleaning lady asked as Fahim's socks skidded on the polished floor.

"None of your business," he snapped angrily.

He buried his face under his pillows and tried not to cry.

Yasmin Hassam had grown up in the United Arab Emirates. She'd always expected to marry, bear children, and become a loyal wife. While she often found herself hating Hassam Bin Hassam, she'd never considered divorcing him.

"Did you eat breakfast?" Yasmin asked as she walked into her son's bedroom and found him curled under the pillows in his uniform.

Fahim rolled onto his back and saw that his mother

had positioned a headscarf over her swollen eye, but no amount of makeup could disguise her fat lip.

"Look at the state of you, Fahim," she said brightly, as she pulled a silk square from a pocket and spat on it before zooming in to wipe chocolate sauce off her son's lips.

Fahim hated mum spit, but after the beating she'd taken, he didn't want to make her life any more difficult.

"I got my own breakfast," he said, trying not to sound shaky. "I thought you must have gone into the office to help Dad with his work, so I left you to it."

Yasmin nodded. "Your father is snowed under at the moment. It'll be best if you give him and Uncle Asif a wide berth for a day or two."

Fahim wanted to ask about the conversation he'd overheard about the airliner, but he knew his mother wouldn't tell him, and a big chunk of his brain wanted to shut it out and pretend that he'd never heard.

"Get your shoes on," Yasmin said as she glanced at her watch. "You know what the traffic's like. If you want, we can stop on the way and get McDonald's."

Fahim managed a half smile, but as he stood up and grabbed his school shoes from under the bed, his mother noticed that his hands were trembling.

"Sweetheart," Yasmin said as she pulled her son into a hug. "It's just a school interview; you've got nothing to be scared of."

CHAPTER 7

RESPECT

"Sit down," the headmaster of Warrender Prep said as Fahim and Yasmin Hassam entered his cramped office. The school building dated from the 1700s, and the low autumn sun caught the dust hovering in the air above the headmaster's desktop.

"Sorry to have kept you waiting, Mrs. Hassam. Will your husband be joining us?"

Yasmin shook her head. "I'm sorry, Mr. Ashley. His business keeps him very busy."

"I can believe that." Mr. Ashley smiled. He stroked his thick gray mustache before gathering up his black teacher's gown and taking his seat across the desk.

"Fahim has something to tell you," Yasmin said as she gave her son a nudge.

The boy looked at his bare knees and spoke stiffly, betraying the fact that his mother had taught him the line on the drive to school. "I want to say sorry for my behavior on Wednesday last week. Although I was provoked, my reaction was incorrect, and I sincerely apologize to all the staff and pupils at Warrender Prep."

The headmaster nodded and said, "Thank you, Fahim," before reaching across his desk and grabbing a thick folder which contained the youngster's personal record. He looked up at Yasmin. "The problem is that this is not the first such incident involving Fahim. He was also suspended last term, and this incident was *exceptionally* nasty."

"He has a lot of problems with teasing," Yasmin explained. "He's a quiet boy at home. I never see him giving trouble to anyone."

"Martin Head suffered three broken fingers when Fahim bent them back," Mr. Ashley said.

Fahim looked guiltily at his mother, who knew exactly who he'd learned that trick from.

"What have you done about the bullying?" Yasmin asked firmly. "I know what Fahim did was wrong, but you can't ignore the root of it."

The headmaster tipped back his seat and took a deep breath. "Warrender Prep is a small school, with a friendly atmosphere. I have questioned several boys in Fahim's class, and frankly, I find it difficult to believe that there is a campaign against Fahim on anything like the scale that he is suggesting: either because of his ethnic origin or for any other reasons."

"They're hardly gonna admit it to you, are they?" Fahim said bitterly. "And it's not like it's big things, beating me up or that. It's just loads of little digs. Like saying that there's a smell of curry when I get changed for rugby, or calling me towel head, or saying I'm a suicide bomber."

"They've also been hiding his things," Yasmin added. "Last term I had to buy three new pairs of sneakers. Then on the last day before the summer holidays, someone put the three missing pairs back in his sports bag."

"I don't deny that boys of this age can be mischievous." Mr. Ashley nodded. "But the correct path is to report matters to the staff. There is *never* an excuse for violence."

Fahim surged forward in his seat. "When I told Mr. Williams about my sneakers going missing the second time, he told me I'd lost them, and he made me play basketball barefoot. Then they all trampled my feet."

"Don't shout, Fahim," Yasmin said gently as she pulled her son back into his seat before looking at the headmaster. "Do you see now how upset this bullying is making him? I'm sure it's part of the reason he's been having nightmares and other problems. Two nights ago I found him at the bottom of the stairs, soaked in sweat and shaking like a leaf."

"I've received the report from the educational psychologist Fahim saw on Friday," Mr. Ashley said as he pulled a stapled document out of the folder. "Dr. Coxon notes that Fahim regularly acts up and seeks attention in class. He also seems to act with unnecessary aggression to mild provocation, and the standard of his academic work has declined over the past year. Fahim's problems at home, including nightmares and sleepwalking, suggest that he needs to begin regular sessions with a therapist and may even benefit from drug therapy to improve his concentration."

"I'm not mental," Fahim protested. "I'd be fine if everyone stopped having goes at me."

Yasmin looked uncertain. "I suppose we could try to see if therapy helps, but I'm much less sure about drugs. I've read stories about them turning children into zombies."

Mr. Ashley closed the folder. "You can further discuss Fahim's emotional needs with Dr. Coxon if you wish. However, Warrender Prep has a demanding curriculum designed to prepare boys for leading public schools, such as Eton and Rugby. I've discussed this with my colleagues, and we no longer feel this school can provide the best education to someone with Fahim's particular needs."

It took Fahim a few seconds to untangle the words and realize that the headmaster was expelling him. Yasmin looked crushed, but Fahim had grown to loathe Warrender Prep, and he felt like a huge weight had been lifted.

"Bloody good," Fahim roared as he stood up and eye-balled the headmaster. "Your school is shit, anyway."

"Manners, Fahim," his mother said fiercely, but the boy wasn't having it.

"I don't care if *you* believe me or not," Fahim yelled. "They *did* hide my stuff; they *did* bully me just like I said. You and the other teachers did nothing but try to cover up the reputation of your nice *friendly* school."

Fahim expected his mother to whack him around the head, but as he looked across, he saw that she actually looked quite proud of him. He didn't want to see Mr. Ashley's stupid face anymore, and he strode out of the office and into the school's main lobby. He found himself surrounded by three hundred years of history: lists of names on the wall, from former headmasters to honored dead in the First World War, and glass cabinets filled with trophies, dusty pennants, and moth-eaten rosettes.

"Bloody school," Fahim shouted, startling a pale-faced ginger boy called David who was in his class. David sat on the spongy chair outside the nurse's office, dressed in games kit and suffering with a badly scraped calf. He was a skinny kid who copped as much trouble from Martin Head and his mates as Fahim did.

"What's up?" David asked.

"Just got expelled." Fahim grinned.

David was shocked. "Sorry to hear that," he said stiffly.

"I'm not sorry," Fahim answered as he realized to his surprise that nobody had come out of the headmaster's office behind him. He could hear his mother's voice, and although he couldn't understand her words, he could tell from her tone that she was giving the headmaster a piece of her mind.

"It's cool that you busted Martin's fingers," David said. "He thinks he's *so* big. Now he can't even write."

Fahim shook his head as he eyed a small green fire extinguisher strapped to the wall. "He is big," Fahim said. "That's our problem."

David tutted. "Remember that time he booted Greg in the guts? And all he got was a detention. It's total favoritism, just because he's captain of the rugby team."

"You know what?" Fahim said as he ripped the fire extinguisher from its Velcro harness. "Screw this place."

David yelped with shock as Fahim smashed the end of the metal extinguisher through the glass front of the main trophy cabinet. Then he dragged it out and totaled the face of a grandfather clock, before swinging at the photo frame with the 1994 South East Counties champion under-twelve hockey squad sitting inside it.

Mr. Ashley steamed out of his office, but was so stunned at what he saw that he stopped, as if he'd smacked an invisible wall.

"Fahim," Yasmin shouted desperately as her son attacked the final cabinet, shattering the glass and taking out the wooden shelf inside. Half a dozen trophies and a rack of war medals clattered to the floor. "Are you crazy?"

"What do I care?" Fahim screamed as the headmaster tried to grab him. "I'm treating this school the way it treated me."

"Give me that now, Hassam," Mr. Ashley shouted.

"Stick it up your arse," Fahim sneered. He grabbed the hose and squeezed the trigger.

The headmaster stumbled backward and wrapped his arms over his face as clouds of white powder blasted him.

"Please, Fahim," his mother shouted in despair.

She was tearful, which made Fahim feel bad, but he was livid about the way he'd been treated, and he didn't want to give the headmaster the satisfaction of catching him. As Mr. Ashley erupted into a coughing fit, Fahim turned and sprinted up the main staircase.

The extinguisher was heavy, but rather than drop it, Fahim launched it at the stained-glass window on the landing. There was a huge crashing sound as the extinguisher punched a hole in the leaded glass.

After climbing the rest of the stairs, Fahim turned into the main first-floor corridor, with classrooms on either side of him.

"After the little bugger," the headmaster roared as he struggled to the top of the stairs. He couldn't give chase because he was still coughing.

The long hallway had an echo, and the headmaster's voice attracted the attention of several staff. A petite French teacher was first into the hallway, and she made a lunge, but Fahim was running at full speed and she couldn't get hold of him.

The next teacher was a scarier prospect. Mr. Linton taught science, but he doubled as a rugby coach, and he'd tackled plenty bigger than Fahim in his time. His huge right arm locked around the eleven-year-old's waist and swept him off the floor.

"Let go, you nonce," Fahim shouted.

Linton had hitched him off the floor, but as his left hand came around, Fahim sank his teeth into the teacher's white lab coat.

"Calm down," Linton shouted as he tried pushing Fahim's mouth away. But the boy kicked, spat, and sank his teeth deeper as some of the Year Six kids from Linton's science class began filtering into the corridor to see what was going on.

Another teacher charged in and grabbed Fahim by his

ankles so that he was suspended between two men with his teeth still sank into Linton's upper arm. The science teacher was in considerable pain and lunged with his free hand, knocking Fahim's head away and forcing him to open his jaws.

"I hate you," Fahim screamed wildly. "I hate this school. You can all rot in hell."

Fahim was snapping like a turtle, and Mr. Linton didn't want to get bitten again. He let the boy go and stepped backward. The other teacher still held Fahim in the air by his ankles, and the back of Fahim's head hit the wooden floor with a thud. The writhing and spitting stopped instantly.

"Blast," Mr. Linton stuttered, cupping a hand over the blood seeping through his lab coat before kneeling over the unconscious boy.

"He was practically foaming at the mouth," the other teacher said as he drew a cell phone from his jacket and dialed 911. "What else could we do?"

By this time, Yasmin had reached the scene, and she collapsed in front of her son. "Idiots," she screamed. "What have you done to my boy?"

CHAPTER 8
SPECULATE

Dr. McAfferty had dished out punishments to most of the kids on campus, and at some time many of them—including James and Lauren—had cursed his judgment. But Mac's days as chairman were far enough in the past for everyone to have put a rose-tinted glow around his memory, and Mac *had* been very good at his job. He always listened to your point of view and was big enough to admit being wrong on the rare occasions when he was.

It was evening now, and the news that Mac had lost his wife, daughter-in-law, and two of his grandchildren was common knowledge on campus. It had affected everyone in some way, and even the cherubs who'd joined after Mac's reign ended had picked up the bad vibe.

The dining hall was usually filled with the sound of kids letting off steam at the end of a long day, but on this Monday night it was like someone had turned the volume down to number three and all but the youngest cherubs kept an eye on News 24.

Men in suits sat in the TV studio talking about who could have been responsible. Someone had dug up archive footage of the plane, and a few of the bereaved had been brave enough to speak for the cameras. James kept looking up, hoping for a real breakthrough, as he sat between Dana and the others eating spaghetti Bolognese.

"I hate twenty-four-hour news," he complained. "All they do is yap, yap, yap, but they won't know anything for weeks, and by then they'll be covering some other story."

"Hello," a small boy said brightly, squeezing into the gap between James's and Dana's chairs.

"Joshua." James smiled as he looked at the son of Chairwoman Zara Asker. "You're getting so big!"

Joshua Asker was two months shy of his fourth birthday. He'd decided at a very early age that James was the greatest person in the universe.

"James," Joshua said seriously. He clearly had something important to ask, but he was excited and could hardly spit out the next word. "After dinner."

Everyone around the table looked at the youngster, and James put a reassuring hand on his shoulder. "Don't worry, they won't bite."

"After dinner," Joshua repeated, "will you come to the lake with me and Daddy and Meatball?"

James smiled and pointed at Dana. "Can she come with us?"

Joshua thought for a couple of seconds before nodding. "But you've got to play with me," he said. "No kissing."

Dana burst out laughing. "Don't worry, I won't kiss James. He's disgusting."

James took this as a cue to lean across and peck Dana on the cheek. Joshua screwed up his face and put his hands over his eyes.

James spoke to the whole table. "Who else fancies a walk down to the lake after dinner?"

Callum and Shakeel had too much homework, but Connor and a few others said yes. As soon as Lauren found out that the Askers' dog, Meatball, was on campus she joined the plan, along with Bethany and a few members of their crowd.

It was only a walk, but Joshua had put himself in charge. He went off to put his coat and hat on before coming back and ordering several people to eat faster. All the while he grazed from the bag of stale bread one of the chefs had given him to feed the ducks in the lake.

In the end, Joshua and Meatball led out a pack of eleven cherubs for the two-kilometer walk toward the lake. Joshua's dad, Ewart Asker, trailed the group with his daughter, Tiffany, asleep in a carriage. It was a nice evening, although the breeze had some bite to it.

While Lauren and the younger cherubs ran around throwing sticks for Meatball and mucking about, James found himself strolling along the concrete path beside Ewart with his hands in the pockets of his hoodie. He'd had a few run-ins with Ewart over the years, but they got on better these days.

"Has Zara heard anything about the crash that's on the news?" James asked.

"Not that I'm aware of," Ewart said, shaking his head. "All I know is that she went down to London for an emergency meeting of the anti-terrorist committee."

"So they definitely think it's a terrorist thing?"

"They've got to work on that assumption," Ewart said.

"Poor Mac," James said as he took a deep breath and stared thoughtfully at the sky. "His wife was only sixty-two. They could have had years together."

"That's sad." Ewart nodded. "But at least she'd lived some kind of life. Angus and Megan weren't even teenagers."

"Did you ever meet them?"

"Just the once," Ewart said. "Mac had a barbecue a few summers back, and they were running around in the garden with all his other grandkids."

"I heard that he's got six kids and at least a dozen grandkids," James said. "I guess it's *some* consolation that he's got other family."

"There's something else I wanted to ask you, actually," Ewart said. "A sort of favor."

James was curious. "What?"

"Joshua has always liked you. With us being away on missions, Zara having Tiffany and then getting promoted to chairwoman, we've never had a chance to get the kids christened."

Meatball whizzed between them, in pursuit of a rubber ball with a bell jangling inside.

"Crazy dog." James grinned.

Ewart cleared his throat before continuing. "Zara and

I were cherubs, so neither of us has family. We'd like to ask if you'd be interested in becoming Joshua's godfather."

James was flabbergasted, but he broke into a big smile. "Yeah, I guess. . . . I mean, I'd be honored. To be honest, I never really thought you liked me much."

"Meh," Ewart shrugged. "You and I have had our share of problems, but you saved my life. That counts for a lot. And you've always had time for Joshua when a lot of kids your age would have told him to buzz off. He doesn't have any older brothers or cousins, and when you go on a mission, he always asks when you're coming back. You mean a lot to the little fella."

"He's really grown lately," James said. "I haven't seen him for a couple of weeks and I'd swear he's gotten bigger."

"He's had a little spurt," Ewart agreed. "Unfortunately, he's starting to ask some pretty awkward questions."

James smiled. "What, like where babies come from and stuff?"

"I can handle those." Ewart smiled back. "But he asks questions about campus. Like, he asked why nobody on campus has a mummy or daddy, and he asks where we are when we go away on missions."

"I guess he's getting to the age where he can't come onto campus."

Ewart lowered his voice. "Zara and I are in discussion with the ethics committee about changing CHERUB's admission policy."

"So that your kids can become agents?" James asked.

Ewart nodded. "And children of other ex-cherubs and members of staff. It's always been a struggle to recruit enough agents. This might be a partial solution."

James didn't seem sure. "But wouldn't you feel different? I mean, would a parent feel right sending their kid off on a dangerous mission? And wouldn't it be weird if some kids on campus had parents while others were orphans?"

"There are obviously issues to resolve," Ewart sighed. "No doubt this is the last place some ex-cherubs would want to send their children, but even though you spend time away on missions, your kids get an outstanding education. And besides, if I wasn't prepared to send my own child on an undercover mission, why should I be happy to send you, or Lauren, or Dana?"

"I see your point," James said.

Joshua stopped on the path in front of James and placed his hands on his hips.

"You're boring, James," Joshua complained. "Play with me."

James grinned. "How about if I turn you upside down and dip your head in the lake?"

"You're silly." Joshua smiled, shaking his head as he walked toward the carriage and grabbed a football from the storage tray.

"Okay, I'll play." James nodded.

"I'll be Arsenal," Joshua said.

"Oh, you reckon." James snorted. "*I'll* be Arsenal; you can be the Chelsea girls' team."

"No way," Joshua growled, stamping his foot determinedly.

Ewart shook his head. "James, I can't believe you've turned my only son into an Arsenal fan."

"I tell you what, Joshua," James said as he put his foot on top of the ball. "We'll both be Arsenal and I'll do this."

James took two steps back from the ball, then made a run up and booted it. The ball swung through the air and hit Lauren hard in the back, making her stumble forward.

Joshua thought this was hilarious, but Lauren didn't. She turned around and steamed toward her brother with her fists bunched.

"It was an accident," James lied, giving Joshua a wink.

Lauren stopped walking and wagged her finger. "Your *face* will look like an accident if you try that again."

Fahim felt like a bowling ball had been dropped on his head from a great height. It took a few seconds to feel around the single bed, half focus on the tattered wooden cabinet beside it, and work out that he was coming around in a hospital.

Memories of smashing the trophy cabinets and the tussle with the science teacher bloomed, then lodged in his brain like fishing hooks. Acts that made sense when Fahim was angry seemed insane now his mood had leveled out.

"Hey," Yasmin said gently. She dabbed her son's face with the tips of her fingernails.

Fahim tried turning his head, but the tiny movement created an eruption of pain in his temples and a heave from his stomach. Yasmin slid an arm behind his back and raised her son off his pillow as she slid a bedpan into his lap, but the sick was already dribbling down his chin.

Fahim's eyes shut and his head flopped forward as he

momentarily lost consciousness again. He inhaled some of the vomit, and Yasmin shouted for a nurse as her son came back to life with a start, before breaking into a desperate coughing fit.

"Stand clear," a nurse shouted, pulling on a disposable glove as she dashed toward the bed. She plunged her fingers into Fahim's mouth to clear the puke from his airway, as Yasmin backed up in a state of shock.

CHAPTER 6

HEAD

James and Dana had been going out with each other for ten months—nine and a half more than most people had predicted. Things had settled into a routine, and some aspects of their lives had merged. CDs, T-shirts, and socks were shared. James kept a Mach-3 razor in Dana's room, and although Dana gave the impression she didn't give a damn about her appearance, you wouldn't have known it from the half-used creams, sprays, and powders that littered the shelves in James's bathroom.

It was past eleven, and James was snuggled up next to Dana on his bed, with half their clothes off and their backs against the wall.

"I'd better go," Dana said as she pulled a dead arm out

from behind James's neck and rubbed her muscle to bring it back to life. "I've got combat training first thing."

James had early training too, but he'd gotten comfortable, and his neck felt cold without Dana's arm to rest on. "Don't go," he moaned softly as he grabbed Dana's wrist. "You can stay here. Who'll know?"

"Don't think so," Dana said before pausing as her yawn got out of control. "I won't get any sleep with you tossing and turning."

"Just cuddles," James said, pressing his bare toes against Dana's bum as she pulled up jeans and a pair of boxer shorts.

"Don't," Dana giggled, waddling forward with the trousers halfway up her leg. "I swear to god, your feet are *always* freezing."

"So you're wearing my boxers now?" James noted. "I wondered where they'd all disappeared to."

"I've started to like them," Dana said. "They don't ride up your crack like panties."

"Maybe I should give your underwear a go." James grinned.

Dana laughed. Ignoring her balled-up socks, she slid bare feet into her boots. She was only going to her room upstairs, so she let the laces dangle.

"I think those little pink numbers with the frilly green edges would suit me."

"Definitely." Dana nodded. "Might take some explaining when you're getting changed in front of the lads, though."

James put on a soppy voice as Dana headed for the door. "Please stay."

"Not while you're still a child," Dana teased. "I can't be corrupting your innocence."

"Come on," James groveled. "I'm sixteen in less than a month, and everyone on campus thinks we're already at it anyway."

"But we're not," Dana said firmly as she headed for the door. "And I told you I'll make it worth the wait."

James had lost his virginity on his last mission, and Dana had lost hers to an older guy on campus before she started going out with James, but they'd agreed that they weren't going to risk what remained of their CHERUB careers by starting up a sexual relationship until they were both sixteen. Or more accurately, Dana had decided and James had been in no position to argue because at the time he'd been skating on thin ice after cheating on her.

James grinned. "When it's my birthday, I'm gonna be knocking on your door at one second past midnight with a big string of drool hanging out the corner of my mouth."

"You're such a romantic." Dana smiled as she leaned over James and gave him a good night kiss.

It was a mild concussion, and the hospital was short of beds, so Fahim was discharged at 11:15. His father pushed him through the hospital corridors in a wheelchair, but he managed to walk the few steps from the chair to the car and made his own way upstairs to his bedroom when he got home.

Despite heavy eyes and a pounding head, Fahim couldn't sleep. He laid on his back, staring at the ceiling and listening to the distant drone of his father's voice in the hallway downstairs. Hassam regularly worked beyond midnight, placing calls to employees and business acquaintances in Pakistan and Indonesia. Fahim had never nailed down exactly what his father did, and whenever he inquired, Hassam always gave the same answer: *I have fingers in many different pies.*

Until he was almost ten, Fahim misunderstood the phrase and came to imagine that his father owned a factory that made frozen cakes. He was constantly disappointed that he never got to taste samples.

"Try to sleep," Yasmin said, startling her son.

Fahim always heard footsteps on the wooden floor of his room, but his mum had made it to his bedside without him noticing. The after-effects of the concussion left him able to see and hear, but his brain felt sluggish and seemed to focus tightly on one thought or sound, to the exclusion of everything else.

"Earlier . . . ," Fahim began as he looked at his mother. His throat ached from the suction tube that had been forced down his throat after he'd been sick for a second time.

"We'll talk about schooling when you're better," Yasmin said softly. "Now you have to rest."

"This morning," Fahim insisted. "I heard Dad hit you. Why were you talking about that aeroplane? What's it got to do with you?"

"It's complex . . . ," Yasmin stuttered uncomfortably. "Modern lifestyles are difficult. . . . Your father had a traditional upbringing, and I'm afraid I don't make a traditional wife. You know he has a good heart. He loves us and provides everything we need."

Fahim despised it when his mum made it sound like it was her own fault that she got knocked around, but that wasn't his main concern.

"The aeroplane," he repeated. "You changed the subject."

There was a pause, during which Fahim tried to read his mother's face. Was she thinking up a lie, trying to protect him, or just struggling to find the right words?

"The plane that crashed was refitted by a company that belongs to your grandfather," Yasmin explained. "Your father arranges transport for some of their supplies."

Fahim wasn't entirely satisfied with the explanation. "But you sounded so worried."

"I remembered that we'd done some business with Anglo-Irish Airlines, that's all. Your father was right— it's his business and I totally overreacted."

"The way you were talking earlier, I thought Dad was a terrorist," Fahim admitted as he broke into a relieved smile.

Yasmin raised her eyebrows and gently stroked his shoulder. "You really thought that, silly boy? No wonder you worked yourself into such a state earlier."

James felt pretty good as he fell asleep. The work-experience thing hadn't gone as planned, but he was clever, good-looking, and still only fifteen years old. He had a comfortable room and enough money to make life pleasant, while his occasional stints helping out the training instructors, and his natural ability in math, meant that he was coping with classes—although nobody would have accused him of being top of the class. He had loads of good friends, a little sister who was basically cool, and he was nuzzling a pillow that smelled like the girlfriend he loved.

Unfortunately, James Adams wasn't the only person on CHERUB campus who'd noticed the comfortable little rut he'd drifted into.

"Get up, you scum-sucking, pinko-loving, marigold-sniffing son of a bag of horseshit," said a deep voice as his bedroom door crashed open and a flashlight blasted his eyeballs.

James was muscular, and at seventy-three kilos, he weighed as much as many grown men. But that didn't stop a colossal set of arms from plucking him off the mattress and driving him down against the springs with such force that two wooden bed slats cracked beneath him.

"Jesus," James groaned as a hand pressed down on his forehead.

"Fairycake-eating, panda-shagging greaseball. I'm gonna pee in a bucket and tip it on your Weetabix."

Another voice came from behind. It was friendly, but its owner was clearly getting a rise out of seeing James suffer. "All right, James?"

It's hard to make sense of anything when an enormous psycho is pitching you around like a squeaky toy in the mouth of a pit bull, but after a second James realized the second voice was Dave Moss. Dave had been the senior agent on two of James's earlier CHERUB missions, but he'd left to go to university, and James hadn't seen him in almost two years.

"I see you've met my good pal, Jake McEwen," Dave said. "Although he prefers it if you ditch the first name."

"Call me Jake and I'll rip off your testicles and feed them to your sister," McEwen explained.

James had never met McEwen, who'd left campus before he was recruited, but he'd heard all about him. McEwen's name was engraved on dozens of trophies in the dojo, and legend had it that McEwen had floored the legendary training instructor Norman Large with a single karate blow when he was thirteen years old.

"Dave," James spluttered.

He could only manage one word, but it meant a lot. It meant: *Hello, Dave, I'm surprised to see you*; it meant: *Dave, I thought we were mates. Could you please tell me what the hell is going on?* And above all else it meant: *Dave, I think this nut job McEwen is going to kill me, and I wonder if you'd be kind enough to stop him.*

But before James could get any more specific, McEwen had crammed a rubber gag into his mouth, then flipped him around, pressed a colossal knee against his back and ripped a set of handcuffs from his belt. James continued to struggle by tucking one of his wrists under his body.

"Gimme that hand, Marigold, or I'll rip your shoulder out of its socket and stick my boot so far up your arse that you'll taste black polish in the back of your throat."

James realized that heroism was going to get him nowhere, and he let out a huge groan before allowing McEwen to lock on the cuffs and drag him to his feet.

"One black T-shirt, one pair of shorts, and his boots," McEwen said.

James stood by while Dave Moss flicked on the light and picked two items of clothing and James's muddy boots off the floor. With the light on, James saw that

Dave had let his hair grow way down his back and had a long beard to go with it. With his army boots and white CHERUB T-shirt, Dave looked like a cross between a Hell's Angel and Jesus.

"There's a rumor going around campus that you're getting soft," Dave explained gently. "So Mr. Kazakov has devised a little tune-up exercise."

"Enough chitchat, you lollipop-sucking flower-arranger," McEwen said as he shoved James in the back. "Let's get you out to the training compound where no one can hear you scream."

CHAPTER 10

DISCIPLINE

Fahim was still awake half an hour later when his parents began arguing downstairs. He couldn't hear properly from his bed, so he crept closer to the doors and opened them a small crack.

"The boy needs discipline," Hassam said determinedly. "I'll speak to my father."

Fahim's heart rate surged when he heard this.

"I'll ask them to recommend a school," his father continued, "somewhere close to my family."

"We've always agreed that our son would stay here and have a proper English education," Yasmin said firmly. "I want him here, not thousands of miles away in Abu Dhabi."

"I can't bear to look at Fahim," Hassam shouted. "With his Nikes and his PlayStation, growing fat on Rolos and chocolate chip cookies. He knows nothing of his own culture or people."

Yasmin laughed. "And how are his Nikes and PlayStation different from your Rolexes and BMWs? You pretend you're such a good Muslim when you visit your father, but you don't own a prayer mat, you don't observe Ramadan, and you've never even set foot inside a mosque in this country."

"You can't speak to me like this," Hassam shouted again, pounding his fist into his palm and making Fahim shudder with fright. "Until now I've left the boy's upbringing to you, but he's turned into a Westernized brat."

"You only want him to go to school in Abu Dhabi to curry favor with your father. Our son isn't a pawn."

"If it's *my* will, Fahim will go to school in Abu Dhabi. How can it make him worse than he is already? How much will it cost me to repair these trophies and stained-glass windows?"

Yasmin took a deep breath. "If you send my son away, I'll go to the police and tell them everything I know about that aeroplane."

Fahim gasped. His mother had lied to him—or at least not told him the whole truth. He heard a slap, and his mother screamed in pain.

The violence always turned Fahim's stomach. Tears welled as he pushed open his bedroom doors. But the cries that usually lasted half a minute at most went on far longer and grew more desperate. Each moan ripped at his soul.

Fahim wasn't strong enough to stop his father, but he hoped his presence might shame him into stopping. He walked unsteadily out of his room and leaned on the banister as he stumbled down the curving staircase. It felt like forever, battling to stay upright, with a swaying head and eyeballs refusing to focus.

"Leave her alone," Fahim shouted when he reached the archway into the living room.

Yasmin was down on the floor, crying. The coffee table was tipped over, and a slick of glossy magazines spilled across the rug.

"Do you spy on me now?" Hassam roared as he saw Fahim in the doorway. He was a powerful man, well past reasoning. Sweat drizzled down his face, and his hairy fists seemed eager to inflict more pain.

"I overheard the screaming," Fahim blurted. "She's half your size. Why can't you leave her alone?"

"Don't interfere, Fahim," Yasmin sobbed as her nose rained red spots onto the rug.

"Get back to bed," Hassam ordered, pointing back to the staircase. "Do you want to feel my belt?"

"For god's sake, he's sick," Yasmin wailed. "Leave him alone."

Hassam turned around and kicked his wife in the stomach. She howled with pain as she doubled up close to the leather couch.

"You will both learn to respect me," Hassam screamed, as he unbuckled and ripped his belt from his trousers. "This is my home. I'm the head of this household."

Fahim turned to run, but there was no power in his legs, and the metal buckle caught him on the shoulder blade, tearing his skin. The pain made his head tilt back in a spasm, and the boy landed heavily on bare knees as the second swipe caught the back of his head.

"There will be discipline in my house," Hassam boomed. "I can't tolerate this behavior."

Fahim sobbed and shivered as he crawled on the cool marble, but his father kept swinging with the belt.

"For god's sake, you'll kill him," Yasmin shouted, as she crawled forward and wrapped her arms around her husband's legs. "He's eleven years old."

Fahim moaned with relief as his father backed off. "Get up to your room," he ordered. "And stay there until I call you."

A CHERUB agent's worst nightmare is being singled out for an individual training exercise. Usually, this only happens when you break the rules or drop below the required level of physical fitness. James was in good shape and fairly sure that he hadn't been caught breaking any rules, but it was still a relief when McEwen opened the back door of a minibus and James saw that he wasn't alone.

"Get in, Marigold," McEwen said as he took off the handcuffs.

James stepped into the van, and Dave Moss threw his boots, shorts, and T-shirt after him. "Put 'em on," he said grudgingly.

The van was used exclusively by the training department, mainly for ferrying around kids in basic training. The carpet and seats were caked in mud, and a hint of sweat lurked in the air. James found a cramped seat and nodded to Gabrielle and a couple of other familiar faces as he pulled his black CHERUB T-shirt over his bare chest. After his head popped through, he looked up front and saw the chief instructor, Mr. Pike, in the driver's seat, as well as his sister, Lauren. She was smaller than anyone else. That's when James realized what was going on.

"We're all black shirts," he said.

"Looks like it." Gabrielle nodded.

James looked out the window and saw another minibus with black shirts onboard and the instructor Mr. Kazakov in the driver's seat. Dana was one of the last to get dragged out of bed. She sat next to James as McEwen and Dave Moss climbed aboard and slammed the back doors behind them.

"Ready to roll, Mr. Pike," McEwen said exuberantly.

They waited a few minutes while the last black shirt was brought down and thrown in the other van, then Pike sped away with Kazakov's van close behind. They took a right turn as they passed around the back of the main building.

Dana looked up from lacing her boot and gave James a relieved smile: a left turn would have taken them through the gardens toward the exit for an off-campus training exercise that might have lasted days. The right turn meant they were staying on campus, where exercises rarely lasted more than twenty-four hours.

The first part of the drive was through the open part of campus, which contained all the buildings as well as the athletics track, and fields marked out for other sports, such as rugby and football. For the remaining two kilometers, the vans crawled along a dirt path around the edge of the basic training compound. It was hard to tell at night because it was pitch-black outside the headlight beams, but James was fairly sure that they were travelling across an area of campus into which he'd never ventured before.

This was confirmed when they branched off to the right and found themselves driving parallel to the back wall of campus. In the open part of campus, you could go right up to the fifteen-meter-high walls, but out here in the wilderness, there were ten meters of gravel between the wall and huge coils of barbed wire that were three meters high. The gravel was crisscrossed with motion sensors, to detect anyone who breached the wall, and signs urged intruders to wait for the security team or risk being blown up by unexploded tank shells—for official purposes, CHERUB campus was designated as an army firing range.

"I haven't been up here since I was about nine," Dana said quietly, not wanting to give one of the instructors an excuse to tell her to shut up.

"What's here?" James asked.

"Trees," Dana said. "But I loved exploring when I was a red shirt, and they used to let us camp out overnight. . . . Mucking around in tents, making little fires and cooking hot dogs and stuff."

"Isn't it dodgy letting little kids out here on their own?"

"Hardly." Dana smiled. "The whole of campus is rigged up with cameras and sensors, and they always made us take walkie-talkies, just in case."

The road ended at a rectangular clearing. It was half the size of a football field, with tall weeds growing in cracks between the tarmac. At the far end was a concrete storage shed, beside which was a fragrant pile of manure used by the campus gardeners, and a deceased digger with flat tires and a decade's worth of rust.

As James stepped out he saw an electronic surveillance post bristling with aerials, where the sections of perimeter wall joined at right angles. They were in the farthermost corner of campus, almost three kilometers from the front entrance and his bed.

"Christ, it's gotten cold," Dana said as she tucked her hands under her armpits.

James's attention turned to a group of white shirts sitting in front of the shed. All aged between eighteen and twenty-two, they wore combat trousers and body armor, and there were ATVs lined up alongside them. James recognized a few of them from his early days at CHERUB, including Paul and Arif, who'd helped him learn to swim when he first came to campus.

"I think they're the enemy," Dana said as Lauren came to stand next to James.

Like everywhere else, kids on the CHERUB campus hung out with people close to their own age. Most black shirts were at least fourteen, and this left Lauren— two weeks shy of her thirteenth birthday—feeling pretty awkward. Although she enjoyed rubbing certain people's noses in her exalted rank, being a black shirt put her in difficult situations with older agents who she outranked, and she often wished that she could be gray or navy like all her friends.

"You cold?" James asked as he looked at Lauren's skimpy running shorts.

"Bit," she admitted with a nod. "You got any idea what we're in for?"

"It's happened before," Dana said. "They pick out all the black shirts, or gray shirts, or all the twelve-year-old girls or whatever for an exercise, but they change the rules every time, so you never know what to expect."

"Gather around," Mr. Pike shouted. "Instructor Kazakov will brief you on your exercise."

Pike was as physically intimidating as any of the other CHERUB instructors, but he was a fair man, and James found his presence reassuring. On the other hand, Kazakov was ex–Russian Special Forces and had a large sadistic streak.

"We've been getting complaints," Kazakov shouted.

As the Russian spoke, the crowd continued to gather. James noticed a bunch of eight- and nine-year-old red shirts, who must have been huddled around the back of the shed. Each of them wore body armor and had a compact rifle slung over their small shoulders.

"Black shirts," Kazakov shouted, before spitting on the ground between his tatty Russian army boots. "You strut around campus, thinking that you rule the roost. You boss around the red and gray and navy. You don't train hard because you already think you've made it. Well, tonight you're getting a long overdue kick up the backside.

"I'm sure you'll recognize some of the retired cherubs in their white shirts. Some have been helping with the recent basic training, or working on campus until they return to university. A few others came here especially for this exercise. We have sixteen whites altogether, to compete with the sixteen black shirts who are currently on campus."

James whispered to Dana and Lauren, "Look at the gut on Dave Moss. He can't have done any training since the day he left CHERUB. We'll run rings around them."

"What was that, Adams?" Kazakov said, walking up to James. "Would you like to share?"

"Just clearing my throat, sir," James said.

Kazakov grabbed him around the neck and choked him. "Is it clear now?"

"Yes, sir," James croaked as his face turned bright red and he started coughing.

Kazakov let go and shoved him backward. "I do not expect backchat," he shouted. "The next black shirt who speaks out of turn will spend next weekend scrubbing the mud out of the minibuses with a toothbrush.

"The objectives for black shirts are simple," Kazakov continued. "You have shorts, T-shirts, boots, and we will be issuing safety goggles. You must make it from here back to the main building. Once you're inside, you can get into bed and enjoy the rest of your night's sleep.

"Unfortunately, the white shirts will be trying to stop you. Each time they capture you and put on handcuffs, you will be brought back here to start again. They will be equipped with rifles, two hundred rounds each of simulated ammunition, night-vision equipment, full-body armor, radios, ATVs, and most importantly, Mr. Pike and I will coordinate their movements with full access to the campus security system, including all cameras, heat sensors, and motion detectors.

"We have also picked some of our crack-shot red

shirts. There are two dozen of them positioned in strategic locations around campus. They are not authorized to capture and return you to the starting position, but they will be acting as scouts, positioning traps and, of course, shooting at you with simulated ammunition. The exercise will end at 0700 hours. Any black shirt who doesn't make it to the main building before then will be expected to complete a ten-kilometer run with a thirty-kilogram pack before breakfast every morning for the next ten days. All other standard safety and containment rules apply. Any questions?"

Gabrielle raised her hand. "Sir, we don't have any protection. Won't the simulated ammo tear us to shreds?"

Mr. Pike took the answer. "The Simunition is grade three. It's not as powerful as the ammo some of you might have used over at the SAS training ground in conjunction with full-body armor. However, it will still hurt a great deal if it hits bare skin. I would seriously recommend doing everything you can to avoid getting shot, and you must wear your goggles at all times."

"Okay," Kazakov said as he went along the line of black shirts, holding out a sack filled with goggles. "When I blow my whistle, you can start to run. I'm giving you forty seconds, then I blow again, and the white and red shirts will be on your arse."

James snapped on his goggles as Kazakov raised the whistle to his lips.

CHAPTER 11

DITCHED

James, Dana, and Lauren ran at full pelt. Forty seconds is scant advantage when your opponents have ATVs that do sixty kilometers an hour and weapons that can knock you flat on your arse from two hundred meters.

"I've got an idea," Lauren gasped as they ran. "I spent months digging ditches out behind the training compound. I know them like the back of my hand, and nobody's gonna be keen to follow us through a bog."

"Sod wading through all that mud, though," James said. "I say we keep it simple: run flat out and hope we get lucky."

"We'll get nailed in two seconds," Lauren sneered as the trio cut off the path into the trees and began crackling through dense undergrowth. They had no flashlights, and a million things scratched at their bare legs.

Something cracked from the trees above, and James yelped in pain.

"Red shirt," Dana gasped as they all dived for cover.

"No way that's forty seconds," Lauren complained.

Dana shook her head. "I think you'll find that forty seconds is however long the person with the gun says it is."

James inspected his arm. The simulated rounds were fired out of real rifles, but they were made from a compressed powder that broke up on impact. It was excruciating if you took a direct hit, but he'd been lucky. The round had caught him at an acute angle and only brushed his arm before deflecting upward into the branches.

James and Dana made it into a gap between the trunks of two trees and tried looking back to see who was shooting at them. They'd been out in the dark long enough for their eyes to acclimatize, but they still couldn't see the sniper up in the canopy. Worse still, there was a pair of ATVs roaring down the path.

Another shot thudded into a tree trunk, flooding the sky with frightened birds.

"Sod this," James said. "I'm never doing the instructors a favor again, that's for sure."

"I'm splitting off and going for the ditches," Lauren said. "The white shirts will work in pairs, which means they can't go after all of us if we split up."

"Maybe we should go that way," Dana said.

But James was resolute. "It stinks out there, and the bugs eat you alive."

"I guess I'll stick with James," Dana said. "Good luck, Lauren."

Lauren smiled. "A pound says I beat you home."

As Lauren rustled away through the bushes, there was a flash from the front lights of two ATVs sweeping by on the dirt path. The ATVs were useless among the trees, so James and Dana weren't surprised that they were heading for open ground.

"They're gonna nail our arses when we try to cross the rugby fields," James said.

But at least the noise of the bike engines gave them an opportunity to scramble out of the undergrowth without the sniper being able to hear them moving off.

"Just hope the red shirts don't have night vision," James whispered.

"Of course they do," Dana said irritably. "How the hell do you think he shot at us?"

The sniper wasn't a he. Siobhan Platter was nine years old. She'd spent two years on CHERUB campus, during which she'd earned two black belts and two first places in the red-shirt target shooting tournament. Knowing that the black shirts would have to cut off the path before the ATVs came after them, she'd positioned herself high up in the fork of a tree fifty meters from where they'd set off.

With a straight shot at James's back, she'd hoped to get at least three hits. The first in the back would knock him down, the second and third would be aimed at his legs. Then she could radio through to the white shirts, and with luck, they'd pick him up before he had a chance to run off the pain.

But Siobhan hadn't accounted for the effect adrenalin can have and the way that a live target in your scope messes with your brain.

After the disappointment of missing her target, Siobhan overheard Lauren saying she was going for the ditches. The lone twelve-year-old seemed like a much more attractive target than fifteen-year-old James and sixteen-year-old Dana.

She unhooked the safety harness from around the trunk and fixed night-vision goggles over her eyes before stepping down onto a thick branch. By this time the ATVs were coming, and she knew that their noise was her best shot at jumping out of the tree without James and Dana hearing.

Siobhan landed on a tree root. The weight of her rifle and the equipment in her backpack made the touchdown hard on her knees, but she screwed up her face, squeezed her mouth shut, and resisted the urge to groan.

Fortunately, James and Dana were more concerned with making it quickly to the main building than in going after the sniper. Siobhan slung her rifle over her shoulder and began moving swiftly east. As she jogged, she reached up and turned the knob on the side of her goggles, switching the sensor from light amplification to heat detection. This made it harder to see where she was going, but the infrared camera revealed tiny differences in temperature, including the difference between the warm surface soil and the slightly cooler soil turned over by Lauren's boot.

It wasn't easy because undergrowth covered much of the ground, but there was enough open mud for Siobhan to stay the trail.

"This is SP," she whispered into the radio mic hanging in front of her face. "I'm tracking Lauren Adams east. She's planning to use the ditches and cut through the basic training compound."

Mr. Pike's measured voice came back at her. "Good work, Siobhan. Try keeping Lauren within visual, and we'll arrange for someone to nail her when she comes out of the compound."

Siobhan was flattered by the instructor's compliment, but after fluffing her golden shot at James, she was determined to do more than follow Lauren through a succession of muddy ditches, and then let someone else grab all the glory by taking her down.

James and Dana faced a trade-off between risk and speed. Keeping to the undergrowth was safe but took forever. Marked paths were faster but the chances of being spotted much greater. After crawling for five hundred meters their limbs were covered in grazes, and Dana had a coating of mud where she'd skidded down a hill into a bog. Under normal circumstances, James might have taken the mickey, but he was tired, and all he wanted was a warm duvet to curl under.

"Red shirts up ahead," Dana whispered as she peeked out from behind a bush.

James shook his head with contempt as he saw the two young boys standing in a clearing for all to see. "How dopey can you get?" He smiled.

"They've got two guns, night vision, and packs full of ammo," Dana said. "Grabbing that lot would definitely improve our odds of making it across the open ground."

James nodded. "I say we creep around from opposite sides and nail them in a pincer."

Dana kept low as she moved toward the two red shirts. One boy spoke into his radio, giving the impression that he was lost, but a second before James and Dana were ready to pounce, the boys turned purposefully and started walking down a path.

Being older and far larger than their opponents, James and Dana were sure they'd be able to emerge from cover and grab the red shirts before they could turn and shoot. Without communicating, they dived out of cover and scrambled out to jump on the red shirts.

James made it onto the path first, but as he crossed the line between two trees he heard the high-pitched gasp of a red-shirt boy. "Spring it!"

James didn't see the lattice of ropes shooting out of the mulch to form a barrier, and he ran straight into them. As he tipped forward, Dana was knocked back by another set rising up behind him. The ropes snagged Dana's boot and dragged her painfully onto her bum. For a moment James thought it was two separate barriers, but the ropes closed around as his feet came off the ground.

"Net," James shouted, grabbing at the sides and trying to clamber out over the top.

As James fought hopelessly, Dana's situation was more precarious. She was outside the net, but her boot was snagged and she was being dragged into the air.

"Pull it higher," a young voice shouted from somewhere in the trees.

There was a pulley in the trees above, which lessened

95

the burden, but the red shirts still struggled to raise the weight of two teenagers.

James realized that he didn't have a hope, but Dana did, and he twisted around so that he could get his hands on her boot. Her arms were within touching distance of the ground, but her entire body weight dangled from one twisted ankle, and she moaned in pain each time the red shirts dragged her higher.

"Hang on," James gasped as he tugged at the ropes, trying to free Dana's boot.

He jolted as one of the red shirts, who'd been in the clearing, shot him in the arse from close range.

"Undo my lace," Dana shouted before yelping as the other red shirt shot her in the left tit.

James unknotted Dana's lace and began loosening her boot. The swinging net lurched another meter into the air as a second shot hit him in the thigh.

Certain basic rules applied to all CHERUB training, and one of them was that you weren't allowed to hurt someone after they were caught.

"I'm captured," James shouted indignantly. "Stop shooting me."

Another bullet hit him in the arse. "You're assisting another participant," one of the red shirts pointed out. "You've not properly surrendered."

James was irritated by the red shirt throwing the rule book back in his face, but he finally got the laces of Dana's boot loose enough for her foot to slide out through the net.

Dana fell from two meters up. Her muscular arms and shoulders absorbed most of the impact, but her head still hit the dirt with some force, and her goggles grazed the skin above her eye socket.

She rolled head over heels and sprang to her feet as the two red-shirt boys who'd led them into the trap fired a dozen rounds at her. Luckily, her powerful presence spooked them, and most of their shots disintegrated harmlessly into the ground or the undergrowth.

A third red shirt shooting from behind had no such problems, and slammed four agonizing shots between Dana's shoulder blades in under two seconds.

"Jesus," Dana screamed, stumbling forward as she looked up at James's outline balled in the net more than four meters off the ground.

She considered a rescue, but with a twisted ankle, a missing boot, and shots coming at her from all directions, there wasn't any realistic chance.

"There's at least five of them," James shouted, thinking of the three red shirts shooting, plus at least two more who were somewhere in the bushes, hoisting up the net.

Dana was injured, and the three red shirts probably could have overpowered her, but they were happy enough to have one victim and didn't fancy their chances against the heavily built teenager.

As Dana ran away through the bushes, the red shirts all stopped shouting and shooting, and James found himself high off the ground, with a sharp stinging pain in his arse and a gentle creaking of the net as it swung from the branches.

The girl who'd done such a good job shooting Dana in the back moved directly under the net and spoke into her headset. "This is LW calling any white shirts. Our honey trap just caught a fairly dim-witted bee, and we'd appreciate it if someone came down and took him off our hands."

James was pretty furious at being up in the net, and having a nine-year-old girl insulting him didn't improve his mood.

"Hey, little girl," he shouted. "I happen to have a privileged position helping out the training instructors. So you watch that mouth, because some day soon you might find yourself on a training exercise where your arse belongs to me."

"Did I ask for your opinion?" the girl laughed as she aimed the gun up and shot James in the arse again.

"Hey," James screamed. "Stop that. It's not allowed and you know it."

The girl tutted. "Why don't you write a letter to the United Nations?"

CHAPTER 12

TREK

Siobhan was only a few weeks shy of her tenth birthday, and if everything went to plan she'd be a qualified CHERUB agent before Christmas. She was confident and fit, but she was also three years younger than Lauren and inevitably that made her slower.

She flipped up the night-vision attachment on her goggles and was surprised by the reminder of how black it was. There was no moon and the nearest source of artificial light was downhill, behind half a kilometer of trees.

"Base, this is SP," Siobhan whispered as she flipped the switch to activate her mouthpiece. "I'm two hundred meters from the rear of the basic training compound, but

I think I've lost Lauren Adams. Have you got any sensors or cameras around here that can help me out?"

Kazakov's voice came straight back in her earpiece. "I've got your location on satellite tracking. I'll see what we've got and get right back."

Siobhan flipped her night vision down again as she waited, but before the response came, she heard a squelching sound like someone dropping into a ditch less than twenty meters in front of her. She suspected that Lauren was long gone, but another black shirt could have wandered into the area.

Dead leaves and branches crackled underfoot, but even with the infrared on its highest setting, there was no sign of recent soil disturbance around the mouth of the ditch.

She kept her rifle poised as she swung left and right, seeking a target. It hadn't rained for a few days, and the water in the ditch had been stagnant long enough for insect larvae to hatch. One landed on her nose, and she squished it before flicking it away from her finger.

Siobhan didn't like the insects or the dank smell. Pursuing Lauren through the least pleasant part of campus wasn't nearly as good an idea as it had seemed fifteen minutes earlier. As she was about to back off, Kazakov's voice crackled in her earpiece.

"I just checked the sensor logs and the motion-detection system triangulated someone up close to your position less than a minute ago. You'd better go take a look."

"Okay," Siobhan said reluctantly. "Will do."

Now she was spooked, because it's almost impossible to move without disturbing the earth and leaving a thermal trace. The ghostly presence sent a shiver down her back.

Siobhan crushed another midge crawling over the back of her hand as she moved right up to the edge of the ditch. As she crouched over the water, she heard a splash and before she knew it, something had gripped her ankle, and her boot was sliding down the embankment.

She kicked and wriggled and clawed at the mud, but her opponent was too heavy, and she found herself plunging into the ice-cold water. Icy hands moved on to the back of Siobhan's neck and thrust her head under the swirls of mud, then held it there for several seconds.

"There's a reason not to mess with me," Lauren snarled as she dragged Siobhan's head out of the water. "I'm a black shirt, you're a red. You should have stuck to picking your nose and finger painting."

With that, Lauren bundled Siobhan against the embankment and smeared her face through the stinking mud before turning her around.

"You like that, red shirt?" Lauren sneered.

Lauren had spent three months ditch digging as punishment and she'd got immune to the smell, but this was Siobhan's first experience, and she sobbed as the filthy water dribbled out of her mouth.

"Poor little red shirt. Are you crying for your teddy, Siobhan? You're almost ten. If this makes you cry, you won't last one day of basic training."

Siobhan sobbed again and Lauren started to feel guilty. She was in a mood because she'd been dragged out of bed, dumped on the far side of campus, and shot at. None of this was Siobhan's fault, but it felt damned good having someone to take out her anger on.

"I want everything you've got," Lauren said. "Night vision, backpack, weapon, and gun."

She ripped the headset from Siobhan's ear. The set hadn't responded well to its excursion underwater, which disappointed Lauren, who'd hoped to gain valuable intelligence by listening in to the radio traffic between the instructors and the white shirts.

Siobhan rubbed her eyes. When she managed to open them up, she was surprised to find Lauren stripped to her boots and underwear, with mud smeared thickly over her face. Lauren had been lucky enough to find a discarded gardener's sack in which to keep her clothes dry. The mud on her face made her skin harder to see and lowered her skin temperature, making her harder to spot with the infrared.

Lauren stuffed her dry clothes in Siobhan's backpack, on top of the spare Simunition, then checked her rifle and night-vision goggles, both of which had survived their encounter with the muddy water.

"What do I do now?" Siobhan sniffed.

Lauren tutted; red shirts weren't forced to go on training exercises. "You volunteered for this, didn't you? What are you bawling for?"

"I . . ."

"If I were you, I'd run back to the junior block before you freeze to death in those wet clothes," Lauren said.

"Okay," Siobhan said weakly as she dug a foothold in the muddy embankment and grabbed hold of a tree root to haul herself out.

Lauren didn't have a lot of sympathy, and she muttered to herself as she waded through the ditch toward the basic training compound, dressed in boots and underwear, with the rifle balanced on her shoulder above the waterline. "What kind of stupid kid volunteers for a training exercise, then breaks down in tears as soon as she gets her head dunked? She's been on campus for two years; it's not as if she doesn't know how it works. . . ."

Lauren agreed with every word she was saying, but it didn't stop her from feeling bad. No amount of reasoning would make her feel okay about making a nine-year-old cry.

Running with one boot on made Dana lopsided, but she didn't want to take it off because then she'd have two damp, freezing-cold feet instead of one, and she'd double the risk of slicing herself open on a thorn or a broken bottle.

She thought about giving herself up so that she could start again with James, but so far all the evidence pointed to Lauren's theory being correct: the red shirts and white shirts were working in teams of two or more, which made it impossible for them to track everyone. You just needed a bit of luck. . . .

She found an old path through campus that had been barricaded here and there with logs and water traps. It was designed for training runs for younger red shirts and new arrivals who required a gentle introduction to assault courses.

Keeping to such an obvious route was a risk, but she ran as fast as the darkness and her missing boot would allow. Within ten minutes of James's capture, she was at the top of the knoll overlooking the lawns around the campus lake and the games fields beyond it.

It was lighter here. CHERUB had an energy efficiency policy, but lights had been left on inside some of the changing rooms. The lake itself was surrounded by illuminated booths containing life-saving equipment and emergency telephones.

Dana shielded herself behind the last line of trees. There was no sign of the white shirts, but she knew they were out there, squatting on rooftops ready to shoot her in the back before the ATVs rode out to scoop her up.

She thought about her training. The only things that came to mind were the urban warfare tactics she'd learned at the SAS training compound a few kilometers away: keep low, move from building to building, and leave yourself exposed to enemy fire for the shortest time possible. But while the urban warfare compound had no open spaces wider than a four-lane road, there were hundreds of meters between some of the buildings on CHERUB campus.

Still, it wasn't like Dana had a choice. She stood up and eyeballed a group of trees halfway between the lake and the edge of the woods. Beyond that was a shelter and the changing room at the edge of the lake. She wondered about swimming across. It was a fair way, but she wouldn't be seen in the dark, and she'd emerge less than fifty meters from the back of the dojo.

Dana lay on her belly and crawled as fast as she could. Once she was thirty meters out into the long grass, she decided that it was safe to stand up and break into a crouching run. But although she hadn't been spotted, she'd been detected by a motion sensor at the edge of the woods, and Kazakov had radioed all the white shirts. As Dana made it to the first group of trees, she heard the buzz of ATV engines.

"Shit!"

The three vehicles stormed out of the trees and came roaring downhill toward her, headlights ablaze. She broke into a run toward the lake, but the bikes had a top speed of over sixty kilometers an hour, and she didn't have a hope in hell.

She found herself trapped in no-man's-land, halfway between the lake and the trees, with three ATVs in a triangle around her. Getting hit by an ATV can kill you, and the white shirts had strict orders not to use them as offensive weapons. Instead, the three riders closed slowly with their guns drawn.

"Kneel down and put your hands on your head," Dave Moss shouted as he cruised downhill astride his ATV.

Dana thought about running, and she might even have tried if she'd been a hundred meters from the main building, but she was still more than a kilometer away, and there was no realistic chance of outrunning three riders over open ground.

As Dana knelt down with her hands raised, the rider coming up from the lake drove to within five meters and hurled a set of handcuffs into the grass in front of her.

"You know what to do, Dana," she said. "No sudden moves, or we'll shoot the shit out of you."

CHAPTER 19

AMBUSH

Lauren's journey wasn't pleasant, but as she'd predicted, nobody wanted to follow her through the mud. The ditches were clogged with litter and debris, which made it impossible to walk barefoot. When she clambered out near the western edge of the basic training compound, her first task was to remove her sodden boots and pour out the water.

She ran barefoot to a storage shed and used a standpipe on the outside to scrub away the worst of the mud and an assortment of beetles. She deliberately left the dirt on her face, because her pale skin would catch the light. After cleaning the night-vision goggles with her dry T-shirt, she quickly donned it, along with her shorts.

After a glance around to make sure nobody was coming after her, Lauren kept low as she headed across the dry earth, but she was alarmed by the loud squelching of her sodden boots. She suspected someone might be stationed at the entrance of the training compound and also knew that the central part of the training area was saturated with video cameras. Luckily, Lauren's days of clearing ditches had taught her about a rarely used side gate that led out of the training compound and into the undergrowth beneath the tall obstacle where cherubs were trained to overcome their fear of heights.

She moved swiftly, with the night vision over her eyes and Siobhan's pack on her shoulder. But even with the red shirt's equipment, Lauren didn't fancy her chances of covering the open ground between the woods and the main building on foot.

The obvious answer was to grab one of the campus golf carts. The white shirts might shoot at her, but damaging other vehicles was expensive as well as dangerous, so it was banned in training exercises. If she got into a cart, she'd be able to cruise all the way back to the main building, unless she got shot up so badly that she fell out.

There were two dozen carts around campus, which the staff used to move quickly between different areas. Kids were only supposed to use them under special circumstances, like if someone was injured or there was a heavy load to carry.

Lauren hoped one of the electric carts would be parked behind the gardeners' storage building, but she faced two problems. Firstly, the staff were always bitching about who used the carts for what, and sod's law dictated that whenever you really needed a cart they'd all be parked on the opposite side of campus. Secondly, the enemy would know the value of the carts, so even if she found one, there was likely to be a crew of red and white shirts waiting in ambush.

A little concrete strip was situated behind the gardeners' shed, and Lauren smiled as she poked her head out of the undergrowth and eyeballed one of the larger pick-up-style carts that were used by the maintenance staff.

Before breaking into the open, Lauren turned up the sensitivity of her goggles and made a careful study of her surroundings in night-vision mode, before flipping the switch and repeating the process with infrared. There were a few boot marks in the mud at either side of the concrete, but they were small prints and widely spaced, suggesting a pair of red shirts who'd been running after someone rather than the more cautious movements of someone setting a trap.

Lauren's boot squelched as she stood up. She kept low as she rounded the back of the cart and pulled out the recharging plug before swinging into the driver's seat. Her nose caught the stench of rotten food, and she felt queasy as she glanced in the back and saw thousands of flies partying on orange peel and moldy bread. It seemed that the cart had been used for a refuse run, and nobody had bothered to hose it out after a bag burst.

Whatever it smelled like, it was a ride, and Lauren dropped the handbrake and pressed the accelerator. The cart jerked forward about five centimeters before the motor gave out. She drifted to a halt less than a meter from her starting point.

"Knob," Lauren steamed as she hammered the steering wheel. The cart *might* have broken down, but more likely it had been sabotaged by the white shirts. This meant that even if she found another cart, it would probably be in the same condition.

Being right next to the gardeners' shed, Lauren considered grabbing one of the ride-on mowers inside, but their top speed was less than eight kilometers an hour, and while ramming a golf cart with an ATV would be considered a serious breach of the rules, there was no reason why someone couldn't run up alongside and knock her off a slow-moving lawnmower.

Lauren was exposed for as long as she sat in the cart, and there was a chance she'd been spotted on a video camera, so she dived back into the undergrowth and crawled fifty meters, ending up in one of the landing nets beneath the height obstacle.

"Use your training," she whispered to herself as she racked her brains. "Think, think, think."

She didn't fancy her chances over open ground against a team of ATVs. On the other hand, by following the ditches and crossing the training compound, she'd emerged on the opposite side of campus, far from the other black shirts, and this gave her an outside chance of making it. Plus, this side of campus was more built up than the area around the lake.

Lauren considered each stage of her route. She'd have to run two hundred meters across open ground, and the first place she'd be able to shelter was around the back of the vehicle workshop.

A smile broke over Lauren's muddy face as she thought

about the evening before and James's hundred-kilometer-an-hour racing cart.

The white shirts took their time rescuing James from the net, and McEwen didn't bother letting him down gently.

"You extra-soft-toilet-tissue-using, wormlike bag of gloop," McEwen screamed as he gave James an almighty kick up the arse.

"Hey, there are rules," James yelled. "You can't kick me."

"Do I look like someone who gives a shit?" McEwen grinned, pointing his rifle at James's nuts. "Get moving."

The delay in letting James down meant that Dana actually returned to the starting point in the far corner of campus before him. James gave her a kiss before throwing over her boot.

"What's the situation?" James asked as he looked around and saw several other black shirts preparing to set off for a second run. The instructors, Kazakov and Pike, were monitoring communications from the warmth of their hut.

"It's grimmer than a shit sandwich," Dana reported. "At least half of us have been captured once already, it sounds like several others are pinned down under fire from the red shirts, and I've not heard from anyone who's made it more than a few hundred meters on to the open ground. There's at least ten ATVs out there, and the red shirts are lined up on the edge of the woods, acting as scouts and snipers. A group of six black shirts set off a few minutes ago, but I knew you were due back, so I told them I'd wait."

"Do you think a bigger group might get somewhere?" James asked. "We could wait for more people."

Dana raised an uncertain eyebrow. "I guess if they all rushed out at once, most of them would get picked up, but one or two might get away. But it's going to get harder as the night goes on. I mean, once people start escaping, there are going to be more white shirts after fewer targets."

"See your point," James said with a nod.

"The only good news is that a few of the red shirts have had their equipment taken, and two more were in an accident with an ATV, so this time there should be fewer guns pointing at us."

"What about Lauren?" James asked. "Any sign of her?"

"Not that I've heard," Dana said as she looked at her watch. "It's slow going through those ditches, though. I expect she's only just reached open ground."

"There's no point trying to run out in the open with no equipment," James said, frustrated. "Ambushing and nabbing equipment is the only way for us to go."

Dana nodded. "Lure in one of the ATVs and knock the rider off, but it won't be easy. So many of us black shirts got caught so quickly that we're all gonna be trying the same kind of tactics."

"We might as well be moving as standing here," James said, and Dana nodded.

They headed toward a white shirt called Jennie Ross. She stood at the edge of the clearing with a clipboard and a pen behind her ear.

"Ready for another shot?" she asked cheerfully. "Agents were made of tougher stuff in my day."

"Seems the birds were a lot uglier, though." James grinned.

The white shirt took a whistle out of her jacket. "You've got forty seconds' immunity from when I blow the whistle." Then she turned and shouted into the trees, "Two more suckers heading out on my mark."

CHAPTER 14

SPEED

A shot cracked the air and hit the ground a meter past Lauren. She dived behind a line of shrubs as a second shot whacked the heel of her boot, then looked up and peeked between the branches. Night vision showed her a single red-shirt sniper lying on the flat roof of the vehicle workshop.

Lauren thought about starting a shoot-out, but the red shirt had the dual advantages of body armor and a radio to call for backup. So she shouted out, trying to sound younger than she was.

"Don't shoot," she squeaked. "I'm a friendly but my headset has broken."

She watched the red shirt swing around suspiciously

and raise his hand. "How many fingers am I holding up?" he asked.

Lauren smiled; the youngster hadn't considered that another red shirt might have had their night-vision goggles snatched.

"Three fingers," Lauren shouted as she stood up and gave a friendly wave. Although she was smaller than any of the other black shirts, she was still bigger than any red shirt, and she hoped that the boy wouldn't work this out until she got up close.

"How'd you bust your radio?" the red shirt asked.

"I fell in a ditch, and it got a soaking," Lauren explained as she jogged up to the side of the building. Even if the red shirt realized who she was now, he'd have to lean awkwardly over the gutter to get a shot in.

"What's happening on the radio?" Lauren asked. "Have you had contact with any black shirts?"

"It's dead over here," the red shirt said dejectedly. "They sent me to check on anyone coming through the training compound, but all the action's on the other side of campus."

"Same here," Lauren said. "I haven't seen a sausage. I might head over there; do you want to come with?"

The red shirt swung his legs over the side of the roof and dropped down. Before he got his balance, Lauren launched a vicious karate kick. Her boot thumped the little red shirt's stomach and he doubled over.

"By the way, I lied," Lauren smiled as she swept the red shirt's feet away and pinned him down in the gravel.

The red shirt cursed his luck: he'd fallen for Lauren's ruse because her voice seemed familiar. But she wasn't a fellow red shirt; she was the girl who helped the little kids in the junior block. He made a desperate grab for the transmit button on his microphone, but Lauren ripped the headset away from his mouth before digging the point of her elbow against the back of his neck. Shards of gravel dug into his face.

"Glad you volunteered for this little game?" Lauren snarled. "I want your jacket, your ammunition, and everything else you've got. Then you'd better walk back to the junior block, cos if I see your face again tonight, I might not be such a sweetie pie."

"Okay," said the kid, making the gravel shuffle as he tried to nod.

Once she'd stripped the red shirt's equipment and sent him on his way, Lauren fixed on the headset so that she could listen to all the communications going back and forth between the white shirts and the instructors. Finally, she squeezed into the red shirt's coat. It was too small to button up, and short on the sleeves, but it had a fur lining, and it was bliss to have something covering her arms.

Despite the red shirt's solemn promise, Lauren knew he was angry and would probably try reporting what had happened. She had to move fast, so it was a relief that the back door of the vehicle workshop had been left unlocked. This was common on campus, where burglars were unheard of and rogue cherubs knew they'd be caught on CCTV if they tried stealing anything.

The first thing she passed was the burned-out shell of Shakeel's cart. It sat on bare wheel rims, filling its surroundings with a vague odor of burned plastic. James's team's cart was up against the wall at the front, and to her relief it hadn't been stripped down after the race.

After flipping on the lamp over a workbench so that she could see, Lauren found the switch for the electronic door at the front and clambered into the seat. As the aluminum door rolled noisily toward the ceiling, she pressed the start button, and the motorbike engine blasted into life.

Lauren had learned to drive when she was ten years old and got scheduled for at least an hour's driving practice every month. CHERUB didn't encourage agents to go out joyriding, but driving was a vital skill that most agents would use to escape from a sticky situation at some point in their careers.

CHERUB had a variety of shared cars, and Lauren had sat behind the wheel of everything from Mercedes and Range Rovers down to Minis and mopeds. The one thing all of them had in common was that the manufacturers had invested millions in their development, making sure all the components worked together and that the steering and handling were expertly tuned.

By contrast, Lauren was now driving a golf cart that had been converted by her brother and three of his mates. If you did anything more than gently dab the accelerator, the back wheels spun like crazy. The brakes had been designed for sedate progress around a golf course, and she was stunned when she first used them and found that nothing happened for almost a second. When she squeezed harder, the beefed-up rear brakes bit, sending a shower of sparks flying out from the rear wheels and hurling her forward in her seat.

The most random element was the cornering, which reminded Lauren of Meatball chasing a ball across Zara's kitchen floor and crashing into all the cabinets. But for all its faults it was a ride home, and once Lauren got to grips with its eccentricities, she realized that it was a very fast one.

Not wanting to risk an accident, Lauren kept the speed down. This also meant that the engine stayed quiet and she could hear the voice traffic going between the red and white shirts and the instructors in her earpiece.

For a black shirt it made grim listening. Over the space of three minutes Lauren heard white shirts capturing Kerry, Gabrielle, and two other agents, while another group lay in wait, ready to ambush the group of six who'd set off before James and Dana. Kazakov sounded like he was enjoying himself and several times he complimented his team on keeping a clean sheet: meaning that nobody had made it back to the main building.

Lauren was confident of becoming the first as she cruised the path at the side of the rugby fields, with just the tennis courts between herself and the back of the main building. She'd be indoors in under two minutes; showered and snuggled under her duvet in fifteen if she didn't hang about.

A shout came up over the radio. Lauren recognized the voice of a red-shirt girl called Ryan Smythe. "I'm eyeballing James Adams and Dana Smith in the trees by the lake," Ryan yelled. "I can shoot if you like?"

"Hold on that," Mr. Pike replied calmly. "Do we have anyone available to intercept?"

McEwen answered, "I nailed that groin kisser once,

and I'm on the ATV ready to get him again. Dave Moss is riding with."

"Okay, Ryan," Pike said. "I want you to keep them in your sights and report any movement."

Lauren felt a twang of conscience. If the white shirts had disabled all the electric carts, she had the only available means of besting white shirts on the ATVs. James was her brother, and parts of her wanted to help him out. On the other hand he was also the git who'd kicked a football at her and left a dirty great red mark on her back earlier in the evening.

Her heart leaped as she slowed to a halt. She was less than a hundred meters from the back of the main building. Did she really want to risk it all for the sake of being a hero? And would James do the same for her if their roles were reversed? She liked to think that he would, but was less than convinced.

She looked at the fuel gauge taped to the dashboard and part of her hoped it showed empty, but it was three-quarters full.

"Can't believe I'm doing this," Lauren grunted as she jabbed the throttle and jerked the steering wheel. The cart almost threw her out as the back wheels squealed, and she spun to face in the opposite direction.

Lauren had a big speed advantage over the white shirts, but the ATVs had four-wheel drive and big tires designed for mud and hills, whereas her cart had a low chassis and titchy wheels. It was meant to run on flat paths and trimmed grass.

She blasted away from the main building, hardly able to believe she was being so nice. After half a kilometer she was alarmed by the outlines of two ATVs on a hilltop, but they didn't come after her. She was heading away from the main building, and they must have thought she was a member of staff.

Judging from the radio traffic, it sounded like a massive fight had broken out in the bushes. The group of six black shirts had gotten hold of some weapons and were in a shoot-out with white and red shirts. Pairs of white-shirt units were moving in to collect them, and Lauren knew she had a chance to help.

She pressed the transmit button and spoke into her microphone, deliberately talking quietly so that her voice was hard to recognize. "I'm over on the west side," she lied. "Five black shirts just came out the front of the basic training compound. I need urgent assistance."

"Can you confirm your ID and location," Kazakov answered.

"Sorry, base, can't understand . . . Weak signal . . . My earpiece got some water in it earlier. I *repeat*, I'm close to the exit of the training compound. I see five black shirts coming toward me, but I can't take all of them out on my own."

Kazakov started to panic. "I want all units patrolling the lake to move west and intercept by the training compound. All rear units move forward to the lake. Don't you dare let anyone through, because there'll be no safety net behind you."

Lauren grinned as a sequence of *will do*s and *roger that*s came through her earpiece. The two ATVs she'd passed moments earlier roared away from the hilltop, heading for the lake, while in the distance she could hear a whole fleet moving toward the training compound. It made her feel pretty good, but if one of the nuttier white shirts like McEwen got hold of her after that stunt, they'd kick her arse whether it was against the rules or not.

It took another two minutes to pass the last of the football fields. She took a right and sped down the track leading toward the lake, all the time trying not to think about how she could have been tucked up in bed by now.

CHAPTER 15

LAKE

James and Dana crouched in the trees, watching the ATVs roar past in the darkness.

"They're heading for the training compound," Dana whispered.

"You think it's Lauren?" James asked.

Dana shook her head. "They wouldn't send all that lot after one person."

They could hear the six black shirts and the white shirts fighting in the woods less than a hundred meters away. James and Dana considered joining the fray, but both sides seemed to have guns and Simunition, while all they had was a big stick and a ropey plan.

"If half the ATVs have gone west and loads of other

white shirts are in a rumble over there, we could try making a break for it," James suggested.

But Dana didn't sound keen. "After my last attempt, I don't fancy our chances on foot. We should stick to our plan. One of the ATVs has got to come up close eventually."

Over the next couple of minutes they heard more shooting and watched a bunch of black shirts break out of the trees and make a run downhill toward the lake. They had no vehicles, but most of them had grabbed weapons from the red shirts, and some even seemed to have retrieved well-fitting clothes and body armor from the whites.

As the massed group sprinted around the edge of the lake, a single ATV closed in on James and Dana's position. Dave Moss had gone after the nonexistent group in the west, leaving McEwen to hunt James and Dana alone.

McEwen was confident that with a gun and body armor, he'd be able to capture them both, but as he stood astride the ATV and glanced around to eyeball them with his night vision, he was stunned to see the pair running right at him. They were two meters apart, and they held a thick branch between them at shoulder height.

McEwen ducked and went for his rifle, but he was too slow. The branch smashed into him. As he tumbled off the ATV and on to his side, his boot caught the hand throttle, and the ATV engine roared. Dana moved fast, landing heavily on McEwen's stomach and knocking the wind out of him.

"I'm under attack," McEwen shouted into his mouthpiece. "Get some backup over here."

McEwen was much bigger than Dana, and she knew he'd beat her if she gave him time to catch his breath. Kevlar armor covered all of McEwen's vulnerable body parts, so Dana went for his goggles, punching them with such ferocity that the plastic bridge between the two sides cracked and blood spewed out of his nose.

"Where are you, James?" Dana screamed as she looked around briefly before grabbing the handcuffs off McEwen's belt and locking them over his wrists while he was dazed.

Getting the better of McEwen felt good, but they needed the ATV to get home. James had made a lunge as it began to roll, but it was heavy, and his fingers had no grip after being out in the cold. He ended up sprawled in the grass.

As he scrambled to his feet, the rolling ATV's front end turned gently into the slope and gathered speed as it rolled downhill toward the lake. James broke into a sprint, but couldn't make up any ground. His last hope was the hedgerow along the lakeside. With luck, it would be enough to stop the ATV, or at least slow it sufficiently for him to catch up and grab hold of it.

The muddy front tires reared up as evergreen leaves rustled and branches crunched. All four wheels were off the ground as James made a desperate final charge. He reached out to grab the fender over the back wheels, just as the front wheels tilted forward and raised it beyond his grasp.

The gravel path between the hedge and the lake was fairly flat, and the ATV crept toward the water less than two meters away. James vaulted the breach in the hedge, confident that he had time to catch up and grab the handlebars before it crashed into the lake, but as he moved out, a simulated round thumped him in the back.

James collapsed as a second slammed the back of his bare leg. He spun around and saw Ryan Smythe and another red-shirt girl running downhill toward him. After straightening his safety goggles, James ducked behind the bushes as the front of the ATV tipped over the edge of the lake. The water was almost a meter below the embankment, and the ATV teetered precariously.

The red shirts were too titchy to risk hand-to-hand combat, but they stood their ground until they spotted Dana charging down the hill toward them. One girl made a run for it, but Dana flew in with a two-footed tackle and knocked Ryan flying.

"Goggles and rifles, short arse," Dana yelled as she held Ryan down. "Make it snappy, or I'll throw your butt in the lake."

James thought about going after the red shirt who was running away, but Dana had now floored McEwen and a red shirt. He figured they had two rifles and two sets of night-vision goggles, so he decided to rescue the ATV bike. However, the red shirt who was on the run knew the ATV would enable James and Dana to get back to the main building. When she noticed that James wasn't coming after her, she dropped into a firing position and took aim.

The ATV was an easy target, and James turned around in time to view the rapid succession of shots. The first hit the back wheel, but the rest punched the metal bodywork. The simulated rounds turned to powder on impact, but had enough power to give the ATV a final nudge into the water.

James dived for cover as rubber and metal hit the surface of the lake. Ducks started quacking as a huge splash spilled up the embankment, giving James a soaking. Even if they could drag the ATV out without getting shot to pieces, the engine would be flooded.

"Why didn't you grab it?" Dana screamed as the two red shirts sprinted up the hill.

James was half drowned and limping from where he'd been shot in the leg. "What do you think I was trying to do?" he shouted bitterly.

The red shirts had made it back to the trees, and the one who still had her gun took a shot. Dana ducked down and fired back, but James noticed a pair of ATVs coming toward them. Lauren's fake radio announcement had only fooled the white shirts for a few minutes, and now they were all heading back to the lake.

"Run," James shouted as Dana fixed on Ryan's night-vision goggles. "Where's the other pair?"

"McEwen's goggles smashed," Dana explained. They started running along the edge of the lake. It was pretty open, but there were a few bushes to shield them.

"We could try swimming across," James said. He realized it wasn't his greatest ever idea, but he forgave himself when he recognized a pungent waft of exhaust fumes. "My cart," he shouted.

But only Dana could see the cart charging downhill toward them, with two ATVs close behind.

"I think it's Lauren," she shouted.

James couldn't believe it, but saw for himself when

the headlights from one of the ATVs caught his sister's face. Dana sprinted uphill with James behind, stopping only to take a couple of shots at the chasing ATVs.

"Care for a ride, old bean?" Lauren asked, skidding to a halt.

"I bloody love you." James smiled. He grabbed the front passenger seat while Dana squatted down in the rear storage compartment and grabbed on to the poles holding up the roof.

The ATVs were almost on top of them, and the little cart struggled to get any grip on the shaggy grass as Lauren tried steering back uphill.

"Gimme a gun," James shouted.

Dana passed her rifle back, but she was out of ammo and it took another couple of desperate seconds for James to fit one of the spare clips from the red shirt's backpack. Dana had to duck as he fired backward at the chasing ATVs. Their riders were alone, and it was impossible for them to shoot and drive at full speed, but they continued to get closer, and while you weren't supposed to ram other vehicles on training exercises, everyone knew that rules get bent whenever a surge of adrenalin kicks in.

"Right in the face," James howled as a pellet smacked the rider of the closest ATV in the goggles. She held on to the handlebars, but the ATV wobbled, and she couldn't keep up the chase with the powdered remains of a Simunition cartridge blocking her view.

The second ATV had always been less of a threat, and as soon as they reached the concrete path, Lauren hit the accelerator and the cart roared clear. The ATV rider realized it was hopeless and gave up.

It was a violent ride, especially for Dana, who was getting thrown all over the place in the back.

"Don't rev it so hard," James shouted over the engine noise. "There's no safety cutout. You could blow the head gasket, and you *don't* want to be onboard when that happens."

Lauren eased off, but she surprised James by taking a left off the path back to the main building.

"What are you doing?" James screamed. "It's the Japanese garden. It's a dead end."

As Lauren slowed down, a volley of shots pelted the cart's roof from a sniper position on the porch at the front of the dojo.

"What's going on?" Dana yelled.

"I just heard on the radio," Lauren replied before yelling into the dark: "Do you want a ride? I can't wait all night."

Seconds later, two crouching figures emerged from the side of the dojo. They seemed to be unarmed, and bullets came from at least two firing positions as they ran. James recognized Gabrielle first as she clambered in the back and squeezed up to Dana. The other girl was James's ex, Kerry Chang, but she hesitated because there was nowhere to sit.

"Get on his lap," Lauren ordered.

Kerry was quite small, but her head was still pressed against the roof of the cart. James locked his arms around her waist as her sweaty back pressed against his face. It had been ages since he'd been so close to his first proper girlfriend, and her smell brought back memories.

"All safe?" Lauren said as she turned the cart and sped away.

The five bodies made the cart heavy, and Lauren almost tipped it as they went around a corner. Now she was back where she'd been ten minutes earlier, on the main path through campus, heading toward the tennis courts.

They were picking up speed, but when she squeezed the brakes nothing happened.

"Slow down," James shouted. "Are you nuts?"

"I'm trying," Lauren screamed. "Why did you design such crappy brakes?"

James couldn't see because Kerry was in his lap, but the golf cart's speed topped out at fifty kilometers an hour, and the needle had gone beyond that.

"We're overloaded, and the brake pads must have overheated," James said. "Pump the pedal hard and keep pumping."

The wire fencing around the tennis courts passed in a blur as they headed for the rear of the main building. Lauren kept stamping until something happened. At first she thought it was the brakes, but Dana and Gabrielle started screaming. The back axle had buckled, and the rear of the cart was scraping the path, throwing up showers of orange sparks and making a grinding noise that woke up half of campus.

Then Lauren screamed as hot sparks sprayed up her bare legs. She looked down and saw a hole beneath her feet where the pedals had been. It was a dramatic failure, but the disintegrated chassis came to a halt less than five meters from the back wall of the main building, and the only casualties were a selection of rose bushes.

The traumatized black shirts jumped out, straightened

their goggles, and grabbed their guns, except for James, who stayed in the passenger seat, horrified at the disintegration of his cart.

Dana cracked him around the head. "Come on, dickhead. You can mourn later."

By the time James was out of his seat, Lauren, Gabrielle, and Kerry had already run half of the fifty meters toward the nearest entrance. Dana heard the roar of an ATV engine. It was way off in the distance, but it still gave James a jolt, and they went sprinting after the others.

A blast of warm air hit James as he stepped into a darkened hallway. Kerry and Gabrielle wore massive grins and took turns hugging Lauren. When they let go, James couldn't help smiling at her.

"You're totally the best sister," James said as he pulled Lauren into a tight hug.

Lauren smiled back. "And just you bloody well remember it next time you feel like booting a football at me."

CHAPTER '16

PRETEND

Fahim had barely slept, but sunlight blasted through the crack between his bedroom curtains. The huge house felt like a mausoleum. He'd heard Sylvia the cleaning lady arrive at eight, and she was vacuuming downstairs, but there'd been no sign of his parents, and he was afraid to leave his room.

When his bedroom door finally clicked, Fahim was delighted by the rattle of cutlery on a breakfast tray, but he was alarmed to find his father holding it. Even when he worked from home, Hassam usually wore a suit, but today he was dressed in jeans and a Ralph Lauren polo shirt.

"How's my boy?" Hassam said cheerily.

"Not too bad," Fahim replied as his heart started to drum. "Is Mum around?"

Hassam straddled the question. "I made you breakfast. You must eat well to recover."

He rested the tray on the edge of the mattress, and Fahim couldn't fail to be impressed. There were two soft-boiled eggs, a small fruit salad, orange juice, iced water, and toast.

"Thank you," he said politely.

"All my own work," Hassam said. "I think it's the way your mother would do it, but if something isn't right, just tell me . . ."

"I'm sure it's fine, Dad."

Hassam's presence felt creepy, but his father's outbursts were often followed by guilt-fueled attempts at reconciliation. Over the years it had taken many forms: from expensive toys and fancy sneakers through to theme parks and family weekends in Paris. When he was younger, Fahim got excited by all this. In a perverse way, he'd even look forward to family fights because of the gifts and attention lavished by both parents afterward. But at eleven years old he was past the stage where LEGO compensated for watching his mother get slapped around, and there were items in his room that he never touched because they reminded him of something awful.

Hassam hovered anxiously as his son cracked the top off a boiled egg and dunked a finger of toast into the runny yolk.

"Your mother left last night," Hassam said awkwardly.

Fahim was startled. He'd often urged his mum to leave

or get a divorce, but he'd always assumed he'd go with her if she did.

"Forever?"

Hassam gave an eerie smile. "Your mother needs time alone. She's packed some things and booked into a spa."

This didn't seem so bad, and Fahim nodded. "She deserves it" was all he could think to say.

"You with the trophy cabinets and me with . . . with what happened last night. We both see the red mist and shoot off like fireworks, don't we?"

Fahim resented his father's attempt to shift blame on to him, but he swallowed his indignation and forced a weak smile. "We should both learn to hold our breath and count to ten," he said.

Hassam roared with laughter and gave the big toe poking from the duvet a friendly squeeze. "You and I can go into town. Remember that leather jacket you saw? And wasn't there some radio-controlled car you were after? I bet it would run well on the big patio out back."

"My head's killing me."

"Not today, *obviously*," Hassam said. "But tomorrow . . . Actually, I have a meeting, but definitely the weekend."

Fahim turned to straighten his pillows, giving his father a glimpse of red where his shoulder had bled in the night.

"I'll get Sylvia to put fresh sheets on," Hassam said, his tone firming slightly. "If she asks, tell her you had a nosebleed. Okay, sport?"

Fahim almost choked on his egg. His father only ever called him "sport" when he was papering over cracks.

"I guess," Fahim said. The blood had made his father

feel guilty, and he decided it was a good time to ask a bold question. "What about my school? I don't want to live in the Middle East."

Hassam raised an eyebrow and was clearly a touch irritated, but his words came softly. "Your mother and I don't agree on this, but I won't force you to go abroad if you don't want to."

"Thank you," Fahim said.

"Your friend from before you went to Warrender Prep. The one who came here to play sometimes in the holidays. I forget his name."

"Louis."

"Yes." Hassam smiled. "Louis just moved to Burleigh Arts and Media. Maybe we can get you in there, and we'll see how things go."

Fahim had never wanted to go to Warrender Prep, with its compulsory sport on a Saturday and outrageous amounts of homework. He broke into a genuine smile at the idea of going back to an ordinary school with his closest friend.

"Really?" Fahim said, but he immediately felt cross with himself for letting his father see that he could be bought off.

"Burleigh got a decent OFSTED report. I'll give them a call later this morning and ask about admissions."

Lauren wasn't sure why she'd been summoned to the chairwoman's office, so it was a relief when Zara opened her office door with a smile.

"Come in, Lauren," she said. "Take a pew."

The office was fitted with modern furniture. An LCD

picture frame had a place of honor on Zara's glass-topped desk, running a slideshow of Ewart, Joshua, and Tiffany.

"Did you enjoy the training exercise last night?"

Lauren shrugged as she rolled her chair closer to the desk. "I wouldn't *exactly* describe getting dragged out of bed at midnight and being handcuffed and thrown out in the cold as my idea of fun. I guess it went okay, though, but I've got a couple of little burns on my legs."

Zara smiled. "We vary all our training programs to ensure the element of surprise, but last night's exercise was designed from scratch by Mr. Kazakov. Overall I think it worked well, although it sounds like the balance of power tilted too heavily toward the red and white shirts."

Lauren nodded. "You can't run across the open part of campus with ATVs chasing after you. You haven't got a chance. Maybe if you kept the golf carts working or something."

"I think Mr. Pike has already decided that if we run a similar exercise again, we'll ban the use of powered vehicles and issue bicycles instead. It's fairer; it cuts down the risk of accidents and the chances of a three-thousand-pound ATV ending up at the bottom of the lake."

"That's my brother's fault." Lauren laughed. "I didn't much like having to duff up the red shirts, either. I mean, some of them were only eight, and Siobhan burst into tears on me. It was horrible."

"Interesting point," Zara said as she jotted it down on a notepad. "I'll pass that along, although all the red shirts were volunteers, and they were all told they could go back to bed whenever they chose. They knew it would be a challenging night going up against black shirts, and the red shirts I've spoken to seem to have enjoyed themselves, despite a few cuts and bruises.

"Anyway, Lauren, I appreciate your feedback on the exercise, but the outstanding thing that came out of last night was your performance. You were the youngest on your team, but you had the savvy to use the ditches and go after James's cart. Then you took a risk and rescued several of your teammates. Mr. Pike and I were hugely impressed."

Lauren broke into a giant smile, but made a point not to tell the chairwoman that getting James's cart was more an accident of geography than part of any grand plan.

"Thank you, boss," she said, beaming.

"It also goes to show that you can shine, even when you're with a group of the best agents on campus. You seem to have behaved yourself over the last couple of months, and I've heard good things about your work helping out in the junior block. I spoke to little Coral this morning, and she's settling in brilliantly now."

"Cool," Lauren said. "She's such a little sweetie, and really clever, too."

"Taking all facts into consideration, I've decided to notify the mission controllers that your suspension from undercover operations has been lifted. You're now free to go on any job they pick you for."

Zara stood up and offered her hand. Lauren grinned helplessly as she shook it.

"Thanks, boss!"

A more serious look came across Zara's face as she held

on to Lauren's hand. "Don't let it go to your head. I'll be keeping a close watch on your behavior on campus. If I hear of any more scheming, plotting, or stirring, I'll be left with no option but to boot you out."

Lauren's smile had disappeared by the time Zara let go. "I know I can't risk it," Lauren said seriously. "No more scheming on campus, I swear."

Rather than use the shower in his en suite, Fahim went down to the health studio on the ground floor and took a soak in the giant Jacuzzi. A quarter of an hour dunking his head underwater and mucking about with the water jets soothed him, and he came out of the steamy bathroom dressed in a luxurious robe with a pink glow to his shriveled skin.

Hassam was in his office, and the cleaning lady was upstairs, so Fahim felt lonely as he padded barefoot down the marble hallway. A glance into the living room surprised him. His father had righted the coffee table and replaced the magazines, but the rug was gone, and when he stepped onto the carpet, he was surprised to find it damp underfoot.

Fahim curled his toes, and a creamy foam of carpet shampoo squeezed up through the gaps between them. He enjoyed the novelty of this and did it again with his other foot. Remembering his mother's bleeding nose, he figured his father had scrubbed the blood off the carpet and probably rolled up the rug so that it could be taken away and cleaned professionally.

As he turned to go back to his room, he noticed a white lump on the carpet next to the chunky base of a floor-standing lamp. He crouched forward, but recoiled when he saw that it was a tooth.

All of Fahim's life, his mother had smiled at him with the same slightly crooked front tooth with three distinctive chips in the enamel. Now, she was gone and she'd left part of her smile behind. It disgusted him at the same time as he felt an odd compulsion to examine it.

"Are you doing something in here?" Sylvia the cleaning lady asked.

Fahim was startled. He slipped the tooth into the pocket of his robe before spinning around. "Nothing much," he said.

"I've changed your bedclothes. Now, I've got to set to and clean up your father's mess in here. If I leave that shampoo to dry in without diluting it, it'll dry up as stiff as a board."

"Right," Fahim said awkwardly. "I suppose he doesn't clean carpets very often. I was going back to my room anyway."

The tooth was still a shock. Fahim desperately wanted to speak to his mum and check that she was okay. He dashed to his room, taking two stairs at a time, then sat on the clean bed and took his cell phone from the shelf above.

After dialing his mum's number, he waited a few seconds. To his surprise, he thought he could hear her distinctive ringtone. He stepped back onto the balcony overlooking the entrance where the ringing grew louder.

Fahim leaned over the railing to make sure nobody was coming before heading briskly down the hallway and through the open door of his mother's dressing room. It was a small room—at least by the standards of this house—with a sink, a dressing table, and fitted wardrobes running the length of one wall.

He tracked the ringing phone to a handbag—the one his mother had taken to Warrender Prep the previous afternoon. He pulled it out and glanced at the display: *Fahim calling*.

It was odd that his mum hadn't take her phone. It seemed even odder when he noticed her purse, her house and car keys, and the wallet in which she kept her credit cards.

Fahim realized his father was lying to him. How could his mother have run off to stay at a spa with a bloody mouth, no car keys, and no credit cards with which to pay the bill?

Had his father done something horrible—like killed her, or hurt her so badly that she was in the hospital somewhere? Fear welled up until Fahim felt like he had a table tennis ball lodged in his throat. He raced back to his bedroom, then lay on his bed, digging his fingers into a pillow as his whole body trembled.

Fahim was terrified about whatever had happened to his mum, but he was also angry with her: she'd told him the whole aeroplane thing was a misunderstanding, but then he'd overheard her threatening to go to the cops. She'd lied, his father had lied, and Fahim hated being trapped in a situation he couldn't understand or control.

"Why can't I just have normal parents?" he moaned to himself.

He racked his aching head, searching for a plan. His mum always told him to stay out of the fighting, but what if she needed his help? What if she really was dead, or if she was scared and didn't come back for weeks or months?

Hassam might have been remorsefully boiling eggs and offering presents this morning, but his mood would swing back eventually. Without Fahim's mum to defend him, another beating and a one-way ticket to Abu Dhabi was just a matter of time.

Fahim rolled off his bed and kept his cell in his shaking hand as he stepped across to his PC. Windows was on standby, so it took seconds to bring up Google on his web browser. The number had scrolled across the screen on all the TV news bulletins about the air crash, but he couldn't remember it, so typed *plane crash hotline* and clicked the gray search button.

The first link brought up a picture of a telephone and a giant 1-800 number in the center of the screen. He slid his phone open, peeked between the doors to make sure nobody was coming up the stairs, then dialed as he walked back to the bed.

It rang several times before a recorded message came on, telling him that the hotline was receiving an unprecedented number of calls and that an operator would be with him as soon as possible.

As a string quartet blared in his right ear, Fahim wondered if he was doing the right thing. If his mother was dead, he really had to speak to someone. But what if she was alive? She was opposed to whatever it was his father had done, but she clearly knew all about it, and what if that made her an accessory? What if his mum ended up being sent to prison because he'd snitched to the police?

The music in his ear stopped.

"Anglo-Irish incident hotline, Detective Love speaking. How may I help?"

What kind of person snitches on their own mother? Fahim thought before stuttering into the phone.

"I . . . I don't know for sure, but I think my dad . . . I think . . ."

The telephone operator spoke soothingly. "Why don't you calm down and start from the beginning?"

"No . . . It's just a prank, I'm sorry," Fahim stammered before sliding his phone shut, throwing it on the bed, and staring at it like it had burned his hand.

His face was red, and he dripped with sweat, but whatever his father had done, he didn't want to risk betraying his mum.

CHAPTER 17

MAC

Thirteen days later

Getting invited to the mission preparation building on CHERUB campus usually meant you were being offered a job. Lauren had walked the gently curving corridors many times and always with the same mixture of excitement and anxiety. This Monday morning was different, because she'd been invited by Dr. McAfferty and felt awkward about seeing him.

"Can I come in?" Lauren asked, poking her head into Dennis King's office.

King was one of CHERUB's two senior mission controllers. His post warranted one of the large offices at opposite ends of the building, but his job involved organizing all the routine missions, such as security checks or sizing up potential cherubs on a recruitment mission.

"Morning." King smiled as he looked at Lauren over the rims of his reading glasses. "Don't stand on ceremony. Go on through. Mac's waiting for you."

One end of King's office was an alcove with floor-to-ceiling windows in which were usually placed suede sofas and a coffee table. These had been cleared out to make a space for Dr. McAfferty to work. His desk had been extracted from a classroom, and CHERUB's retired chairman could barely be seen behind mounds of meticulously stacked paperwork, cross-indexed with hundreds of Post-it flags.

"Ahh good," Mac said with a smile. He placed a hand onto his back as he stood up and shook Lauren's hand. "I was just looking at your file, and it seems congratulations are in order."

Lauren was slightly perturbed at finding Mac in a cheerful state.

"Wasn't your thirteenth birthday last week?"

"Oh that," Lauren said happily. "It was great. I went shopping with the girls on Saturday afternoon, then we had cake and stuff in the dining room, and a corridor party in the evening."

"Sounds fun," Mac replied. "I remember when you first came to campus and you were nine. You've really changed."

Mac grabbed his back again and groaned as he sat down. This surprised Lauren because although Mac was in his late sixties, he was in good shape, and he'd regularly run on campus, right up until he'd retired.

"Are you okay?" Lauren asked warmly as she sat in a plastic chair.

"My wife was a potter," Mac explained. "A good one, too. She won all kinds of prizes and even wrote a couple of books on it."

"I remember." Lauren nodded. "You used to have that huge bowl in your office."

"My youngest daughter followed in her footsteps, and I said she might as well take her mother's clay oven. But it weighs about a ton, and I did the old back in by lugging it out to the car with my son-in-law."

Lauren smiled because Mac was smiling, but she felt really uncomfortable. She didn't know what to say, but at the same time, didn't feel she could ignore what had happened to Mac's wife and grandchildren.

"I'm really sorry about your family," she said, feeling a touch of heat in her cheeks. "Everyone was. It must have been awful."

"It certainly has been," Mac said. "But life goes on, and we had some relief this morning. It looks like the FAA is going to release all the bodies so that they can be flown home for a proper funeral."

"Great," Lauren said, although she immediately felt like she'd said the wrong thing. *I'm glad*, or *That's good* would have been okay, but blurting out *great* felt totally dumb. There was nothing great about it.

"I got so many messages from people on campus, and Zara was wonderful. She was driving me everywhere. In the end I had to tell her to go back to campus and get on with her job."

Lauren nodded. "I'm so glad they picked her as your replacement. She's really nice."

"Have you heard what I've been doing on campus?" Mac asked.

"Only gossip, though obviously everyone knows it's to do with the air crash."

"Although I'm retired from full-time work, I still have seats on several intelligence committees, and I do regular advisory work for the government, so I still had my security clearance," Mac said. "Whenever there's a major incident, someone at CHERUB has to shadow the investigation and see if and where there's a situation in which agents such as yourself might be useful. It's not the most exciting part of a mission controller's job, but I didn't fancy sitting at home brooding, so I asked Zara if she'd let me butt in. You can see the results in front of you."

Mac panned his arms around at the mounds of papers.

"And as I'm sitting here, I take it you're on to something?" Lauren asked.

"I might be," Mac said cautiously. "It's a lead, but it could easily turn out to be a hoax or a cry for attention."

"What kind of lead?"

"A phone call," Mac explained. "Over eight hundred were made to the anti-terrorist hotline in the days after the air crash. Every call they receive is recorded and categorized *A* through *D*. *A* basically means *send the cops out to arrest the bad guys now*. *B* is a serious lead that will be followed up within a matter of days or hours. *C* is a lead that's put on the back burner and may be investigated if more information comes to light. The majority of hotline calls are graded *D*, which basically means they're regarded as prank calls, nutters, and time wasters.

"I was going through the *D*-graded calls when I came across this one," Mac said as he clicked an icon on his laptop to play a sound file.

A boy's voice came out of the speaker. "*I . . . I don't know for sure, but I think my dad . . . I think . . .*"

Then the operator's voice. "*Why don't you calm down and start from the beginning?*"

And finally, the boy again. "*No . . . It's just a prank, I'm sorry,*" and the call ended with a *click*.

Lauren was underwhelmed, and Mac laughed at her expression. "You don't look wildly impressed."

"Well, it's not much to go on," Lauren said awkwardly.

"From tiny acorns mighty oaks may grow." Mac smiled. "Of course, most acorns end up as squirrel food, but every investigation has to start somewhere, and this particular lead intrigues me."

"When we did forensics training, they used the example of a murder that was solved by a tiny flake of paint found on a wooden post," Lauren said.

"A detective called Mark Love took the call," Mac continued. "He categorized it grade *D*, and the lazy sod didn't even bother doing a background check on the incoming number. It intrigued me because if there's one thing thirty years of working on campus has taught me, it's that there's often more to what children say than meets the eye."

"Like what?" Lauren asked. She leaned forward curiously, but couldn't help wondering if Mac's judgment had been affected by his grief.

"How old did that boy sound to you?" Mac asked.

"Twelve or younger," Lauren said. "The voice hadn't broken . . . I mean, it could just as easily be a girl."

"I've done background checks," Mac said. "But you're right, I wasn't sure about the sex at first either. The thing is, pranks are generally called in by teenagers, and he sounded too young. What about the accent?"

"Definitely Middle Eastern," Lauren said.

"Anything else? What about the sound of his voice?"

"He's scared," Lauren acknowledged. "So what else did you get from the background checks?"

"The phone was an unregistered pay-as-you-go, but it had been topped up several times using a debit card belonging to a woman named Yasmin Hassam, and on one occasion, by a credit card belonging to a Hassam Bin Hassam, who turns out to be her husband. The couple have one son, Fahim Bin Hassam, who is eleven years old. The family lives in Hampstead in North London, less than two miles from where you grew up."

"Not far, but it's dead snooty. You wouldn't find the likes of me and James living round Hampstead."

"I guess you wouldn't," Mac agreed.

"So Fahim's the caller?"

Mac nodded. "I don't have definitive proof, but it's the only reasonable assumption."

"So what do we know about the Bin Hassams? Do they look like potential bombers?"

"Yes and no," Mac said. "Hassam runs a trading company called Bin Hassam Dubai Mercantile, or BHDM, with his younger brother, Asif. As far as I can tell, the brothers' main business involves bulk-buying empty space on container ships leaving ports all over the world and using it to move anything they think they can sell at a profit. A lot of it is junk. Usually Chinese manufactured, stuff like the sets of cheap steak knives or tools you might find in a market or everything-for-a-pound store.

"There are a lot of these trading companies operating out of Dubai because the emirate offers low taxes and one of the world's biggest container ports. Some trading companies are reputable, but an awful lot of them have shady reputations. BHDM has been prosecuted for tax evasion in India and Germany. Over here, they're on a customs and excise watch list of companies suspected of fraud."

Lauren shrugged. "So they're a couple of dodgy businessmen, but is there any evidence linking them to terrorism?"

"The British intelligence service drew a blank, but the TSA does have the name Asif Bin Hassam on their no-fly list."

Lauren leaned back. "TSA?"

"Sorry," Mac said. "The United States's Transport Safety Administration."

"So the Bin Hassams must have been up to something," Lauren guessed.

"It's not as positive as it sounds," Mac said warily. "No-fly lists were introduced in 2003, and the name itself is a misnomer because people on the lists *are* allowed to fly; they just have to undergo rigorous extra security whenever they pass through an American airport. The major problem is that it's a list of names only; there are no dates of birth or physical descriptions, and Asif Bin Hassam is a common Arab name."

"So anyone of that name just gets automatically nabbed by airport security?"

"Exactly," Mac said. "Senator Ted Kennedy—JFK's brother—had problems because a terrorist suspect used the alias T Kennedy. That name was removed from the list, but there have been several other high-profile cases."

"Did you ask the FBI why Asif Bin Hassam is on the list?"

"They added the name to the list after it was received from an anonymous Pakistani informant," Mac said. "That's the only information they have."

"But you *still* think we're on to something?" Lauren asked.

"Yes," Mac said firmly. "And this is what makes it look really interesting."

Mac handed Lauren a small pile of photocopied credit-card statements and cell phone bills, with Yasmin Hassam's name at the top. There were more than a dozen phone calls each day, and the money being run through the credit card made Lauren's allowance look extremely humble.

"What was the date of Fahim's call to the hotline?" she asked.

"Tuesday, September eleventh; two days after the plane went down."

"There're no phone calls or credit-card payments after the tenth," Lauren gasped. "It's like Yasmin Hassam disappeared off the face of the earth. Did you check the airports?"

"And the ferries," Mac said. "If Yasmin left the country, she used a false passport."

"And on the day she disappears, her son rings the anti-terrorist hotline, scared out of his wits," Lauren said.

Mac smiled and raised a finger. "So now you're not so sure that this old codger has gone off his rocker?"

"Suppose not," Lauren said. Then she shook her head desperately. "I mean, not that I ever was."

"There's just one problem," Mac said as he threw more papers across the desk. "Fahim was expelled from his school on the tenth, and that's the educational psychiatrist's report on him."

Lauren scanned through a three-page document and read aloud some of the sections highlighted by Mac. "Fahim suffers from emotional insecurity and constantly craves attention. He seems mildly paranoid and believes that everyone is out to get him. . . . Fahim is disruptive in class and prone to fighting and facial tics. . . . His parents report regular night terrors, panic attacks, and sleepwalking."

"And he's the bedrock on which my hunch is based," Mac said uneasily.

"Tiny acorns," Lauren said as she put the report down on the desk. "It's not much, but when you put it all together, I guess it's worth looking into."

CHAPTER 18

WORK

James and Kerry had both passed CHERUB's advanced driving course, but they were still too young to drive legally, and Meryl rejected James's suggestion that they drive to Deluxe Chicken and park up a couple of streets away.

Instead, they had a cover story that they were Year Eleven pupils from a school more than thirty kilometers from where they'd be working. After being dropped at a bus stop in a village three kilometers from campus, they had to suffer a forty-minute journey on a crowded bus. The only people who used it were either too old or too poor to drive, and James found it a depressing experience.

The driver had a face like thunder, nobody smiled,

and even when James hopped out to help an old dear bring her shopping basket on board, all he got was a suspicious look like she was expecting to get mugged.

"Everyone loves teenagers in this country," James tutted as he crashed back into his seat in the row behind Kerry.

She smiled, which was a rare thing in James's presence. He'd broken Kerry's heart when he dumped her for Dana, but it had been almost a year, and James couldn't understand why things hadn't thawed out. Especially as Kerry was going out with Bruce—who was more or less James's best friend now that Kyle had retired from CHERUB.

"You heard from Bruce at all?" James asked.

Kerry nodded. "He told me to say hello. He thought it was pretty funny us two getting the same work experience."

"Is he doing okay?" James asked.

"Seems to be. He's annoyed about the weather, though. You expect it to be hot if you get sent down under, but it's the middle of their winter, and he says it's just drizzle all the time."

James smiled—this was the longest conversation he'd had with Kerry in eleven months. "What was your first-choice job?"

"Stern and Frank, the merchant bank."

James nodded. "I thought about applying for that one. It looked cool, and you got to stay in London for two weeks."

"It was the most popular option," Kerry said.

James nodded. "I heard it's not all it's cracked up to

be, though. Last year they were in the middle of some big corporate merger, and they had Katie Price ferrying documents around between buildings until about one in the morning."

"That's true," Kerry said. "And they told her to make sure she was in at seven-thirty the next morning. But I'd still rather have experience working for a merchant bank on my CV than two weeks of serving fried chicken and coming home smelling like Jumbo Rooster fries."

"Guess you can't win 'em all," James said as the bus pulled up and a woman with a double stroller and three chocolate-smeared kids struggled on board and started looking for her purse.

"They always do that," Kerry moaned. "Why can't these morons get their fare money out while they're waiting?"

The leisure park was on the outskirts of a market town fifteen kilometers from campus. There was a bowling alley, a twelve-screen cinema, and a skating rink that had burned down in the nineties and never got rebuilt. The sprawling lot had spaces for six hundred cars, and Deluxe Chicken was one of half a dozen stand-alone restaurants in a roadside strip that included all the big names in fast food, as well as a car wash, an arcade, and a pub that served pints in plastic cups so that nobody got cut in the fights that erupted on Friday and Saturday nights.

One of the doors at the front of Deluxe Chicken was boarded up. James gave it an almighty tug, but it didn't shift. Kerry banged on the front window to catch the attention of a young woman mopping the floor inside.

James guessed she was about twenty. Beneath her messy Deluxe Chicken shirt, she had a black miniskirt on, and shapely legs leading down to ankle socks and battered pink Reeboks.

"We don't serve breakfast at this branch," the woman shouted as she tapped on the face of her watch.

Kerry shook her head and yelled: "Work experience."

"What?" the woman said, cupping a hand around her ear as she moved closer to the glass.

"Work experience," Kerry repeated.

The girl smiled and pointed toward the counter inside. "Go around the back and ask for Gabriel."

"Thanks," Kerry said, giving a thumbs-up.

The alleyway between Deluxe and the pizza place next door was covered in shattered beer bottles, and they had to straddle a giant puddle of dried-out sick.

"Nice neighborhood." James smiled, but he recoiled when he saw that Kerry was giving him the evil eye. "What?"

"You know," Kerry said sourly.

"Obviously," James said. "*That's* why I asked."

"Oh, you're so innocent. I saw you eyeballing that girl's legs."

James tutted. "Get over it, Kerry."

"Not on my watch," Kerry said as she wagged her finger. "If you so much as wink at her, Dana's gonna know all about it."

"You're paranoid," James said. "I'm not a sex fiend, you know."

They reached the open back door of the restaurant. The tiled floor was covered in shoe prints, and an unhealthy grinding noise was coming out the back of a walk-in freezer.

"Hello," Kerry said loudly, putting on her polite voice. "Anyone in here?"

A wiry mixed-race man looked at them as they came into the dilapidated kitchen. They both saw *Gabriel, Manager* written on his name tag.

"Afternoon," Gabriel said sarcastically as he glanced at his watch. "Nice of you to stop by, but weren't you due here at ten? That's more than half an hour ago."

James got the urge to pop him one, but Kerry was determined to play the good girl.

"There's only one bus an hour, and it was running late," she explained.

"I'd appreciate it if you could get the earlier bus tomorrow," Gabriel said snidely. "Your training takes place on top of all my other responsibilities."

James shook his head. "I tell you what, why don't you take it out of our wages. . . . Oh wait, it's work experience, so we're not getting any."

Kerry jabbed him in the ribs and whispered, "Don't start."

"This is a place of food preparation," Gabriel announced pompously. "The golden rule is hygiene, hygiene, hygiene. If chicken isn't cooked and prepared according to the Deluxe Chicken guidelines, the result could be a nasty dose of salmonella for our customers, plus bad publicity and a hefty fine for the company. I want you to grab a shirt and hat, then scrub up your hands. There's a workbook I want you to go through, and once you've completed the questionnaire, you'll get the first star on your name badge. That star is transferable to any Deluxe Chicken branch, anywhere in the world."

"Supercool," James said.

Ten minutes later they sat at a table in the restaurant, James with a coffee and Kerry with hot chocolate. They each had a pencil and a workbook with smiling cartoon chickens on the cover and the slogan *Welcome to the global Deluxe Chicken Family.*

"Okay, Kerry, see if you can handle this one," James said, before reading aloud in an upbeat American accent. "'You have now read and studied the section on hygiene and safety. Now please answer the following six questions. Number one, after using the restroom, all members of staff must: (a) *turn out the bathroom lights*, (b) *return to work as quickly as possible*, or (c) *carefully wash and dry their hands using soap and hot water*.' Which one do you think?"

Kerry tutted. "James, we've just got here. Stop pissing about."

"It's so lame," he said, before reading out another question. "'If you find a spillage of liquid in the customer area of the restaurant, should you: (a) *place a safety warning cone over the site of the spillage and ensure that a crew member clears the spillage quickly*, (b) *ignore it because it isn't your responsibility* or (c) *pull down your pants, grab your ankles and do an enormous shit in the puddle*.'"

Kerry kept a stony silence.

"I made that last one up, by the way."

"You never grow up, do you?" Kerry said irritably. "If you get fired from this, Meryl Spencer will have you running punishment laps or scrubbing toilets on campus. And then we'll all have to listen to poor James whining about how unfair life is."

James shook his head as he waggled his cartoon chicken in the air. "Only you could take this seriously. This booklet must have been used by thirty other people; you can see the marks where the answers have been rubbed out."

Kerry managed a smile. "The disturbing thing is, it seems quite a few members of the global Deluxe Chicken family have been getting the answers wrong."

As James started to crack up, the girl in the miniskirt approached the table. Her badge said *Gemma, Crew member*, and James tried hard not to look at her body. She was sexy in a short-skirt-and-cheap-jewelry kind of way.

"Sorry," Kerry said anxiously, wrapping a hand over her smile. "Didn't mean to disturb you."

"From mopping?" Gemma said as she raised an eyebrow and shook her head. "Don't sweat it on my account. There're only two things you need to know if you wanna work here. The first is that Gabriel is a miserable hard-arsed stickler for the rules. That's because he's twenty-eight years old and he's never gotten within sniffing distance of a woman. The second is that all the urban myths you've heard about people dropping wings on the floor, spitting on your fries, and melting chewing gum in the deep-fat fryers are true—especially if I'm doing the cooking."

James laughed and put his arm up to shake Gemma's hand. "Sounds like you and me share the same work ethic." He grinned as Kerry shook her head and sighed noisily.

CHAPTER 19

TERROR

After fifteen minutes speaking with Mac, Lauren still wasn't sure about the proposed mission. While something clearly wasn't right in the Bin Hassam household, the combination of phone bills, dubious no-fly lists, and a three-sentence telephone conversation didn't make a convincing picture of a terrorist conspiracy. Zara and the ethics committee had signed off on the mission, but Lauren wondered if it was more out of respect for the retired chairman than any genuine belief in Mac's hunch.

"The crash has dropped out of the news," Lauren said as she stared at Mac between two mounds of indexed files. "Is there any information that hasn't been released to the public? I mean, they never seemed sure whether it was mechanical failure or a terrorist attack."

"It's still a tough call," Mac said. "I was patched in to a video conference between the crash investigators and the cops on both sides of the Atlantic last Friday. They're having difficulty reaching any conclusions. They've recovered over eighty percent of the aircraft and all but a handful of bodies, but the section they really need to examine is the piece of fuselage under the wing that blew out first. It would have landed in the sea more than a hundred kilometers from the main crash site and probably sank straight to the bottom of the ocean."

"But after the crash the TV said there'd definitely been an explosion," Lauren said.

"The pilots reported an initial explosion near the center of the fuselage that caused damage to the hydraulic systems and a crack in the left wing, but the million-dollar question is, *what caused it?* A bomb, a pressurized cylinder packed in someone's luggage, a short in the electrical system setting fire to something? It could be any one of a hundred things."

"And didn't they announce that some terrorist group was claiming responsibility?"

"Several groups." Mac nodded. "Terrorists thrive on publicity and you can rely on several claiming responsibility whenever something like this occurs. But none of them have offered convincing evidence to back up their claims."

"So basically it's like the guy said on the first morning after the crash: they're ruling nothing in and nothing out."

"Exactly," Mac said. "But if terrorists were involved, they could strike again. The law enforcement and the intelligence community has to treat the incident as a terror attack until the crash investigators say that it isn't."

Lauren was startled by a boy's voice coming from behind. "Morning, Dr. Mac. Is she with us or not?"

She turned quickly and saw Bethany's eleven-year-old brother, Jake, grabbing the plastic seat next to her.

Mac smiled. "I haven't had time to fully brief Lauren on the details of the mission yet."

"Oh, right," Jake said. "I can go away and come back if you want."

Mac shook his head. "You might as well stay. You can probably learn from Lauren's experience."

Lauren knew she'd eventually find herself on a mission where she was in charge of a younger agent, but she'd always imagined herself in a kindly big sister role with a younger girl rather than on a mission with her best friend's kid brother.

Jake could be a pain in the arse, and Lauren wasn't too impressed that he'd apparently been briefed before her—usually the more senior members of the team got briefed first. On the other hand, it was obvious that Fahim would get on better with a boy of his own age than a girl two years older. Jake was also desperate for his first proper mission, so hopefully he'd be on his best behavior.

"I believe you two know each other quite well," Mac said.

Lauren and Jake both nodded.

"My original plan was to use Jake and Bethany," Mac explained. "But Bethany needs time to recover from her

Brazilian mission, and Zara and I thought that you two were the next best thing.

"Fahim started attending a new school last week. It's one of the worst schools in the borough of Camden, and they're short of pupils, so we'll have no problem getting you in. With luck, Fahim won't have made any close friends yet, either.

"The mission will start off as a routine intelligence-gathering job, and if it goes well, we'll see where it takes us from there. Fahim's father works from home, which means that if you can get inside the house, you should be able not only to search and put surveillance into Hassam Bin Hassam's home, but also get inside his office and possibly access all his computer files. I'll also want you to pump Fahim for information on what he knows about his parents and their possible connections with terrorist groups."

"Assuming he's not an attention-seeking loony who called the hotline for kicks," Jake said glibly.

Lauren found Jake's interruption annoying, but chose not to say anything. "Could I suggest sending in a second boy?" she said. "There's always a chance that Fahim and Jake won't hit it off."

Mac shook his head. "If the terrorist threat is real, another attack could happen at any time, so we're going for an open approach."

"That means we tell Fahim who we really are," Jake said.

Lauren glowered at Jake and stretched out her T-shirt. "I know what an open approach is, Parker. See the black T-shirt? That means I know what I'm doing."

Jake tutted as Mac slapped his hand on the desk to

get their attention. He spoke firmly. "Jake, this is your first shot at a prestigious mission. Lauren, you're just back after a long suspension for misbehavior on campus. I would have thought you'd both have the common sense to get along with each other and make the best of this mission. Wouldn't you?"

"Yes, sir," Lauren and Jake both said.

"If this mission is going to succeed, I need to know right now that you're both mature enough to put aside any petty squabbles that you might have. Is that crystal clear?"

After another round of *yes sirs*, Lauren posed a question. "Isn't an open approach risky, though? Especially when there's no definite link to terrorism."

"The risk is very slight," Mac answered. "It's similar to the risk we take every time we bring a candidate to campus to undergo recruitment tests, and it's easily outweighed by the benefits. We know Fahim has already toyed with the idea of going to the police, and an open approach is faster.

"Instead of taking a week or more to form a friendship and infiltrate Fahim's home, we can approach and lay our cards on the table within forty-eight hours of the mission starting. If he refuses to cooperate, we can apply pressure by telling Fahim that the police will be forced to arrest his father and ask why he called the hotline."

"It's better to be friendly, though, isn't it?" Jake asked.

"Always." Mac nodded. "A contact who wants to cooperate is more reliable than someone acting under duress. I only want you to turn the thumbscrews if you can't win Fahim's trust."

"Gotcha, boss," Jake said.

Lauren was less than thrilled by the limited evidence behind Mac's mission, but Jake's obvious excitement made her realize how jaded she'd become with experience.

Mac continued. "Another factor in our favor is that Fahim is an isolated figure. Yasmin Hassam has disappeared. Fahim's only other close family member is his father, and his history of emotional problems means that he'll hardly make a credible witness if he claims that he was approached by child spies."

"So when do me and Jake move into position?" Lauren asked.

"ASAP. We've sorted accommodation close to where Fahim lives. That way you'll be able to travel back and forth to school on the same bus as him."

"And who's our mission controller?" Lauren asked. "You?"

Mac nodded. "I haven't worked as a mission controller for close to twenty years, but everyone else is snowed under, and I'll be able to continue working through the daily intelligence briefings relating to the crash while you're out at school."

Jake broke into a smile. "You're too old to be one of our parents, though. We'll have to say you're our granddad."

Mac had just lost a grandson, and Lauren thought Jake was being insensitive, but Mac seemed to see the funny side, and he gave Jake a gentle crack on the knuckles with his ruler.

CHAPTER 20

CLEAN

On a weekday the lunchtime rush didn't amount to more than ten people in the Deluxe Chicken restaurant, and the queue at the counter rarely extended beyond three.

"Hello," Kerry said brightly as she stood in front of a cash register in her nylon shirt and paper hat. "Welcome to Deluxe Chicken, may I take your order?"

The customer resembled a hot-air balloon swaddled in a leather jacket, and her body spray overpowered the smell of cooking fat.

"I want two Deluxe Mega Meals, one with Fanta, one with baked beans," she said. "And I've got the half-price coupon from this morning's paper."

Kerry looked at the hand-torn square of newspaper,

then turned around and peered through the aluminium shelves stacked with fries and chicken pieces.

"Excuse me . . . Gemma, Gabriel?" Kerry shouted, but they'd all disappeared.

She looked frantically at the grid of buttons on the register. Then she noticed one for discount and pressed it, but the screen said *enter code*, and she didn't know what that meant and she didn't want to mess it up.

"I'm sorry," Kerry said to the customer. "I don't know which button to press to get the discount on the register."

She walked around behind the counter, where she found Gemma, James, and another assistant called Randall crouching behind the area where the burgers and chicken were prepared with grins on their faces.

"Stop taking the piss and come help me," Kerry said fiercely.

James laughed as Gemma stood up and walked around to the counter. She gave the waiting woman a sarcastic smile.

"Sorry to keep you waiting," Kerry apologized.

Gemma snatched the coupon and started reading it slowly.

The customer looked angry. "I've got to get back to work in fifteen minutes; can't you get a move on?"

"Okay," Gemma said as she leaned over Kerry's till. "See at the bottom of the coupon where it says 'PROM6.' That means you press the promotions button, then the number six. Discount is for special orders, and only the manager can authorize that."

Kerry did as she was told, and the register cut the

price of one meal in half. Then she turned around and searched the racks desperately.

"Where are the beans?" Kerry shouted.

Randall stood up and shrugged. "Ready in five minutes."

According to the Deluxe Chicken training manual, you were never supposed to deter customers from buying by saying how long an order would take. You were only supposed to say "ready in a moment,' but Kerry didn't feel comfortable lying.

"Five minutes," she said.

The customer sucked air between her teeth. "Just gimme two bloody Fantas, then."

Kerry assembled the order for the impatient customer, by which time another was waiting. Randall was working the prep station, cooking pieces of chicken and making up the sandwiches, but Kerry was annoyed that she was doing all the serving while James and Gemma mucked around at the back.

Luckily for her, Gabriel stepped out of his office as two more customers joined the queue.

"Let's hustle, people," Gabriel shouted, then he glowered at Gemma. "Why do we have a queue of customers and only one register open? Randall, move your arse. Kerry, good work, keep it moving. James . . ."

The scrawny manager had taken a dislike to James backchatting him when he'd first arrived.

"James, I seem to be getting a lot of negative vibes from you," Gabriel said. "I don't think you've got the correct attitude for serving customers, so I want you to get a bucket of hot water and a broom, then you can go out into the alleyway, wash up the puke from the weekend, and sweep up all that broken glass."

James was furious at being picked on and considered telling the manager where to stick his job, but he knew he'd be in deep shit with Meryl if he got fired from work experience after less than three hours, so he filled a bucket with disinfectant and hot water and sauntered outside while moaning to himself about the crummy job he'd landed.

Back in the restaurant, the queue died down once Gemma started serving, so Gabriel invited Kerry across to the second prep station. This was only used on Friday and Saturday evenings, when the restaurant was packed with bowlers and cinema-goers.

"You seem like a smart girl," Gabriel said. "Would you like me to show you a few things?"

Kerry smiled and nodded keenly. James shot her a dark look as he came back inside carrying a pail filled with broken glass.

"Ah, James," Gabriel said smugly. "When you're done with that, you can pick up the litter and wipe down the tables inside the restaurant."

Kerry couldn't resist poking out her tongue at James as he went back out into the alleyway.

"This is a standard cooking station used in Deluxe Chicken restaurants all over the world," Gabriel explained, loving the sound of his own voice as he stood a little too close to Kerry for comfort. "Three deep-fat fryers—for chicken burgers, chicken pieces, or fries. A salad and relish station where we make up our sandwiches and baguettes, and over your head, two microwaves, to ensure that all sandwiches are delivered at an acceptable temperature.

"Your basic ingredient is frozen chicken. All the boxes come from the walk-in freezer, and on each one you'll see there's a colored square. Simply match the colors on the box to the colors on the fryer dial, and the computer automatically sets the right cooking time."

Kerry looked at the solid layers of milky fat in the fryers. "How long does it take for the fat to heat up?"

"About fifteen minutes from cold. While the oil heats up, the operator is expected to fill the containers with salad and condiments from the fridge and make sure that the preparation surfaces and the inside of the microwaves are wiped down with antibacterial gel."

Gabriel went on in this less-than-riveting fashion for another ten minutes, but being keen to make a good impression, Kerry nodded, smiled at her boss's feeble jokes, and asked lots of questions. Gabriel had an annoying habit of standing too close and Kerry found this creepy, but she ignored it right up until the moment when he planted a hand on her bum.

"Get that off," Kerry snarled. "Now."

Gabriel smiled. "Just being friendly, honey," he said, as he gave her cheek a gentle squeeze.

Kerry stepped back and put her hand up behind her boss's head. She bopped his forehead against the front of a microwave oven with such force that it broke off the bracket holding it to the wall.

"Hey," Gabriel shouted, wagging a finger in Kerry's face. "I know karate."

"Really?" Kerry said indignantly. "So do I."

James heard the commotion and came running inside to find Randall and Gemma watching in amazement.

"You lay one more finger on my arse, you skinny perv," Kerry hissed, "or anyone else's for that matter, and it'll be more than pieces of dead chickens sizzling in your deep-fat fryers."

Kerry was tempted to break Gabriel's pointing finger, but she didn't want to do any permanent damage, so she shoved him backward into the refrigerator.

"You know karate?" Kerry growled, goading Gabriel on as she moved into a fighting stance. "Come on, then, skinny. Show us your moves."

Gemma jumped up in the air and clapped her hands noisily. "You tell him, sister," she shouted. "I already warned him I'd get my Danny in here to give him a slap if his busy hands came near me again."

Gabriel was in a daze from his encounter with the microwave, and he didn't fancy his chances. "Get back to work," he steamed as his bandy arms flailed in the air. "All of you."

Then he dashed into his little office and slammed the door.

Gemma ran over to Kerry. "Are you okay?" she asked sympathetically.

"I'd bet I feel better than his head," Kerry said as she broke into a sly grin.

"All right, sis*taah*." Gemma grinned as she gave Kerry a high five. "I thought you were a square, but you showed him."

"I hate people like that," Kerry said as James stepped

up to the microwave and admired the crack Gabriel's head had made in the clear plastic door. "First day on the job when you're vulnerable . . . I mean, I know how to defend myself, but there's a lot of people out there who don't."

CHAPTER 21

SCHOOL.

The Emergency Relocation Unit is a subbranch of the intelligence service that makes short-notice housing arrangements for everyone from CHERUB agents to protected witnesses. Within two days of Mac telling them that he'd need an apartment close to Hassam Bin Hassam's Hampstead home, the local estate agencies had been scoured, and the team had discreetly signed a lease on a three-bedroom apartment in a luxury block.

Mac dealt directly with Jake and Lauren's enrollment in school. Over the years, CHERUB had become adept at manipulating school staff and computer systems to ensure that young agents ended up sitting in the same classroom as their targets.

Three hours after briefing on the mission, Mac was driving Lauren down the motorway with Jake in the back and their luggage stacked in the trunk. He drove fast because he had to buy ties and badges for Lauren and Jake from the school uniform shop and then meet with their new deputy head at five p.m.

Lauren had slept in loads of places since she'd joined CHERUB, but she always found it hard to sleep on her first night in a new bed. No amount of experience seemed to quell the butterflies that came at the start of each mission. If anything, after being shot at, kidnapped, blasted with pepper spray and nearly getting blown up, her nerves had worsened.

Mac cooked a full English breakfast, but Lauren only managed to rearrange the food with her fork a few times before downing a couple of mouthfuls of egg and pushing away the plate.

"My cooking not up to scratch?" Mac asked as he scraped the plate and loaded it into the dishwasher.

"New mission nerves," Lauren explained.

Mac nodded and glanced at his watch. "Pretty standard, I think."

"I'm always fine once the mission starts and you know what you're getting into," Lauren said. "It's fear of the unknown, I guess."

"How about you, Jake?" Mac asked. "You holding up okay?"

Jake sat at the kitchen table wolfing down his food, dressed only in the football shorts and grubby white socks he'd worn the day before. He was small for his eleven years, with spiky black hair, big brown eyes, and a boyishly cute face.

"I never get nerves," Jake said, his cheeks bulging with bacon and toast. "I've been trained. I know what I'm doing—more or less."

Lauren gritted her teeth. Jake was so full of himself it made her want to scream.

"You should take it more seriously, Jake," she warned. "If training goes wrong, you might break a few bones or have to repeat the exercise. If you mess up on a mission, you, me, and possibly lots of other people could end up dead."

"Yeah, yeah," Jake said dismissively. "I've been hearing the same lecture since I was five years old. I'm not stupid, you know? I just can't see the point in worrying about stuff you can't control." Then he looked over at Mac. "Here, Doc, your scrambled eggs are way better than the ones on campus. You got any more to spare?"

Lauren groaned to herself as she headed down the hallway to put on her school uniform. It would be a miracle if she got through the mission without giving in to the urge to crack Jake around the back of the head.

Fahim couldn't get into Burleigh Arts and Media where his friend Louis went because the school had a waiting list. Instead, he had to get a bus to the opposite end of the borough and attend Camden Central. It was the kind of inner-city school that sends shivers down the backs of posh parents.

Fahim hated it but didn't dare complain. He suspected his father still wanted to send him off to be educated in

Abu Dhabi and he didn't want to provide any excuses.

There were a few kids in Fahim's class who were okay, but lonely Year Sevens had a rough time in the public spaces. The five-minute walk from the bus stop to his homeroom was always precarious, and he'd evolved a strategy to minimize the risk. He walked fast, keeping his hands in his blazer, and his face aimed straight ahead.

Lauren and Jake had gotten an early bus to make sure that they spotted Fahim as he left his bus.

"Looks chunkier than in that picture from his old school," Jake noted as they got off the bench under the bus stop and began following a few paces behind. Their job was easy because the streets were full of kids in black uniforms and blue ties identical to their own.

"He looks depressed," Lauren said. "Definitely a fish out of water."

Fahim *was* miserable. His father kept inventing reasons why he couldn't speak to his mum and why she wasn't coming back, but Fahim was certain it was all lies. Hassam claimed to have spoken to Yasmin on her cell phone, but Fahim knew the phone sat in her dressing room with a dead battery.

At first, Hassam said Fahim couldn't talk to his mum because she was in the countryside and the reception was bad. A week later, he claimed that Yasmin had rushed off to Dubai to look after a sick relative. But Fahim knew the code to his father's safe, and he'd snuck inside while he was at a meeting and found all of the family passports inside.

Fahim had no friends at his new school, and he shut down all thoughts about his mother because they made him want to cry. In his darkest moments, Fahim had considered killing himself. He'd also thought about killing his father or going to the police, but he was scared of the consequences.

With his mother out of the picture and his father locked up, he'd end up being adopted by his grandfather or his uncle Asif. Either option was a one-way ticket to the kind of ultra-strict upbringing endured by his cousins.

"What a tub of lard," Jake said, grinning at Lauren as Fahim emerged from a newsagent with a Snickers bar and a packet of Skittles.

"Will you shut up for two seconds?" Lauren said irritably.

Jake smiled. "Sorry, you're sensitive about that, aren't you? Bethany told me that your mum was a fatty."

Lauren gritted her teeth. "Jake, if you want to keep your teeth within the vicinity of your head, I'd suggest you don't talk about my mum like that."

"Sorry," Jake said, with an obvious lack of sincerity. "Don't overreact, will you?"

By this time they'd reached the school gates. In 2003, Camden Central had opened its doors to both sexes in a desperate bid to attract more pupils, but there were still five boys for every girl. Apart from a few kids who hadn't gotten into their first-choice schools, everyone came from sink housing estates nearby. Most faces were black or Asian, and Lauren felt uneasy. White girls were a novelty here, and she could feel boys eyeing her up from all directions.

"Bend over and show me some of that arse," a Year

Eleven shouted as one of his mates blew kisses and another grabbed his crotch and thrust his hips at her.

Lauren felt her cheeks burn and consoled herself with the thought that her combat skills would shatter their oversized egos if they tried anything more than verbal insults. But she regretted being proud of her legs and picking the shortest skirt she could find from the uniform storeroom on campus.

"Where are you going?" Jake said, grabbing Lauren's blazer as they went up four steps and passed through the school entrance.

She'd been flustered by the boys and hadn't noticed Fahim taking a right turn. The narrow corridor echoed with raucous lads, and a kid screamed as a football blasted against a door centimeters from his head.

"So close," someone shouted. "You're lucky."

"Fahim," a muscular Asian boy called Alom shouted.

Alom's mates chanted, "Fahim, Fahim, Fahim," as Fahim got grabbed by his collar and bundled against the wall. They were all in Year Nine, and Fahim had the dejected look of someone who knew he was beat.

"Skittles," Alom said happily as he extracted the red packet from Fahim's blazer.

He ripped them open, tipped back his head, and poured them decadently into his mouth. About half of the Skittles made it between Alom's lips; the remainder bounced off his face and clattered down to the tiled floor. Lauren and Jake stopped walking and leaned against the wall like they were waiting for class.

"Faaaahim!" another bully shouted as he jabbed Fahim in the ribs.

"Here's the . . . ," Alom said as he struggled with a mouth crammed with Skittles. "The thing is, Fahim, I seem to have lost my appetite."

He gobbed the multicolored clump of chewed-up Skittles into his hand and broke into an evil smile.

"I tell you what, Fahim, why don't *you* eat them?"

Fahim looked desperately up and down the corridor, hoping for a teacher to save his butt.

"I insist." Alom grinned. "Eat them up, or I'll be seeing you again outside school."

A tense crowd had gathered around Fahim, including a few of his fellow Year Sevens. Jake reared forward, but Lauren pulled him back.

"If we save him now, he'll owe us big," Jake said.

"Use your brain," Lauren said. "There'll be a riot if you start on that lot. At best we'll get busted for fighting, at worst one of those nuts will pull a knife out of his jacket and stick it in your back."

The crowd had started to chant "Eat, eat, eat . . ." and Fahim looked close to tears.

"I'll beat you, Fahim," Alom threatened.

The rest of his gang closed in so that Fahim could smell their breath. Everyone quieted down as Fahim took the blob of spit-soaked Skittles from Alom's beefy hand. He opened his mouth and raised it to his lips.

"Chomp it down, fat boy."

As the blob was almost entering his mouth, Fahim thrust his palm forward and screamed out: "Bollocks."

The Year Nine backed up, but Fahim got Alom in the chin with the blob, then mashed it down the front of his shirt, leaving a multicolored trail. Everyone was stunned by this turn of events, and Fahim used his bulk to surge forward. He shoved desperately through the crowd as it let out a collective gasp.

"Crazy dog." Lauren grinned.

But the Year Nines weren't so happy. "You can run, fat boy," Alom shouted as he stared aghast at his stained shirt. "But when I catch you, you're *dead*."

Some of the Year Seven kids started laughing. Lauren glowered at a Year Eleven who said, "Hey, baby," as he brushed past. Then Alom completely lost it. He started lashing out and going psycho.

"What are you all staring at? Get out of my face, you Year Seven dicks, or I'll mash you up."

Then he turned and saw that some of his own mates were laughing.

"What's your problem?" Alom shouted. "Why'd you let him run off?"

The gang all shrugged and mumbled stuff about being taken by surprise.

Lauren looked at her watch, then down at Jake. "Go to your classroom and try being nice to Fahim," she whispered. "My homeroom is up on the next floor, but I've got my phone if you need me."

"Cool," Jake smiled. "Fahim might be a fat arse, but you've got to admire his balls."

James felt depressed as he started his second day at Deluxe Chicken. Kerry had come to work in ripped jeans and the mud-encrusted Nikes she used for running on campus. She deliberately broke the rules by leaving her Deluxe Chicken shirt unbuttoned so that you could see one of Bruce's T-shirts with the gory poster from a martial arts movie on it.

She was clearly looking for an excuse for a fight with the manager, but Gabriel cowered in his tiny office pretending to be busy.

This left Gemma in charge of the staff, which consisted of James, Kerry, and a friendly old dude called Harold, who worked three days a week to supplement his pension. A couple more would come in at lunchtime to deal with the busy period.

"Gabriel's scared of you, Kerry," Gemma said happily as the four staff members stood around the kitchen, leaning against the equipment. "He knows if you report him for what he did, he might get fired, and even if they couldn't make it stick, he'd never get promoted."

Kerry had her bum on the service counter—another breach of the rules. "He'd better be scared of me." She grinned. "If he ever touches me again, I won't bop his head against the microwave, I'll stick it inside and give him eight hundred watts."

James was smiling his head off. "I *love* this," he said. "You guys don't know Kerry, but she's always a good girl. This is totally unlike her. It's like that episode of *The Simpsons* where Lisa goes bad and starts smoking and tells Miss Hoover to shove it."

"I'm not *that* perfect, James," Kerry protested. "The way you carry on sometimes, you'd think I didn't even fart."

James wanted to joke some more, but he couldn't take the argument with Kerry any further without using examples of stuff that had happened on campus, and he couldn't do that while Gemma and Harold were around.

James noticed that his ex had been a lot chattier on the bus that morning, and with her boyfriend, Bruce, away on a mission and her best friend, Gabrielle, spending most of her time with her boyfriend, Michael, he suspected Kerry was lonely. She might even be up for an illicit snog if he tried his luck. . . .

But a warning claxon went off in James's head the

instant he thought this. There were lots of good reasons why he shouldn't try getting off with Kerry again: when they were together, their relationship always lurched from one train wreck to the next. He now had a completely cool relationship with Dana, and Kerry was now Bruce Norris's girlfriend. Not only was Bruce one of James's best friends, he was a martial arts expert who would shatter the spine of anyone who touched his girl while he was away on a mission.

Against all this solid reasoning was one undeniable fact: there had been chemistry between James and Kerry since the first day they met. James loved Dana, but that did nothing to alter the tingle down his back every time Kerry smiled in the way he liked, or got her pouty look when things didn't go her way. He could never put his finger on exactly what it was Kerry had, but she had it in spades.

Growing up on CHERUB campus, Jake knew that you got thirty laps for late homework, washing-up duty for backchatting a teacher, and punishments you didn't even want to think about if you were caught doing something more serious. But he'd never been inside a London public school, and it was a big shock.

Kids sat on the desks and carried on talking when the teacher told his class to sit down for morning attendance. People belched out loud and lobbed litter out the windows. When they got to first lesson, Jake sat near Fahim but didn't start talking because he'd been trained not to act pushy.

It took the teacher ten minutes to get the class to settle down, then another ten taking attendance and listening to excuses as to why nobody had done their homework. When he got around to handing out exercise books and a worksheet, half the kids either didn't have pens or claimed not to have pens, and then a bunch of nutters started swinging from the curtains at the back of the room, at which point the teacher went red and started screaming.

Twenty minutes into the lesson, Jake realized that he'd left his timetable in homeroom and had no clue what subject was being taught. Then a bunch of Year Ten girls started battering someone in the corridor outside, and Jake's class threw stuff around and went mental while the teacher stepped out to deal with the girls.

"It's a lunatic asylum," Jake told Lauren when he met up with her in the main lobby at morning break. "How the hell can anyone be expected to learn anything?"

Lauren laughed as she offered Jake half of her Twix bar. "Nobody does learn anything. This school has the worst exam results in the borough and almost the worst in the country."

Jake grinned guiltily. "It's kind of fun, actually."

"Yeah, Jake. Unless you're like the boy in my class who turned up to second period practically crying cos two hard cases kicked him in the nuts and pissed on his bag."

"No way," Jake gasped.

"Yes way," Lauren said. "Remember, the kids in your class have just moved from primary school. They're angelic compared to my lot."

Up ahead there was a massive metallic slam as a group of Year Eight boys bundled into a vandalized locker unit. Year Sevens were refilling Fruit Shoot bottles from the drinking fountain and squirting them at one another.

"I've been watching Fahim," Jake said as he kept a wary eye on the water fight.

"Where is he now?" Lauren asked.

"He stayed back at the end of history to talk to the teacher, but that's the first time I've seen him really speak to anyone. There's a couple of Asian boys in my class, and I think Fahim's trying to get in with them, but they're best mates with each other and they're totally ignoring him."

"Poor Fahim." Lauren nodded sadly. "It makes our job easier, at least."

"I know," Jake said. "Next class is combined science. I don't know what the seating arrangements are like, but if I can get near to Fahim, I might try to be his lab partner or something."

Lauren nodded. "Okay, but however it pans out, we'll introduce ourselves properly after school, so don't lose sight of him then."

Harold said he liked to keep busy, and James, Kerry, and Gemma were happy to let him work the register and wipe down the odd table. A couple of extra staff came in to work over lunchtime, and once the rush was over, James found himself sharing a lunch break with Gemma.

"Where you going, James?" she asked as she pulled on a white puffy jacket.

"Dunno," James said. "Buy lunch or something, I guess. There's a PC World across the street. I might have a wander over there for a browse."

Gemma smiled. "Never had you pegged for a computer geek."

"I'm not," James said defensively. "Just . . . I'll get some money for my birthday in a few weeks, and I was gonna see if there were any decent computer games around."

"Suit yourself," Gemma said as she did up her zip. "I'm going up to the pub on the corner. My Danny works behind the bar, and the grub's not too bad."

James shrugged. "Pubs won't usually serve me. I still don't exactly pass for eighteen."

"I guess not, but where I sit's usually closed to the bouncers. You'll be fine, and they do a wicked chili burger with rice."

The smell of frying in Deluxe Chicken had stunted James's appetite, but the chili burger sounded okay, and the prospect of wandering around shops for an hour wasn't exactly exciting.

When they reached the pub, Danny came out from behind the bar and gave Gemma a kiss. He wore head-to-toe denim and looked like he was touching thirty. There were faded tattoos on his beefy hands, including a couple of handmade prison tattoos and an Arsenal logo.

James followed Danny and Gemma behind the bar and into an area of the pub with dartboards and pool tables that were only open on evenings and weekends. Gemma lit up a cigarette as they sat in the deserted space with pints of beer, waiting for their burgers.

"You're an Arsenal man," James noted as he downed a third of his beer.

"Too right," Danny said.

"You ever go to matches?"

Danny shrugged. "Not in a really long time. When I was your age, I used to go to Junior Gunners. It was such a laugh. Three quid to get in, and then you'd go crawling round all the pubs afterward, come home completely plastered, and get shouted at by your ma. Nowadays, it's fifty quid a game; you've gotta be loaded, ya know?"

James nodded. "I've heard Highbury was pretty mental in the old days. Did you ever see any trouble?"

Danny laughed. "If I couldn't see trouble, I'd start some. One time I got nicked for stealing a couple of Chelsea mugs. Thought they were well hard, but they went down like sacks of shite."

"What did you get?" James asked.

"Caution," Danny admitted, sounding almost embarrassed. "But I was only sixteen. Getting nicked was like a badge of honor. When I finally got sent down a couple of years later, it was for head-butting a priest when I was robbing the registers at Tesco."

"Priest," James laughed.

"I was dead nervous, you see. I saw this bloke all in black in the corner of my eye, and I thought he was a copper . . . Another round?"

James stood up and pulled out his wallet. "I'll get them in."

"Don't worry, son." Danny smiled. "You don't think I'm paying for any of this, do you?"

Danny came back a couple of minutes later with three more pints and three shot glasses filled with tequila.

"Down the hatch," Danny shouted as he emptied the shot glass and drained half of his Guinness. "So when did you last go to the Arsenal, James?"

"Years ago," James said. "I keep meaning to sort it out, but you've got to get a membership card and stuff."

"It gets on my tits, all that." Danny nodded.

Gemma wasn't keen on spending her lunch break talking about football. "Have you still got the picture of our boys?" she asked.

"Sure," Danny said as he pulled his wallet away from his enormous denim-clad butt and flipped it open.

James was surprised to see a picture of Gemma holding a baby boy, while another aged about four stood on the carpet beside her.

"They're cute." James smiled. "You must have been pretty young when you had the first one."

Gemma pointed to Danny. "The dirty sod knocked me up when I was sixteen," she giggled. "My old dad went mental."

"Gemma's dad's a dentist," Danny laughed. "Drives a Lexus, right pompous git."

Gemma nodded. "He won't have nothing to do with me now. I think he wanted me to marry some boring accountant or something."

"Plus, I smacked him one when he got up on his high horse," Danny added.

James was starting to get the impression that Danny wasn't exactly the friendliest person on the planet.

"So, do you go clubbing, James?" Danny asked.

"Too young," James said. "I mean, I've heard the cops keep all the clubs around here on a tight leash."

Danny smiled. "Cops are cops. Put a crate of whiskey in the back of a panda car and they'd let you run a human sacrifice. Do you know the Outrage Club?"

"Isn't that a gay place?" James asked.

"Years back," Danny said. "But these days they're open

to all sorts, and I'm starting up my own night there every Wednesday. Me and a couple of mates work the door, so if you show, I'll make sure you get in. Then there's a DJ who's my mate's little brother. It's not really my type of music, but the students rip up a storm."

"You should come," Gemma said. "Especially if you've never been clubbing before."

"Yeah, I guess," James said as he tried thinking up an excuse to get off campus. "Can I bring my girlfriend?"

"Which one?" Gemma asked cheekily.

James was startled by this. "Dana. I've only got one."

"What about Kerry?" Gemma teased. "You said she's your ex, but I can tell there's still shit going on with you two."

James shook his head as Danny burst out laughing. "Bring Kerry, Dana, and anyone else you like. Maybe you'll be able to get it on with the pair of them."

After rapidly drinking a shot of tequila and a pint and a half of beer, James was starting to feel drunk, and he laughed noisily. "I reckon I could live with that, Danny."

Gemma shook her head and tutted. "In your dreams, James."

Meanwhile, one of the other staff had placed the three burgers on the bar.

"Another pint, James?" Danny asked as James got up to help him carry the food and cutlery to their table.

"Why not?" he slurred, realizing that he'd be smashed by the time he got back to work.

CHAPTER 29

LATE

Jake and Fahim's class took things too far in the lesson after lunch and ended up with their head of year bursting into the art studio and giving them all detention. When the bell rang for the end of school, the twenty-eight Year Sevens had to walk around the corridors and playground, picking up litter.

Jake and Fahim spent the two afternoon classes sitting together, and during detention they were assigned to clear the same section of corridor. When the head of year dismissed them, they headed off to catch their bus. Jake looked at a text message.

"My sister Lauren's waiting for me at the bus stop," he said before pocketing his phone.

But Fahim had other concerns and glanced nervously in all directions as they stepped gingerly through an after-school kick-about on the concrete pitch.

"They've probably gone," Jake said casually. "School finished hours ago."

Fahim wasn't so confident. "You should go," he said. "If Alom finds me, he'll batter me, and if you're with me, his mates will get you."

Jake slid his phone out and typed a quick text to Lauren: LEAVING NOW COULD BE TROUBLE.

"Shit," Fahim said as he spotted Alom and his Year Nine cronies hanging out by some telephone booths fifty meters from the school gate. He gave Jake a shove in the back. "Get away from me."

But Jake shook his head. "We're mates."

"Don't be a tit," Fahim said as the six Asian Year Nine boys spotted him and chanted "Fahim, Fahim, Fahim" as they started jogging toward him. "What difference are you gonna make against that lot?"

But there was no more time to argue. Alom grabbed Fahim by his collar and yanked him up so he was on tiptoes.

"You're coming for a walk," he said as he looked around. "Too many teachers around here."

Two other lads pushed Jake away. "Piss off, white boy."

Fahim sprawled out as the Skittle-stained bully punched him hard in the back.

"Like it down there in the dirt, fats?" Alom grinned as he kicked Fahim in his chubby thigh. "Since you don't like eating Skittles, I'm gonna take you to the park and find a nice juicy dog turd for your dinner."

"Leave him the hell alone," Jake shouted as he hit one of the Year Nines in the guts with an explosive upward punch.

The Year Nine was a beefy dude twice Jake's size, but he hadn't been expecting it, and he made an agonized groan as he hit the pavement.

Jake panicked as the other lad tried to get an arm around his neck. He was a third *dan* karate black belt and expert in the most effective techniques from several other fighting disciplines; but no amount of skill can compensate for being little, and he'd started a fight with six guys who weighed twice as much as him.

"You're an idiot, Jake," Fahim said. "This is my problem."

The most important thing when fighting much heavier opponents is to make sure they don't pin you. Jake couldn't afford to let anyone get close. He stepped backward before launching a roundhouse kick, slamming his second opponent in the stomach.

As two Year Nines lay on the ground, Jake continued backing off as three more stepped over their bodies and rushed him. In the movies, the baddies always have the decency to wait in line and get beaten up one at a time, but that never happens in real life.

As Alom punched Fahim in the stomach, Jake faced off three well-built Asian youths. He looked backward over his shoulder and realized that screaming his head off and running back inside the school was the safest option, but if he did that, Fahim would be left at Alom's mercy.

"Come on then, wankers," Jake said as he ducked into a fighting stance.

"It's the Karate Kid," one of the Year Nines jeered.

But he stopped smiling as Jake lunged and punched him in the mouth. His jaw crunched, but Jake had made a fatal error by going for the boy in the middle. As the youth moaned in pain, the lads on either side got their arms around Jake.

He wriggled for all he was worth, but the lad he'd punched in the guts was back on his feet, and Jake knew he was doomed when they got his ankles and scooped him off the ground. After a moment of indecision, the three lads carried Jake kicking and swearing toward the curb, where they bent him over a metal bollard and started landing heavy punches.

"Leave my little brother alone," Lauren shouted breathlessly as she ran across the street.

Being a girl worked to her advantage. She was the same age as the three lads pounding Jake, but the boys were bigger, and they didn't think she'd do anything except yell at them to stop. This was a serious mistake.

When kids learn karate at the local community center, they're taught techniques that are playground friendly. Cherubs routinely go into dangerous situations and are taught to mercilessly target the weakest areas of the body.

Facing three opponents, Lauren wanted to take down two in one go. She moved expertly, swinging a palm in from either side, slamming two heads together. Both lads collapsed in a daze.

Jake was winded after taking more than a dozen hard punches, but his instincts had been honed by hundreds of hours' of combat training, and he grabbed the bollard tightly before launching a two-footed back kick. His black Nikes hit the third boy so hard that he flew across the width of the pavement and into the breeze-block wall surrounding the school. Furious after the beating, Jake knocked him cold with a kick to the temple.

"Feeling big now?" he shouted before breaking into a coughing fit.

Meanwhile, Lauren had gone after the last man standing. Alom still had hold of Fahim, but his brain couldn't handle what his eyes were telling him.

"Let Fahim go or I'll break your neck," she ordered.

Alom looked at his mates: two in a daze after getting their heads knocked together, one on the ground holding a dislocated jaw, one slumped against the wall with a bloody nose and a split lip, and one who'd run off rather than get knocked down again.

"I don't want no trouble," Alom said ridiculously as he let Fahim go and smiled innocently at Lauren. But he turned around and ran before she got close.

"You okay, Fahim?" Lauren asked.

Jake looked at the carnage as he hobbled toward Lauren, clutching his stomach. A few kids hanging around the school gate had witnessed the whole thing, and he realized that there were going to be cops on the scene and an ambulance for at least one member of Alom's crew.

He turned toward the gate and shouted: "We didn't start this. Anyone snitches and they're dead, you understand?"

Lauren wasn't too impressed with what had occurred, and she glowered at Jake as he came near. "Make a scene, why don't you? We'd better get the hell out of here."

Jake and Fahim were both hurting, but Lauren grabbed their blazers and forced them to walk quickly.

The first bus stop was only two minutes from the school, so they carried on walking toward the next one. This took them past a McDonald's, which was pretty empty at this time of the afternoon.

"Inside," Lauren said stiffly.

Fahim shook his head. "I haven't got any money."

"I'm buying," Lauren said. "We need to talk."

Fahim smiled awkwardly. "I appreciate what you two did, but I'm not stupid. If anyone asks what happened back there, I'm just gonna keep my mouth shut."

But Fahim's smile was fake. He was terrified that news of the brawl would reach home, and if he got suspended or expelled, it would be the excuse his father needed to send him abroad.

"I don't want to talk about the fight," Lauren said as she pulled a twenty-pound note out of her blazer pocket. "You two must at least be thirsty after all that lot."

As Lauren said this, she noticed that Jake was in a state. The Year Nines had landed some bad punches, and his eyes were moist. "Do you want a tissue or anything, Jake?"

"I'm not crying," he said defensively. "Just get me fries and a Coke."

There were no customers waiting at the counter, so it only took a couple of minutes for Lauren to come back with a tray of fries and soft drinks.

"I got six nuggets," she said as she sat with Jake and Fahim in the quietest corner of the restaurant. There were a few kids from a nearby primary school with their parents, and some pensioners drinking cups of tea, but basically the place was empty.

Fahim opened the box of nuggets. "Two each," he said.

Lauren shook her head. "I'm vegetarian."

"None for me," Jake groaned. He was still clutching his chest, and Lauren was getting worried about him. "Are you sure you're okay?"

"Been better," Jake croaked. "Think I'm just winded."

Lauren looked at Fahim and sounded serious. "Fahim, there's something I have to tell you. Jake and I came here to help you."

Fahim looked mystified. "I really appreciate what you did. If Alom had his way, I'd be eating dog turd instead of McNuggets right now."

Lauren shook her head. "That's not what I meant. Two weeks ago, you made a call to the anti-terrorist hotline. You sounded extremely scared about something, and we've noticed that your mum has disappeared."

Fahim's jaw dropped, exposing a nasty-looking mouthful of chewed-up chicken. "Pardon me?"

"I know it's a bit of a shock," Lauren continued as she tried a reassuring smile. "But keep calm and listen carefully. Jake and I work for the government. The intelligence service traced you from your call."

Fahim tapped his head. "You're messing with me. How come you know all this?"

Jake didn't sound too healthy, but he took up the story. "Our people have been running background checks on your father, but rather than send a bunch of police in to arrest him and start asking questions, we wanted to speak to you first and get some more information."

"Was the call a hoax?" Lauren asked bluntly. "Do you

think your dad might have anything to do with the air-liner that crashed?"

Fahim was in shock. He thought about trying to fool Lauren, but the past two weeks had been the worst he'd ever known, and he was desperate to speak to someone about his nightmarish excuse for a life.

Fahim spluttered as he pointed at Jake. "You're eleven. Lauren, you're, like, thirteen. You work for the government. . . . I mean, what are you, kiddie detectives or something?"

"Kind of." Lauren smiled. "Here's the thing, Fahim. All we have to go on is your call. If the cops moved in and arrested your dad with no clue what's going on, they'd probably make arses of themselves. We know you reached out and called the hotline because you wanted to help, but you were scared and you hung up. We under-stand that, but now we're here to help you."

"And we can help find your mum," Jake added.

"Help how?" Fahim asked.

"We want all the evidence you have," Lauren said.

Fahim shrugged. "I don't have evidence. Just some stuff I overheard when my parents were fighting."

"What stuff?" Jake asked.

"Something to do with the Anglo-Irish crash, for sure," Fahim said. "I don't know what they did, but I heard them fighting about it. Then that night they were fight-ing again, and my mum threatened to go to the police and tell them what was going on. When I got up the next morning, she was gone."

"Do you think your dad killed her?" Jake asked.

This wasn't subtle, and Lauren shot him an angry look.

"She doesn't have friends or relatives in this country," Fahim said weakly. "I hope she's alive, but if she is, she must have run off in the middle of the night with a bloody mouth, no phone, and no money."

"What does your dad say?"

"Lies," Fahim said, close to tears. "First, he said she was at a spa, then she was supposedly looking after someone. The last time I mentioned her name, he just glowered at me, like I shouldn't. And he wiped the CCTV tapes."

Lauren's eyebrows shot up. "What CCTV?"

"We've got cameras covering the front door and the outside of our house," Fahim explained. "I waited for my dad to go out and looked for the recordings from the night my mum disappeared, but he'd put in a new set of tapes."

"We know she hasn't used her credit cards or cell phone since the night you called," Lauren said. "Although, if she was involved in a plot to bring the plane down, she might well have another identity."

Fahim shook his head. "She threatened to go to the police. . . . I don't know anything for sure, but she definitely didn't like whatever it was my dad has done. The thing is, I've got no evidence, and the school shrink thinks I'm a nutter, so who's gonna believe *me*?"

"That's where we come in," Lauren explained soothingly. "Tell your dad that we're friends from your new school. If you invite us home, is he likely to complain?"

"He doesn't mind me having mates round, as long as they don't make a racket." Fahim shrugged. "Our house is pretty big, and my dad's usually either out or he works in his office until at least seven."

"So who looks after you?" Jake asked.

"The cleaning lady is around in the morning. It used to be my mum, but now, if Dad's out at a meeting or something, I'm on my own until he comes home and makes dinner. Sometimes that's not until eight, or even later, so he leaves me a note and a ready meal to go in the microwave."

Lauren tried to speak with authority. "Our first step would be to discreetly gather as much evidence as we can. We've already bugged your dad's home and cell phone calls from the exchange. We'll also try to get listening devices in the house to record his conversations, and we want to go through all his documents and computer files."

Fahim looked worried as he bit the end off a couple of fries. "And what about me?"

"What do you mean?" Jake asked.

"Suppose you get evidence against my dad, and my mum doesn't come back?"

Lauren wasn't prepared for this. "Our files say that you have an uncle nearby and heaps of relatives in Pakistan and the United Arab Emirates."

Fahim shook his head. "My uncle Asif and my dad do everything together. If my dad is involved, Asif is too, for sure. If they go down, I'll end up being adopted by my granddad, and I hate it in Abu Dhabi. He's megarich, but he's the most miserable old git you'll ever meet.

"All my aunts and uncles tiptoe around doing exactly what Granddad wants them to do because he's nearly eighty and they want their share of his loot when he dies. My cousins are a laugh, but they get sent away to Islamic schools that are, like, megastrict. They have to learn the entire Koran by heart, and they get beaten if they recite one word wrong."

"What about your mum's family?" Jake asked.

"My mum's parents were from Pakistan, and they came to the Emirates to work as servants. They're piss-poor, and I've never even met any of them."

Mac hadn't anticipated this problem. "So what is it you want?" Lauren asked.

"I just can't help you," Fahim said firmly. "I hate my dad's guts, but if I snitch on him, I'm totally screwed."

"Maybe Abu Dhabi isn't that bad when you get used to it," Jake said.

"It's nothing to do with the country," Fahim stressed. "My granddad's a psycho, and what he says goes. If it wasn't for him, I'd have gone to the cops the minute I realized that my mum was probably dead."

Lauren ran tense hands through her hair and tried to think. "Okay, Fahim, would you help us if we found somewhere for you to live?"

"Like where?" Fahim asked.

Jake smiled. "You could join CHERUB and live with us."

Lauren glowered at Jake. He wasn't supposed to mention the name under any circumstances.

"What's CHERUB? Is that the organization you work for?"

"Yes," Lauren said reluctantly. "But you can't just join. I mean, you need to be extremely fit and speak other languages and pass loads of tests."

"I speak good Arabic," Fahim said. "Practically fluent."

Lauren was furious with Jake. Not only had he mentioned CHERUB by name, but with Fahim's history of psychiatric and behavioral problems, she was sure he'd never get in.

"I'll speak to our boss and see what we can sort out," Lauren said cautiously. "For all we know, your mum's gonna turn up again."

"I don't wanna be dumped in some grotty children's home," Fahim said, and the way he ignored Lauren's comment about his mum made it clear that he thought she was dead. "I want to grow up like an ordinary kid."

"Joining CHERUB is a long shot," Lauren sighed, "but a foster family shouldn't be a problem."

Fahim pondered over the last McNugget. "You're not winding me up because there's no way you could have known about the phone call, but I want to speak to an adult and . . . I mean, I want to know what happened to my mum and if you guarantee that I'll never have to go and live with my granddad, I'll do everything I can to help you."

CHAPTER 24

HOME

It was four thirty by the time the bus came to take Lauren, Fahim, and Jake back to Hampstead. They all went up to the top deck. Jake and Fahim sat at the front, while Lauren found empty seats up the back. She discreetly called Mac and explained the conversation in McDonald's.

"Let me talk to Fahim," Mac said.

There were a few people at the front of the bus, so Lauren called Fahim over. Jake followed down the aisle as Fahim took her phone.

"Hello, Fahim," Mac said calmly. "I understand that your situation is a difficult one, but I'm delighted that you want to help us."

"That's okay," Fahim said as he sat on a seat in the back row. "My life's a mess. I need a way out."

"If you help us to find evidence against your father, I'm prepared to guarantee that you'll never have to go to Abu Dhabi. We can set you up with a comfortable home and provide enough money to ensure that you're properly looked after."

"I know what I heard my parents saying," Fahim said. "But I don't have proof. What happens to me if you don't find any evidence?"

"It would be more difficult," Mac said cautiously. "But our investigation will be thorough, and while I can't say what will happen under every possible circumstance, I give you my word that we'll look out for you."

Fahim had been trapped in a nightmare for two weeks, and it almost seemed too good to be true. "I guess that's fair," he said. "But can I get something in writing?"

"We're part of the secret service, so we can't make a legal agreement," Mac explained uneasily. "But I'd be happy to sit down with you and discuss your needs. However, there's one thing you'll have to consider very carefully."

"What's that?"

"If we set you up with a new identity, there's no going back. The separation from your family and its money will be irreversible."

Fahim didn't hesitate. At eleven years old he cared far more about being a happy child than a rich adult. "As long as I don't end up living with my granddad," he said resolutely. "My family in Abu Dhabi all have two things in common: They're all rich, and they're all miserable."

"Okay," Mac said. "But I really want you to think carefully about this."

"Is there any chance I could join CHERUB like Lauren and Jake?"

Lauren had avoided telling Mac about Jake giving away the name, and the retired chairman practically swallowed his false teeth. "Fahim, CHERUB is . . . There are very stringent criteria for entry."

"Lauren said that already, sir, but would I be allowed to try? Can't I at least get an interview or something?"

"I suppose," Mac said reluctantly. "But I'm not in any position to guarantee entry."

Fahim broke into a big smile. "I understand," he said.

"I'll need a few hours to make arrangements, and then I'd suggest that we meet somewhere and discuss your future properly. I don't want you to rush into decisions that you'll regret, but we do need to move quickly. How about I let you think of any questions you might have overnight, and we'll meet tomorrow morning, before school?"

"That's fine by me," Fahim said. "I can tell my dad that I'm going in early to play football in the playground or something. And I know you just want me to be sure, but I swear I won't change my mind."

"I hope not," Mac said softly. "Could you put Lauren back on, please?"

Fahim smiled as he handed the phone over.

"Hey," Lauren said cheerfully. "Everything sorted?"

Mac growled, "How the *hell* does he know the name CHERUB? Don't answer me while Fahim can overhear, but there's going to be trouble later."

Mac's ire made Lauren's heart skip, but she knew it wasn't her fault. "I'm sure Jake will be glad to explain." She smiled, anticipating the way Mac would lay into him.

By the time Jake and Lauren got home, Jake's chest was swollen, and he was struggling to breathe. Mac took him straight back downstairs and drove to the nearest casualty unit for an X-ray. Lauren had changed out of uniform and was sitting in front of the TV when the pair returned holding boxes of take-out pizza and garlic bread.

Jake had his school shirt unbuttoned and bandages strapped tightly around his chest. Unfortunately for him, severely bruised ribs weren't enough to earn him much sympathy.

"I'm sorry," Jake said weakly as he sat on the sofa chewing a slice of Hawaiian.

Mac shook his head. His voice was calm, but you could tell that he was really angry. "I know this is the first day of your first big mission, Jake. I could have excused one slipup, but two smacks of carelessness."

"I only said CHERUB by mistake. It's one little word."

"Easily done when you're nervous," Mac acknowledged. "But it was a stupid thing to even mention, and you've done enough role-playing exercises on campus to know better. However, it's the incident outside the school that really troubles me. What in the name of *god* possessed you to start a fight against six boys so much bigger than yourself?"

"You might have a black belt, but you're not Superman," Lauren added. "And the way you kicked that guy in the head, he could have ended up with brain damage."

Jake was a sorry figure, with his bandages and his crumpled school uniform. He was clearly shaken up, but Lauren thought Jake was too cocky for his own good and reckoned the dose of harsh reality would do him good.

"You're extremely lucky that Lauren arrived when she did," Mac said.

"But she took ages getting there," Jake said. "I sent her a text."

This was the one area where Lauren realized she was at fault. "I could have stayed by the gates instead of under the bus shelter," she admitted. "But I belted over there as soon as I got his message."

"And was I supposed to stand there and let Fahim get beaten up?"

"You should have waited for Lauren," Mac said. "What do we teach you in training about fights getting out of control?"

"Okay," Jake said bitterly. "I know."

"What do we teach you?" Mac insisted. "Say it."

Jake shook his head, but he didn't dare tut. "Gangs pose a much greater threat in a violent situation because the presence of other gang members means that they all egg each other on."

"I already pulled you off and told you not to butt in at nine o'clock this morning," Lauren added. "What if one of them had a knife? What state would you have ended up in if I'd arrived two minutes later?"

Jake stood up and shouted, "Lauren, piss off, okay? I know I messed up, but have you got to keep rubbing it in?"

"Get your arse back on that chair," Mac barked, finally losing his cool. "Lauren is an experienced agent. This isn't a game, Jake. This isn't you hanging around on campus with your mates. Several people ended up seriously hurt, you and Lauren are lucky to have gotten off relatively unscathed, and for all we know the police are going to want to question the pair of you about the fight. If they want to talk to Fahim and it gets back to his father, he won't let you two anywhere near his house and our mission will be blown before you've even gotten through the front door."

Jake opened his mouth like he was going to say something, but instead he sobbed, "I said I was sorry."

Lauren had never seen Jake as anything other than Bethany's annoying kid brother, but seeing him cry made her feel horrible. She remembered how worried she'd been before her first mission and the sense of relief when she didn't mess up.

"Can I be excused?" Jake said, trying to disguise his tears as Mac handed him a square of kitchen towel to wipe his face.

"Can you sort out the police?" Lauren asked.

"I expect so," Mac sighed. "I've already contacted campus, and hopefully the officers will get a message from above telling them not to investigate the fight too closely."

Jake looked sadly at Lauren. "Please don't tell Bethany about this," he begged. "I don't want everyone on campus ribbing me."

After all of Jake's smart-arsed comments, there was part of Lauren that wanted to see him humiliated. But for their mission to work, the two agents had to trust each other.

"I'll make you a deal," Lauren said. "I'll keep this quiet, but you've got to stop acting crazy and start listening to what I say."

"Okay," Jake said as he rubbed his eye with the back of his hand.

"We all make mistakes, Jake," Mac said, sounding less angry. "The important thing is to make sure you learn from them."

CHAPTER 25

CANDY

Lauren met Fahim as he stepped off the bus in his uniform. They had a full hour until school started.

"Where's Jake?" Fahim asked as they walked toward a diner.

"Battered ribs," Lauren replied. "He's basically okay, but he's not really up to an argy-bargy in school corridors."

"Or another encounter with Alom and his crew." Fahim smiled.

"The school called the police, but Mac squished the investigation," Lauren explained. "Officially, they're investigating conflicting evidence about the fight. Unofficially, the cops will sit on the evidence for a few days before letting it drop."

"Your people can do that?"

Lauren nodded. "You can't stop a murder investigation or something massive like that, but the intelligence services can lean on senior police officers to make sure that our routine break-ins and fistfights wind up at the bottom of the investigator's pile."

"Did you hear any news about the gang?" Fahim asked.

"Jake broke one guy's jaw and the one Jake kicked unconscious will have a headache for a few days. The others were just cuts and bruises."

"The way you two fight," Fahim said, smiling admiringly. "It must be so cool just walking into a room and knowing that you can annihilate anyone if they give you hassle. If I join CHERUB, how long would it take me to get really good?"

"You can pick up most techniques with six months of intensive training, but mastering all of them takes years."

"Can't wait," Fahim grinned.

"You probably won't get in," Lauren warned. "I'm not trying to be bigheaded about myself, but cherubs are handpicked. As well as basic intelligence, you need to be mentally and physically fit. There's a big chance you won't even pass the recruitment tests, let alone basic training."

"I know, Lauren. But I want a shot, and that's all I'm asking for."

"We can promise you that," Lauren said.

The diner was a kilometer away from Camden Central, and it was crowded with builders and taxi drivers eating fried breakfasts, but there was enough background noise to hold a quiet conversation without being overheard.

Mac was seated at a table at the rear of the diner, and Fahim took an instant liking to his bald head and soft Scottish tones.

"I think this is everything you asked for," Mac said as he slid a laser-printed sheet across the laminate tabletop.

A waitress took orders for tea and toast as Fahim studied the sheet carefully. As well as a shot at joining CHERUB, the document promised him a new identity and a home with an adopted family. Money would be available for a private education if Fahim wanted one, and he would be provided for up until he completed university, including a gap year, a second-hand car when he passed his driving test, and a 25 percent deposit on his first home.

"It's the same package that CHERUB agents get," Mac said reassuringly. "If any of your father's assets are seized under anti-terrorist legislation, the money will be put into a trust fund for you. Obviously, none of this applies if your mother is found."

Fahim looked at Lauren. "Do you have a trust fund?"

"Uh-huh," Lauren said. "My mum owned her flat and had another one she rented out. The insurance paid off both mortgages when she died. She also had some antique jewelry in a safety deposit box and a bit of cash. Me and my brother will get half each when we leave CHERUB."

"Okay." Fahim smiled. "Where do I sign?"

"There's no such thing as a contract under these circumstances," Mac explained. "For official purposes, CHERUB doesn't exist. I could go through the charade of writing out a contract, but it wouldn't be worth the paper it was written on. All I can give you is my word."

"And mine," Lauren added. "You'll be looked after, Fahim. I swear on my life."

Fahim hesitated for a moment, before smiling uneasily. "It's not like I have a lot of options," he said. "What about my mum? Are the cops looking for her or trying to find a body?"

"I've put out some discreet feelers," Mac said. "But it's difficult to conduct an investigation without letting your father know that we're on to him. Our first task is to gather enough evidence to arrest your father, then we can launch a proper search for your mother."

"Fair enough." Fahim nodded. He was trying to stay calm, but his emotions crept into his voice. "I couldn't sleep last night, and the more I thought about it, the more sure I was that she's dead. She knows what my dad's like. There's no way she'd just leave me with him, and even if she was in the hospital or something, she'd have found a way to call my cell."

"You might be right," Mac said mournfully. "But I've worked on many investigations over the years, and the one thing I've learned is that you can never be sure of anything until there's hard evidence in front of you."

"I hope you're right." Fahim nodded. "The good news is that my dad's left microwave spaghetti and meatballs. He's got a meeting, and when I asked when he'd be home, he said he had a table booked at a restaurant at seven thirty."

"Perfect." Lauren smiled.

"That's really excellent, Fahim," Mac said. "So when your dad goes out, he just leaves you alone? There isn't a neighbor who keeps an eye out, or anything?"

"The cleaning lady is gone by the time I get in from school, and I've never even met the neighbors," Fahim said. "They're on the other side of a dirty great wall. Dad tells me not to let anyone in the front gates and let the machine answer the phone and not to pick it up unless it's him or Uncle Asif."

The empty house was a golden opportunity to install surveillance equipment. To maximize the effectiveness of the operation, Mac arranged for three extra bodies to drive down from CHERUB campus. These were Bethany Parker, who was on holiday but keen to spend time with Lauren, plus retired agents Dave Moss and Jake McEwen, who were helping out around campus until they went back to university in a few weeks' time.

As an extra precaution, Mac staked out the luxury home from inside a BMW 5-series with blacked-out windows. As Fahim predicted, the cleaning lady left at three followed half an hour later by Hassam and his brother Asif.

McEwen picked Lauren and Fahim up from school in a minivan, which already had Bethany and Dave inside. Fahim's presence meant they couldn't talk openly about life on campus, but Lauren couldn't resist winding up the two white shirts about how she'd outwitted them in the training exercise two weeks earlier.

"Don't tease, sweetcakes," McEwen growled. "You might be a girl, but don't think I won't dip that blonde mop down a shitter if you wind me up."

Lauren turned to see Bethany drawing a line across her throat. *Cut it out, he's psycho,* she mouthed.

Fahim and Lauren jumped out of the minivan half a kilometer from his house. They met Jake on the corner of Fahim's road. He'd spent most of the day lying on his bed, alternating between sulking and playing on his PS3.

"You okay?" Fahim asked. "You were *amazing* yesterday afternoon."

Jake smiled. "It was nothing," he said casually. "I should be okay for school tomorrow."

But his smile melted the instant he saw Lauren. He was terrified that Lauren might have told Bethany about him crying the night before.

"Mind you," Fahim added, "Lauren saved your butt. Another two minutes and those guys would have *killed* you."

"Was there any trouble over the fight at school?" Jake asked.

"Rumors flying about that Alom's mob got their arses kicked," Lauren said. "There was an appeal for witnesses in morning assembly, and a few kids who knew the score hassled me, but I just told everyone to mind their own."

"But we're not in trouble?" Jake asked.

"Doesn't look like it," Lauren said. "I saw Alom in the corridor and he shat himself and ran."

"We're lucky it was outside of school," Fahim added. "If I got suspended, I'd be screwed."

By this time they were up to the gates. Mac lowered the tinted window of the BMW across the street and gave Lauren a nod, indicating that it was okay to move in.

The tall metal gates led on to thirty meters of brick driveway, but Fahim had a key for the metal door built into the brick pillar alongside them.

"I'm home," Fahim shouted as he came through the

front door into the marble hallway. "Anyone in?"

Lauren was intimidated by the echoing marble hall-way and the abstract paintings on the walls. It felt more like a museum than a home.

"Check all the rooms quickly," Lauren said. "Then we'll take out the CCTV so that we can bring the van up the drive."

Fahim was sure nobody was in, but checked every room in the house and the office annex just in case. After the survey, he found a key in a kitchen drawer and opened up a panel built into the wall under the curved staircase. The four VCRs stacked inside were linked to the security cameras outside the house.

"Do you know anything about how it works?" Lauren asked.

"I'm not supposed to touch it," Fahim said. "But it's just like using a normal video, except that the tapes go for seventy-two hours."

Lauren looked inside the cupboard while Jake pulled one of the VCRs out gently and turned it sideways to look at the leads plugged in the back.

"Just phono cables running from the video cameras," Jake said. "Nothing special."

Lauren flipped her phone open and called Mac. "I'm in front of the CCTV system. It looks pretty basic, but I want an okay from you before I disconnect it."

Mac sounded confident. "There's a direct debit going out of Hassam's bank account to the security company for thirty pounds a month. I called them up pretending to be a customer, and that's the fee for their standard call-out package. They'll come out if the burglar alarm goes off, but there's no remote video surveillance or anything like that."

"You're the boss," Lauren said.

She went down the row of VCRs and stopped each tape from recording.

"There will be a gap in the recorded footage, but that doesn't prove anything," Lauren explained to Fahim. "In the unlikely event that your dad does decide to play it back, just deny everything."

Two minutes later, Fahim opened the gate and McEwen drove the Volkswagen minivan up the driveway. Bethany dashed inside while Dave opened the back and took out a pair of laptop computers and a cricket bag filled with surveillance equipment.

"Okay," McEwen said as the team gathered around the equipment in the hallway. "Dave and I will take the laptops around and clone every hard drive we can get our hands on. Jake, I want listening devices in every room. Bethany and Lauren, there's a pair of high-speed document copiers in the back of the car. Go to the office and duplicate anything you find interesting."

"Can I help?" Fahim asked.

McEwen sounded unfriendly. "Are sure you've told Mac where all the computers are?"

"Definitely," Fahim said. "My dad's no computer whiz. I have to install the software and sort out his Internet whenever it crashes."

"Right," McEwen said. "And you gave us the combination of the safe, so the best thing you can do is sit on your can and let us do our jobs."

As Bethany and Lauren ran outside to get the copiers,

Jake unzipped the giant equipment bag Dave had brought in and pulled out a device that looked like a staple gun.

"Come with me if you like, Fahim," Jake said warmly. "Show me where your dad likes to sit, then I'll be able to put bugs in all the best places."

"What is that thing?" Fahim asked as they headed up the stairs.

When they reached the balcony, Jake opened up a catch on top of the device, then swung open a metal panel, exposing a reel of what looked like tiny black needles.

"It's the very latest," Jake explained. "We used to have bugs that were about the size of your little fingernail, but there was still a chance they'd be discovered. These new ones are like hairs: You just line up the gun over something soft, and fire them in. As they leave the gun, a seal is broken, which activates a small chemical battery and it transmits a compressed recording pulse about once every three seconds for the following eight to ten days, depending upon how often people talk."

To demonstrate, Jake lined the gun up over the back of a velvet armchair and pressed down on the handle. There was a pulse of compressed air.

"Now it's embedded inside the cushion. It's flexible, so it won't prick you if you sit on it, and it's sensitive enough to pick up sound, even if it's embedded two or three centimeters inside a pillow or mattress."

"Nifty." Fahim smiled. "It must take you ages to learn how to use all this equipment."

Jake held his thumb and fingers wide apart. "They give you massive fat technical manuals to read. You have to take a test before you're authorized to use any piece of equipment, and there's no room for error. You get a hundred percent, or you fail.

"Of course, something like this is relatively simple. But it takes weeks to learn all the ins and outs of cloning computer hard drives and installing key loggers and stuff like that."

Fahim's eyes were wide with excitement. "All this is so cool," he said, beaming. "I've dreamed of doing stuff like this ever since I watched *Spy Kids*."

Once Jake had injected listening devices into cushions, carpets, and mattresses throughout the house and adjoining offices, he took out a PDA and walked around checking the signal strength.

"The last step is to install a relay box," Jake explained as he dug inside the equipment bag in the hallway. "We'll probably need a pair for a house this size. The relays pick up the weak signals from the tiny needle bugs and boost them for transmission to a master receiver stationed a few hundred meters from the house."

"What about on TV, when you see people sweeping for bugs?" Fahim said.

"Only works with old technology," Jake said as he showed Fahim the two relays, which were the size of drinks coasters but flatter. "The kind of bugs you'd buy in a spy shop transmit continously. Two disadvantages: transmitting all the time uses a lot of energy, which means they have to be fitted into something like a light socket or a clock radio. Continual transmission also means they're easy to detect.

"All our bugs store sound in memory and compress

it into a tiny pulse which lasts less than a hundredth of a second. It's impossible to detect them over the background static created by the earth's magnetic field."

Jake gave Fahim one of the relay boxes, and he turned it over in his hand.

"The best place to put this is in your room, inside a toy or somewhere else your dad never goes. The higher the better if you want a good signal."

"CD case?" Fahim asked. "You know, if you snap out the black bit that holds the CD? It would go inside and he'd never look there."

"Good thinking." Jake smiled.

The relay had a sticky backing, which they peeled off and fitted inside the case of Fahim's Killers CD. Then they placed it on top of Fahim's wardrobe under a stack of board games.

Jake pulled out his telephone and called Mac. "Hey, boss, I need a signal test," he said. "I've installed unit IDs 65341 through 65409."

Mac couldn't help laughing as he pulled a PDA out of the glovebox and tapped the screen with a stylus to turn it on. "Sixty-nine listening devices in one house! Call me an old fart, but I can remember the days when we had to drill holes in the walls to fit devices the size of a fist. . . . I'm getting medium or strong signals on everything except 65389 through 65404."

"More or less what I thought," Jake said. "We need another relay in the office wing. I'll get right on it."

The office annex was a hive of activity. Hassam and Asif Bin Hassam had three PCs and three laptops between them, plus two extra machines in the third office, which was used when they hired a temporary secretary, or when Yasmin did the bookkeeping.

While Dave and McEwen copied hard drives and backup data tapes on to a laptop specially configured to rip data to a bank of high-speed hard-disk drives, Lauren and Bethany worked with the document scanners.

The latest scanners were based around ultra-high-definition video cameras. All you had to do was flash a document in front of the lens, and it would be recorded legibly within a fiftieth of a second. The two girls worked meticulously through the filing cabinets, with the cameras mounted on tripods as they flicked through pages as fast as their hands allowed. But even with near-instant scanning, filming every page in a filing cabinet would take hours, so they had to make educated guesses as to which documents were likely to prove valuable before replacing them exactly as they found them.

"Anyone seen a good spot for a second audio relay?" Jake asked.

Dave pointed toward the drawer unit built into the side of Hassam's desk. "Pull the drawer out and stick it on the back. Nobody will ever look there, and even if someone does, it'll just look like a sticker."

Lauren looked at Fahim as Jake knelt in front of the desk and began fitting the relay.

"You holding up okay?" she asked.

"My heart's racing," Fahim admitted. "But the way you guys work is amazing. You pull all this fancy equipment out, and you know exactly how it works."

"Mac's got the front gate covered," Lauren said reassuringly. "And we've got hiding places and escape routes worked out if your dad does turn up."

"Finished," Jake said, rubbing dirt off his gloved hands as he stood up. "Is there another document scanner, or maybe I could make a cup of tea?"

"There's only the two scanners," Lauren said, "but don't worry. I reckon we'll have filmed all the important stuff within an hour."

Dave clapped his hands. "I'm definitely up for a cuppa. Just make sure you don't spill any on the carpet or you'll give the game away."

"I know, Dave," Jake tutted. "I'm not stupid."

"Just cocky," Lauren said before noisily clearing her throat.

Bethany, Dave, and McEwen were mystified, but Jake knew he was being warned about his attitude.

"Sorry," Jake said anxiously. "I'll make sure all the cups are washed up and put back properly afterward as well."

"It's safest if we take a ten-minute break and drink it in the kitchen," McEwen said. "We've got bags of time."

CHAPTER 26

NITE

It was already dark, and misty rain drifted on the wind. James had his arm around Dana's waist as he walked up to the door of a second-story flat and pressed the doorbell. Kerry walked a few paces behind. She'd invited Gabrielle and her boyfriend, Michael, but they'd dropped out because Gabrielle wasn't well.

"Come in," Gemma said cheerfully, opening her front door, barefoot and dressed in a baggy cardigan. "Bloody hell, James, you look smart. And you must be Dana."

"Hey," Dana said. "Thanks for inviting us."

James wore a Chunk T-shirt, Dana's leather jacket, and black chinos with weathered brown shoes. Dana wore scruffy CHERUB-issue combat trousers and a denim jacket, while Kerry had gone all out to impress with a red micro-dress and white Converse pumps.

"I'm not *quite* ready, as you can see," Gemma said apologetically. "Why don't you go through to the living room? My sister, Mel, will fix a drink."

The trio followed Gemma down a hallway with loud carpet and Tonka toys parked along the baseboard. The TV was playing a *Charlie and Lola* DVD when they got through to the living room. Mel, who looked like a teen-aged version of Gemma, sat on the couch, while two little boys mucked around behind it.

"Mel's babysitting for me," Gemma explained. "I've gotta go upstairs and find my shoes, but make yourselves at home. There's a bottle of vodka in the cupboard. Get pissed ASAP, I say."

Mel looked fifteen at the most, so James was stunned when she stood up, revealing that she was a good six months pregnant.

"I know," Gemma said when she saw James and the girls' startled expressions. "She's beaten my record for getting knocked up, the dirty little cow."

Mel gave her big sister the finger as she pulled down the front of a drinks cabinet. As soon as the two kids heard the door open, they belted out from behind the sofa in their pajamas and demanded Cokes.

"Don't *start* you two or I'll tell Daddy," Gemma growled from halfway up the stairs. "You should have been in bed an hour ago."

"Is Danny here?" James asked as Mel poured vodka and Cokes into plastic tumblers with Flintstones charac-ters on the side.

"Nah," Mel said. "He went over to open the club and help the DJ set up."

Kerry and Dana were both fascinated by the sight of someone their own age who was pregnant, and they cooed over Mel's bump and asked loads of questions. James let himself get swallowed in a leatherette recliner, holding his drink in one hand while putting a Cookie Monster hand puppet on the other and using it to play peek-a-boo with Gemma's youngest.

"You look nice," James said when Gemma came back in a different dress and matching shoes.

"Getting mashed, getting mashed, getting mashed," Gemma chanted to the tune of "Here We Go, Here We Go," before slugging her vodka and Coke down in one go. Then she kissed her kids good night and told them to behave for Auntie Mel.

The Outrage Club was a ten-minute walk across a housing estate into a deserted industrial park. All the businesses were closed for the night, and clubbers were ignoring the NO PARKING FOR CLUBBERS signs and hanging around their cars, getting loaded on supermarket booze before having to pay club prices inside.

The Outrage itself had once been a light industrial unit that made hi-fi loudspeakers, but its transformation into a nightclub had led to a redesign that included a trendy roof garden and fluorescent orange cladding.

"Weird place to open a club," James said.

Gemma nodded. "Started off as a gay venue—still is on weekends. They put it out here cos there's loads of chav palaces in town and all the gays used to get battered at chucking-out time."

James hadn't been to a club before, and he'd imagined a velvet rope and crowds of glamorous people waiting to get in. But this was quarter to eleven on a Wednesday in a small town, so there was just Danny and a couple of hard-looking mates crowding the entrance.

"James, you big homo!" Danny said affectionately, before slapping him on the back. "Good to see you."

"Kids won't go to bed," Gemma moaned, after Danny gave her a kiss.

"Another hour and they'll crash." Danny grinned. "Don't sweat. It's Mel's problem; I'm paying her enough."

As they walked inside, Danny gave them flyers that included free entry and two drinks for the price of one before eleven o'clock. The interior was gloomy, with a floor made from railway sleepers and seventies-style furniture. Much of the crowd was underage, mostly high school seniors and college students. James, Dana, and Kerry were among the youngest, but far from out of place.

The teenage DJ was letting a homemade mash-up CD of garage and seventies rock deafen the crowd while he sat on the steps leading up to the stage, drinking from a bottle of Volvic while girls in short skirts stood around lapping up every word he said. James looked on enviously, knowing that only a tin ear and a complete lack of talent stood between himself and a career at the turntables.

By midnight the club was heaving with students, twenty-somethings, and creepy older guys who seemed to think that Ben Sherman shirts were still fashionable. One of them got short shrift when he tried chatting up Kerry.

When the music got too much, the flat expanse of roof provided a quieter area where you could chill out. There weren't enough seats, so most people stood around, their animated conversations fueled by expensive booze and cheap drugs.

Dana, Kerry, and James had found a table under a heated canopy in the VIP area. Maybe some minor local celebrities had graced it over the years, but on Wednesday nights, VIP status belonged to anyone who knew the DJ or one of the bouncers.

James glanced drunkenly at his watch and saw that it was quarter to two in the morning. It wasn't a particularly cold night, but he was sweaty from bopping downstairs, and he got goose bumps every time the wind blew.

They'd all had a good time, and James particularly liked the fact that he, Kerry, and Dana were all getting along. He'd danced with Kerry, and he was content to sit back while they had boring conversations about girl stuff.

"What do you reckon?" James asked. "Time to make a move?"

Dana's blond hair was straggly from dancing in the heat downstairs, and she'd teased James by letting some random guy write his cell number on her neck. "It's gonna take an hour to sort out a cab and get back to campus," she said before smiling. "And I have a math class in six and a half hours' time."

"You're screwed." James grinned. "We don't have to be at Deluxe Chicken till ten thirty, but I'm not even gonna bust a gut to get there that early. It's not like they're paying us."

Kerry giggled. "We're gonna feel like absolute shit."

"Language, Kerry." Dana smiled.

Kerry slammed her hands on the tabletop. "You all make out like I'm such a princess," she slurred. "But I'm totally not."

James found this hilarious. "When Gabriel touched your butt, it's like he opened a door into this whole new Kerry."

"Blah, blah, blah," Kerry mocked, swaying as she got out of her seat. "My name is James Adams, and I talk utter crap twenty-four-seven. Arsenal, birds, and motor-bikes, blah, blah, boring, boring."

"You're so wasted," James laughed. "I need a piss before we leave, and we'd better say thanks to Gemma if we can find her."

"I'm a ditzy blond boy and I love myself *ever* so much," Kerry continued as James got a little irritated. "But my penis is very, very tiny."

Dana stifled her laughter because she had her cell out and was trying to speak to a cab company.

"Dispatcher said they'll have a car out front for us in five to ten minutes," she said finally.

"I'll go to the gents and meet you both by that pink sculpture thingy," James said.

The spiral staircase that led up to the roof terrace was trendy, but less than ideal when you're drunk and you have to negotiate people sitting on the carpeted steps. When James got to the bottom, a tiny Goth stepped up to him and put her hand on his chest.

"Lookin' nice," she said with a grin.

She looked totally up for it, but with Dana and Kerry present he didn't have a hope. "Sorry, I'm taken," he said.

"Young but cute," the girl snorted as she turned back toward friends who accused her of cradle snatching.

Having a random girl throw herself at you is always good for the ego, but James's mood wilted as he headed into the toilets. They were quite swanky, but a centimeter deep in water from a flooded urinal. This didn't seem to have discouraged a couple shagging in a stall and James couldn't concentrate on peeing because the girl kept saying, "Ahhh big boy," with an accent that reminded him of Schwarzenegger.

It was as much as he could do not to burst out laughing, and he finally cracked up as he emerged into the corridor. One direction led back to the club, but he noticed Gemma and Danny at the opposite end by a set of fire doors. He headed toward them and realized too late that they were having a fight.

"It's not your money," Danny snarled as he shook Gemma by her shoulders.

"I lent you all my savings," Gemma shouted. "You never would have gotten this night started without me. I want my share."

James wanted to turn and leave them to it, but Danny had spotted him.

"Good night?" he asked, acting like nothing was out of the ordinary.

James nodded awkwardly. "Really good, but we've got shit to do in the morning, so Dana booked us a cab."

"Life goes on, I guess," Danny said. "We had our best crowd yet. It's building all the time, and that DJ is the shit! Be sure to tell your mates about us, yeah?"

"Sure," James said. "And thanks for inviting us and letting us into the VIP and stuff. I'd never been to a proper club before."

Gemma looked less tense and managed a smile. "Better than a youth club disco, then?"

James grinned. "There's more sex and drugs at a youth club, but this was classier."

Gemma and Danny both laughed. "Have a safe trip home," Danny said as James started walking away.

He made six steps before Gemma yelled, "Get your hands off me."

James turned back and saw that Danny had grabbed Gemma's wrist and shoved her against the wall. He thought about ignoring it, but Gemma was struggling, and he didn't feel he could leave her.

"Come on, Danny," James said as he walked back. "Calm down, eh?"

Danny narrowed his eyes. "None of your business, kid."

James shook his head. "You're twice her size," he said indignantly. "Whatever you're fighting about might not be my business, but I'm not gonna stand here and let you push her around."

"I'm okay," Gemma said shakily. "Just go back to the girls."

James hesitated.

"Leave before I knock you into next week," Danny said.

James shook his head again and reached out to Gemma.

"Why don't you walk back with me? We can get our cab to drop you off at the flat."

Danny didn't like this one bit. His eyes opened wide and he turned toward James. "You're asking for a slap, you chunk of shit."

Danny was a big man who'd been in his share of scraps, but he moved like a sack of potatoes. He tried shoving James back with his two massive hands, but even though he was quite drunk, James was too fast for him. He ducked down, then brought his knee up to slam Danny in the kidneys. Danny groaned in pain but kept coming forward.

"You're getting it now, ya little bastard."

"Leave him alone," Gemma screamed, but she needn't have worried.

Danny was going in slow-motion compared to the teenagers James met thrice weekly in combat training. As the big man waded in, James flattened his palm and slammed it against Danny's right temple. Seeing stars, Danny collapsed sideways, hitting the corridor wall before sliding down and ending up slumped in the trail of water leaking from the gents' toilet.

"Holy shit," Gemma gasped, leaning over Danny before raising her hands up to her face. "What did you knock him out for?"

"Was I supposed to stand there and let him slap you about?"

Gemma was frightened. "There's four other bouncers out there, James, and they're all Danny's mates. You'd better get out of here, because if they see this, they'll bloody murder you."

"Come with us," James begged. "Our cab should be here any second."

Gemma sounded irritated. "Where am I going to go, James? I live in his house."

"Well . . . ," James said, feeling bad.

Gemma managed a slight smile as she placed a hand on James's shoulder. "I know you meant well, but we're a couple. You flooring him won't do me any good."

A couple of blokes were ambling toward the gents. They were surprised seeing the big man on the ground, but they didn't want to get involved.

"Do you want me to drag him somewhere out of harm's way?" James asked.

"No," Gemma said anxiously. "Find Kerry and Dana and get in your cab, *please*."

"Guess I'll see you at work tomorrow."

Gemma shook her head. "Friday," she said. "Tomorrow's my day off."

James wasn't sure what to feel as he walked off. He thought he'd done the right thing, but Gemma clearly didn't agree, and he was worried about what would happen to her when Danny came round.

"Took you long enough," Kerry said as they met up in the lobby. "Cab's waiting."

"I met Gemma," James said—he would save the rest of the explanation for the ride home.

"What were you talking to that little Goth about?" Dana asked.

James was drunk and distracted, so it took him a couple of seconds to remember the incident. "It was nothing," he tutted. "She just asked if I had a lighter. . . . And you're one to talk, with a phone number written on your neck."

He was pleased that Dana cared enough to be jealous, but he didn't smile until they'd walked past the bouncers at the door and climbed into the waiting Nissan.

CHAPTER 27

SQUAD

Once all the listening devices were in place, there wasn't much for Lauren and Jake to do except go to school and stay friendly with Fahim. Lauren didn't mind because Camden Central was lax and she had to do way less than on campus. Plus, they were in London, so Bethany, Rat, and a couple of Jake's friends had visited on the weekend. Rat didn't know London, so they went on the Millennium Wheel and took in a couple of other touristy places, but mostly they just wandered around the shops and then went to the cinema in the evening.

Mac was almost unbearably sad on Tuesday, when his wife of forty years, plus his daughter-in-law and grandchildren Angus and Megan, were cremated in a private service. Although Mac's father was the founder of CHERUB, and the organization had been a huge part of his life, his family thought that he worked as a weapons evaluation specialist for the army. This explanation covered the fact that Mac worked on a military firing range as well as his regular meetings in London and occasional trips abroad.

Despite his obvious grief, Mac maintained a professional attitude toward the mission. After Lauren and Jake left for school, he'd spend each morning looking for clues in the latest intelligence briefings and reports from the crash investigation team. In the afternoons he'd receive an e-mail report from the MI5 team who were monitoring the surveillance equipment inside Fahim's house.

Lauren was always anxious for news of progress when she got in from school, while Mac enjoyed hearing the kids charging up the stairs to the apartment after spending the day on his own. It was now Friday, nine days after they'd planted the bugs.

"You want cocoa?" Mac yelled as Lauren dumped her backpack and hooked up her blazer in the hallway before wandering through to the kitchen. "Cruelty-free organic milk, as per Madam's instructions."

"Sounds lovely," Lauren said as she grabbed her hot mug and let the steam rise up to her face. "It's a right miserable day out there."

With time on his hands, Mac took good care of the two young agents. There was always cooked breakfast and packed lunches prepared before they got out of bed, hot drinks and a snack when they came home from school, and a good dinner after homework. Mac's cooking was decent, but didn't extend beyond roasts, fish and chips, and other traditional British fare, so they'd also been out for a curry and visited an excellent Italian restaurant in the parade of shops directly below their apartment.

"Where's the little guy?" Mac asked as he sat at the opposite end of the small dining table, facing Lauren. "I made some for him too."

"PlayStation at Fahim's house. They're getting on really well—I almost feel unnecessary."

"That was always likely to be the case," Mac said. "But Jake needed your help at the start, and I'd rather your experience was still on hand. We'll need you again if anything interesting crops up now."

"Any news from MI5 surveillance today?"

"Nothing," Mac sighed. "If Hassam and Asif are part of a terrorist organization, they're hiding it remarkably well."

"If they're cautious, they might stick to speaking in code."

Mac rocked his head from side to side. "That's possible, but you'd think it unlikely when you're talking about conversations between two brothers in their own offices."

"Maybe Hassam is involved but not Asif," Lauren suggested.

"I was wondering that myself." Mac nodded. "But to be honest, I'm starting to think we're flogging a dead horse."

"But Fahim seems pretty certain about what his parents said," Lauren noted. "And there's no denying that his mum vanished off the face of the earth in very dodgy circumstances."

"Perhaps Fahim misunderstood," Mac said. "He seems very bright, but MI5 have three operatives on twenty-four-hour surveillance duty. They've picked up every phone call, listened to every conversation, and read every e-mail. Hassam's DNA and picture have been checked against all known terrorist databases, and he comes up clean, as does his entire immediate family.

"We've opened every file on the hard drives and studied all the documentation you copied. There's evidence of tax fraud in the accounts, but the picture we're getting is of a slightly shady trading company that's bending the rules here and there. Not one word has been said about terrorism."

"What about Fahim's mum saying that the plane was refitted by a company owned by his grandfather?"

Mac shook his head. "The plane that crashed originally belonged to a Japanese airline. It was given an overhaul and fitted with an Anglo-Irish interior in India a couple of months before it crashed. I checked out the maintenance facility's ownership, and none of the major shareholders have links to the Bin Hassam family."

"Isn't that a bit iffy?" Lauren asked. "I mean, why send planes to a developing country for maintenance?"

"It surprised me too." Mac nodded. "But apparently the aviation industry has boomed in India recently. You can easily fly an aircraft to the subcontinent and maintenance work is labor intensive. It costs up to a third less in India than in Europe or America. Most Indian workshops are modern and either owned or co-owned by Western aerospace companies who stake their reputations on highly trained workers and standards equal or better than anywhere else."

"But still," Lauren said, "it must be easier for a terrorist to get hold of explosives and detonators and place them onboard an airliner while it's undergoing maintenance in India than it would be to get a bomb through airport security at Heathrow?"

"Perhaps." Mac shrugged. "Straight after the crash, the investigators sent people across to India to speak with the team that refurbished the aircraft and get copies of their maintenance logs. But none of this alters the fact that after all the information we've gathered and a week of surveillance, the only thing we have linking Hassam Bin Hassam with the air crash is Fahim's claim that he heard his parents mention it during an argument."

"So you think it's all in Fahim's head?" Lauren asked as she pulled off her school shoes and wriggled her toes.

"Fahim *does* have a history of nightmares and erratic behavior," Mac said. "You know him better than me. What do you think?"

"He seems perfectly normal," Lauren said. "I mean, he's depressed, but under the circumstances, who wouldn't be? And when I've had conversations with him about random stuff, he's obviously intelligent—and more mature than Jake, truth be told."

"I was thinking," Mac said as he shook his head. "The reason I first took Fahim's call to the crash investigation hotline seriously was the obvious fear in his voice. But what if he was traumatized by a nightmare and woke up scared and confused?"

"You mean he didn't know what was real and what

wasn't? He was suffering from a concussion. His parents got into a big fight, his mum disappeared, and his brain jumped to all kinds of crazy conclusions."

"Exactly." Mac nodded. "It's possible that his fear after his mother disappeared got jumbled up in his head with the stories he was watching on the news. The psychological report from Warrender Prep School described Fahim as a fantasist."

Lauren shook her head. "He just doesn't seem like he's lying to me."

"In Fahim's head, it might all seem real."

"So what do we do?" Lauren asked. "How can we be sure one way or the other?"

"I think it's time to scale the operation back," Mac said. "You and Jake can head back to campus. We can leave the surveillance equipment in place for another week or two, but I'll ask MI5 to call off the live monitoring. We'll just get one operative to skim through the recordings until the batteries inside the listening devices die off."

"Poor Fahim," Lauren said sadly. "Whatever the truth behind the link to the air crash, he's still lost his mum."

"I know," Mac sighed. "I haven't worked out exactly how, but I'll find a discreet way of informing the police that she's missing. Hopefully, they'll have more luck getting to the bottom of this than we've had."

"We'll have to tell Fahim that we're abandoning him, too," Lauren said. "After all he's been through, it's gonna tear him apart."

CHAPTER 28

TALK

James and Kerry were nearing the end of their two weeks at Deluxe Chicken, and they'd gradually gotten used to the routine and the boredom. They remained on the morning shift, but after they'd seen Gemma the previous Friday, she'd worked different hours from Monday onward and they only saw her briefly in the afternoons before heading back to campus.

Gabriel had also juggled the shifts so he didn't face the embarrassment of dealing with Kerry. Instead, they were supervised by an assistant manager called Wendy. She'd joined Deluxe Chicken as part of a graduate recruitment program, which meant she could expect rapid promotion to manager of a newly opened restaurant. Despite her exalted status, Wendy was in her early twenties and had done enough crummy jobs when she was at university not to hassle her staff unless they were outrageously lazy.

James and Kerry basically turned up, put on their uniforms, and did as little work as they could get away with until it was time to go home. Kerry seemed cheerful, and James was pleased that relations between them had finally thawed out. It reminded him of the days between training and their first kiss when they'd just been good friends.

Kerry was pleased to see Gemma when she came in at noon on the Friday, but the feelings didn't seem mutual.

"Shift swap," Gemma explained grudgingly, without turning to look Kerry in the eye.

"How was the club on Wednesday night?" Kerry asked as Gemma straightened her baseball cap.

"I didn't go," Gemma said. "Mel's boyfriend's on leave from the army, and Danny's mum goes to pilates, so I had to stay home with the kids."

"I was wondering, actually," Kerry said. "You know it's James's birthday next week? I spoke to Dana, and she said it would be really cool if we could all go to the Outrage again, but we obviously can't if Danny's still mad at James."

"Don't even *think* about going there," Gemma said as she finally turned to face Kerry. "He's still in a mood."

"Bloody hell," Kerry gasped as she saw that Gemma had a huge black eye and a fat lip. "Was that him?"

Gemma raised her palms as she pushed past. "Don't start going on about it."

"Screw that," Kerry said as she went after her. "Did that bully slap you around?"

"Who else?" Gemma tutted. "There's nothing you can do, Kerry. I came in to work so I didn't have to sit at home thinking about it."

Kerry was shaking with anger. "You *can't* let him do that."

Gemma put her hands on her hips. "Kerry, my life is none of your business. It's your last day of work experience. You'll head home in a few hours, and after that we'll never see each other again."

"I'll kick his arse myself," Kerry steamed.

"And what good would that do *me*?" Gemma snorted, red with embarrassment and fighting off tears. "He owns our flat; I've got two kids under five and nowhere else to go. He's been off work with headaches and back pain ever since James decked him. He's lost a week's wages, and he's taking it out on me and the kids."

"He hits the kids?" Kerry said incredulously.

Gemma shook her head. "He's got a short fuse. He never hits them, but he goes mental if they act up."

"What about your parents?" Kerry asked.

"Screw them," Gemma said. "You think I'm gonna turn up on their doorstep with two kids and a begging bowl, so that they can say *I told you so*?"

"Can't you go to the housing office or something and try getting another place to live? Maybe it won't be a palace, but you can't carry on like this."

"He's okay mostly," Gemma said, as she dabbed her eye. "He's my man. He's just got a temper."

Kerry shook her head. "How can you defend him? Have you seen your face in a mirror?"

Gemma stepped back and shouted loud enough for the customers to hear. "Kerry, stay out of my life. *Don't* come near the club, and you'd better warn James that Danny is back working in the pub today. James better steer clear, because Danny's steaming and knows it's his last day."

Kerry looked at her watch. "James is on lunch break. He'll be back any minute."

James jogged across the street with a PC World shopping bag flapping in the wind. He was chuffed because he'd found a cheap MP3 player in the bargain bin. Dana had a full-size iPod, but she was on the lookout for a dinky one she could clip to her shorts when she went running, and while Christmas and birthday gifts were expected, James had learned that giving your girl something unexpected earns you untold brownie points.

As he stepped onto the curb, with Deluxe Chicken ten meters away across an expanse of dead shrubs and litter, James noticed Danny coming out of the alleyway that led to the staff entrance.

"Hey, hey, shit face," Danny shouted before swinging a baseball bat at a Deluxe Chicken dustbin, sending its roof-shaped lid spiraling through the air.

Two of Danny's mates stood in line behind him. They weren't as tall, but they had the same kind of leather-jacket-and-fat-neck look about them.

"I don't want trouble," James said, glancing around to see if there was anyone else coming from another direction. There wasn't, and he reckoned he'd easily be able to outrun the three heavies.

"You seen Gemma yet, big man?" Danny jeered. "Last

night, I punched her from one side of my flat to the other. What have you got to say about that?"

"You're a gent," James said, shaking his head. "I hope your two monkey slaves are proud of you."

"Tonight, I might *just* do it again." Danny smiled.

"I don't want trouble," James repeated, backing up slightly. "I know it's all down to your upbringing: your mum being a whore and that."

Danny reared up. "You come over here and say that."

James had no intention of getting into a street brawl with three blokes who'd never get near him, but as he turned to jog away, Gemma stepped out through the front doors of the restaurant.

"Leave it, Danny," she said angrily. "He's only a kid."

"I'm messing with him, sweetheart," Danny said, making it sound like it was all a joke. "Come and give us a little kiss."

Gemma didn't seem too sure, but she stepped across, and Danny kissed her swollen lips. As Danny let go, he grabbed the ponytail coming out the back of Gemma's cap and yanked it down, making her yelp as her head snapped backward.

"Go on, little boy. Run away, run away," Danny teased, twisting Gemma's hair some more with one hand while brandishing the bat with the other. "Why don't you come over and rescue her?"

James pulled out his cell. "I'm calling the cops, you fat freak."

"Your word against mine, James," Danny said. "This little bitch won't take your side if she knows what's good for her."

"Hey," Kerry shouted as she burst out of the restaurant. She was holding something purple, but it was only after she threw it that James realized it was one of the miniature Frisbees that came with Deluxe Chicken's kids' meals.

From less than two meters, it smacked Danny in the forehead. While he was distracted, Kerry bounded forward and nutted him. Danny let Gemma go, then swung at Kerry with the bat, but she dodged before hammering his jaw with her fist.

As Danny's two goons closed on Kerry, James ran forward and bundled them away, before letting go and knocking them down: one with a roundhouse kick, the other with a punch in the guts.

Meantime, Kerry had Danny down on the ground, and she was screaming her head off. "You warped little bully," she spat as she grabbed Danny's tattooed wrist and twisted it behind his back until his arm snapped with a sickening crunch. "See how you like some pain."

James's well-aimed blows had been little more than a warning, but Danny's goons had no appetite for more, and they scuttled away on all fours as Kerry grabbed the baseball bat and whacked Danny in the shin.

"Jesus Christ," James yelled, running toward her. This had nothing to do with self-defense. Kerry was out for vengeance.

"You like beating women up?" she shouted. "You like bragging to your mates about smacking her around? I'll show you, you fat turd."

A second two-handed swing blasted his other shin with bone-crunching force.

"Happy now?" Kerry screamed, looming over Danny with the bat grasped tightly. "The only reason I'm not breaking your other arm is that it'll probably be some poor woman who has to wipe your arse."

James pulled Kerry back nervously. She'd totally lost control, and he thought she might swing at him. But James got his hands around the bat and she let him take it.

"If you ever lay one finger on her again," Kerry warned, wagging her finger furiously, "I don't care if you've moved to Mars, I *will* be there to make your life a misery."

Danny wasn't hearing any of this because he was flailing on his back and moaning in agony from a broken arm and two fractured shins.

James put his free arm around Kerry's back and pulled her into a hug. She was trembling with rage. At the same moment Gemma glanced at Kerry, then hesitantly toward her boyfriend.

Gemma had always defended Danny by saying that he was basically a decent person who suffered from a serious temper. Hearing him brag about beating her up and then using her to lure James had shattered that illusion. She stepped forward and spat furiously on Danny's leather jacket.

"You're an animal!" Gemma screamed, close to tears. "Using me as bait. I'm not a toy, you know."

James's stomach churned as he stepped away from Kerry and surveyed the scene. Danny's two mates were out of sight while a dozen customers gawped from inside the restaurant. Wendy, the assistant manager, had locked the door so that nobody could get in or out, and she stood behind the glass with her cell phone up to her face.

"She's called the cops," James said nervously. "The police station's only up the road."

But Kerry had already seen the police car pulling up at the curb behind him. Another was speeding through the parking lot to cut off the other end of the alleyway.

"Run?" James asked, looking at Kerry.

She shook her head as Danny continued to moan. They might have gotten away, but the news would get back to campus one way or another, and their explanation would look far more credible if they stuck around to explain themselves.

What hadn't occurred to either of them was what the four cops would see as they stepped out of their cars: two smallish females, Danny down on the ground almost passing out in pain, and the powerfully built James standing in the middle of it all, holding the baseball bat.

"Put the bat down," the lead cop shouted, pulling a stun gun from his belt as he charged toward James.

"It wasn't him," Kerry shouted.

James didn't fancy fifty thousand volts, so he obediently dropped the weapon and raised his hands. Two cops shoved him against the brick wall at the side of Deluxe Chicken.

"You're nicked," the cop said enthusiastically as his colleague grabbed James's wrists and snapped on a set of handcuffs.

"It was work experience, for god's sake," Zara Asker shouted. She stood up and rested her knuckles against her glass desk. "Kids getting in trouble on missions I can handle, but you're telling me that James Adams can't even sell fried chicken for two weeks without getting himself arrested?"

"Well, you see," Kerry said weakly, "the thing is . . ."

She'd grabbed a taxi and got back to campus as fast as she could, but she hadn't been able to think up a good explanation before reaching the chairwoman's office.

"Spit it out," Zara yelled. The chairwoman didn't lose her temper often, but you knew all about it when she did. "I've got enough on my plate without this kind of nonsense."

"James is innocent," Kerry blurted. "*I* beat the guy up, but the cops arrested James. He took the baseball bat off me and tried getting me to calm down, but when the cops arrived, they saw him standing there with the bat."

"Didn't you try explaining?"

"I told them I wanted to give a statement, but there were loads of people in the restaurant who all claimed to have seen something different. I even told them that they needed to arrest me instead of James, but they were totally patronizing and told me to go away. I'm quite little, so I guess they took one look and decided that James was the only person with the muscle to beat up Danny."

"Conflicting witness statements are good," Zara said. "What about this Danny? Are there likely to be serious complications?"

Kerry shook her head. "I didn't target his head or any-where *too* vulnerable with the bat."

Zara leaned back in her chair, then looked up at the ceiling like she was stressed out and couldn't believe what she was hearing.

"This is so unlike you, Kerry. What made you attack him?"

"Danny was trying to get a rise out of James and start a fight. But James wasn't biting, so Danny grabbed his girlfriend, Gemma, and gave her a slap. He'd already smacked her around the night before, and I just completely lost my mind."

Zara seemed a touch more sympathetic when she heard that. "And why did this guy want to start a fight with James in the first place?"

Kerry realized she'd talked herself into a corner. "The other night James popped Danny one when he was pushing Gemma around."

"Ahaa." Zara smiled. "Is this when you, James, and Dana said you'd been invited to a party at one of your coworkers' houses, promised to be back on campus by one, and rolled up at the gates at a quarter past three? I believe the report from the security team described all three of you as *smelling like the inside of a vodka bottle*."

"We lost track of time," Kerry said weakly.

"I wasn't impressed, but I let it slide because it was a one-off, and you all got up and went to work and classes the following day. However, I *didn't* realize James had also been in a fight."

"Look," Kerry pleaded. "I'll take whatever punishment is coming my way because I overreacted. But all James did was try to defend a young mum who was getting battered by her boyfriend."

"Fortunately, I know Inspector Marsdell very well. His phone call telling me that James was in one of his cells actually reached campus before you did."

"Oh," Kerry said, startled. "So you knew already? Do you think they'll charge him or what?"

Zara shook her head. "I thought I'd let James stew in his cell for a few hours. Meryl said she'll collect him when she's finished red-shirt athletics training at five."

"There's something else," Kerry said. "Can I get some advice?"

"On what?"

"Gemma," Kerry explained. "She lives with this guy Danny, and he owns their flat. She's got two kids about the same age as yours, and he's knocking her about all the time."

"I see," Zara said. "Doesn't she have parents or friends who can help her out?"

Kerry shook her head. "Gemma refuses to talk to her parents and says she doesn't want help. She spat on Danny after the fight, but then she ended up riding in the ambulance with him."

"It sounds like she really cares about him," Zara sighed.

"But he's beating the crap out of her," Kerry choked. "Maybe I shouldn't have interfered, but I did, and I can't have it on my conscience if Gemma ends up with a fractured skull, or out on the street with two little kids. There must be *something* we can do to help."

"Gemma's an adult. She'll only get out of this abusive relationship if *she* wants to."

Kerry was exasperated. "But I've *tried* telling her, Zara. She just won't listen."

"I bet you're not the first to tell Gemma how to run her life," Zara said. "Hopefully, she'll meet another bloke, or a friend who makes her realize that she deserves better. But when people interfere aggressively and tell people how to run their lives, it puts them on the defensive."

"So what should I do?" Kerry asked.

"I don't think there's much you can do." Zara shrugged. "Except listen to Gemma and offer her emotional support if she needs it."

Kerry sounded annoyed. "So we just wait until Danny gets out of the hospital and starts beating her up again?"

"This Danny sounds like a nasty piece of work, and you *were* severely provoked," Zara admitted. "But you're not the law, Kerry. Nothing gives you the right to go around breaking arms and legs. I don't know if there's much I can do to help Gemma, but there are charities and groups that provide shelter and other help to people trapped in violent relationships. I'll make some calls and arrange to have some leaflets sent to her at work."

"*Leaflets*," Kerry said, tutting contemptuously. "What good will that do?"

"We can't make Gemma do something she doesn't want to," Zara said firmly. "She has to work it out for herself. With luck, she'll study the information and realize that she has other options. As for your punishment . . ."

"So I am getting a punishment?" Kerry sighed.

"You can rely on that." Zara nodded. "I'll have to speak with James and Dana and get to the bottom of everything that's been going on over the last two weeks, but you *will* be punished, and you can expect it to be severe."

CHAPTER 29

SATURDAY

Fahim woke early on Saturday morning. He hated being in the house now that his mum was gone, but his mood was fair because he was meeting Jake at the cinema later on. After eating breakfast, he headed down to the basement and racked up the balls on his father's pool table.

Having a table at home meant Fahim got a lot of practice, and he played well, but there was only the washer-dryer for company, and after clearing two sets of balls, he got bored and headed back toward his room. A shout startled him as he neared the top of the basement stairs.

"Tell me, you little bitch," Hassam yelled as a body thudded against the wooden paneling on the other side of the door.

The tone reminded Fahim of arguments between his parents. He moved his ear toward the door, tantalized at the possibility that his mother had come back. But the desperate reply came from Sylvia, the cleaning lady.

"Let me go," she squealed. "I don't know what you're on about, I swear to god."

"Well, who else?" Hassam yelled. "Do you see anyone else coming in and out of here?"

"Please, Hassam," she begged. "I don't know what you want."

"Skanky bitch," Hassam shouted. "Who put you up to this? Who are you working for?"

"You're talking crazy, Hassam," Sylvia cried. "I clean your house, that's all I do."

Fahim heard a scream and a rip of clothing. Sylvia had been knocked against the wall again, but this time she lost her balance and slapped against the marble floor near the front door. Heart thumping, Fahim turned the doorknob and opened a crack to glance in.

Spots of blood ran from the kitchen and all the way to the front door. Fahim watched his father bundle Sylvia into the small bathroom directly off the hallway. She moaned as Hassam plunged her face into the toilet bowl, then slammed the seat down on her head before pulling the flush.

"Tell me," he demanded. "Who are you working for? Who put you up to this?"

As water gushed over Sylvia's head, Fahim edged cautiously into the hallway. He looked back toward the kitchen and gasped as he saw smears of blood where the cleaner's face had been smashed into a wall cabinet. There was a piece of buckled plastic in the middle of the floor, and he was horrified to recognize it as one of the relays installed by Jake.

Fahim wanted to sneak out and run to Jake and Lauren's flat two streets away, but the walk to the front door was risky because his father was in the toilet right next to it. Dressed only in a tracksuit and socks, he moved quietly down the hallway, dodging the spots of blood.

"Do you want more?" Hassam screamed as he flushed the toilet and banged down the toilet seat a second time. He'd only need to lean out of the door to see his son trying to escape.

"Please stop," Sylvia begged as he tugged her face out of the rushing water.

"Stop," Hassam laughed sadistically. "It hasn't even started yet. Tell me who you're working for before things get much worse."

Fahim thought about grabbing some sneakers from the cupboard by the door, but he was desperate to get out, so he went straight for the door handle. Unfortunately, his father had locked it with the mortise key to stop Sylvia escaping. If he'd done that, Fahim reckoned he'd also have locked the electronic front gate, trapping him inside the house. His only option was to head up to his room and phone for help.

"Oh god," the cleaner sobbed as Fahim belted up the stairs. "Please let me go."

Fahim closed his bedroom door and grabbed his cell, then flipped through until he found Jake's number.

"Come on," he begged as the call rang in his ear. "Pick up the bloody phone, you midget."

Bethany's postmission holiday was over, and she'd started a strict fitness regime that required her to spend Saturday morning in the campus gym. Only Rat managed to persuade his handler to let him off Saturday morning classes for a second week running to visit Lauren and Jake in London.

"Mac makes a bloody good breakfast," Rat said, rubbing his stomach as he knelt on the blow-up mattress where he'd spent the night, squeezing out the air.

"It's a shame about the mission," Lauren said sadly as she lay on her bed staring at halogen lamps on the ceiling. "MI5 have already cut the live surveillance, and it looks like we're heading back to campus on Monday night."

"I guess our missions can't all work out," Rat said. "I'm surprised, though; you were all dead optimistic last weekend."

"We were only following up on Mac's hunch, but Fahim seemed so convinced about what he'd overheard that I was sure the surveillance would pick up some evidence."

"And you or Jake will have to tell Fahim that you're abandoning him."

Lauren groaned at the prospect. "He'll be really upset, and I'll have to do it because Jake has all the sensitivity of a randy rhino."

"Still." Rat smiled. "Once you get back to campus, you'll be able to wind your brother up about how he got arrested while on work experience."

"It's so classic," Lauren laughed. "Only James could do that."

"Kerry's got three hundred laps, a hundred hours' decorating duty, and three months confined to campus with no allowance. James got fifty laps and twenty hours. The police won't be pressing charges, thanks to Zara."

"My room could do with a lick of paint," Lauren decided. "I might put in a request."

Rat shook his head. "It's not that cushy. They're sending them up on the scaffold, painting around the windows on the outside of the junior block. A lot of people are saying it's out of order. They were defending some girl who was getting battered by her boyfriend."

"I'll buy him a brush and some turpentine when we're out later." Lauren grinned. "That'll wind him *right* up."

By this time, Rat had rolled his air mattress, and he stepped out into the hallway and stuffed it inside his overnight bag.

"Still no sign of Mac and Jake," Rat said as he glanced at his watch.

"Not surprised," Lauren replied. "Sainsbury's on a Saturday, the queues will be massive."

Lauren's phone burst into "Sweet Child o' Mine" by Guns 'n' Roses. She rolled nonchalantly off her bed, thinking it was probably Bethany or someone else from campus, but she sped up when she saw Fahim's picture on the screen.

"What's up?" she asked. "Everything okay?"

"That's a *big* bloody no," Fahim spluttered, sounding terrified. "I tried Jake, then Mac, but I couldn't get through. My dad's downstairs knocking seven shades of shit out of our cleaning lady. The front door and the gates are locked down, and somehow my dad's found one of the relays that Jake planted."

"You're kidding," Lauren gasped. "Mac and Jake have gone out, but I'll head straight over there. You keep calm and stay out of the way."

"What's the matter?" Rat asked as Lauren pocketed her phone.

"Problem," Lauren yelled. "Get your clothes on and grab whatever equipment you've got with you. We've got to get to that house."

"Hadn't you better call Mac first?" Rat asked as he slid his feet into sneakers. "Or even the cops?"

"It's less than ten minutes if we run," Lauren said. "Fahim already tried Mac. Their phones must be in a dead spot, but I'll keep trying. If we ring the cops, they'll probably think we're taking the piss, and even if they do believe me, it'll take ages to explain."

"I thought MI5 were running surveillance," Rat said. "Why didn't they pick it up?"

"The operation was downgraded yesterday. They'll have everything recorded, but nobody is monitoring the live recordings—remember?"

"And what are we supposed to do when we get to the house?" Rat asked.

"Christ knows," Lauren said as she grabbed her keys and a backpack with most of her espionage equipment inside it. "But there's nothing we can do here, that's for sure."

After the call, Fahim edged onto the balcony that over-looked the hallway and was surprised to see his uncle

Asif coming through the front door. He was a well-built man, ten years younger than Hassam.

"What's going on?" Asif asked as he opened the toilet door.

"Bitch isn't talking," Hassam said breathlessly.

"They bugged us, that's all that matters," Asif said, eyeing the walls suspiciously. "Someone's onto us, and we've got to disappear fast. There might be other bugs in the house, and if the cops have overheard, they could be closing in already."

"I think it was MI5, or Special Branch," Hassam said. "It looked very high tech."

"How did you find it?" Asif asked as the drenched cleaning woman continued sobbing inside the toilet.

"I could hear this little humming noise: high-pitched and going right through my head. I pulled out the drawer, reached behind, and there it was. Are you set to leave?" Hassam asked.

"Three hours," Asif answered. "My wife's already on her way to the safe house."

"Fahim," Hassam shouted. "Get out here."

"Dad?" Fahim said as he looked down over the railings and pretended to be shocked by both Asif's presence and Sylvia's gasping.

"Get down here now, put your sneakers on. We're leaving."

"Leaving where?"

Hassam roared. "For once in your life just do what I say."

Fahim turned back, hoping to pocket his cell.

"Right now, Fahim. *Don't* make me come up there."

"Won't I need some stuff?"

Fahim glanced at his father's expression and realized he'd be spitting out teeth if he pushed his luck. As he walked down the stairs and grabbed some Nikes from the shoe cupboard, Asif turned to look at the cleaning woman, who was sprawled over the toilet bowl, gasping.

"What about her?"

"She won't talk," Hassam said. "Did you bring the gun?"

Asif pulled a pistol from inside his jacket and handed it to his brother. Hassam clicked off the safety, and the cleaner raised her hands in front of her bloody face.

"Please," Sylvia begged, shaking her head desperately. "I don't know what that thing was. I swear I don't know a thing."

Fahim looked on as he wriggled his foot into a sneaker and found his lips moving. "She's telling the truth," he shouted. "Leave her alone."

"Shut up," Asif ordered. "Wait in my car."

But Hassam turned suspiciously toward his son. One shoe on and one off, Fahim stared his father down.

"What do you know?" Hassam growled.

"It's nothing to do with her," Fahim shouted. "They approached me after Mum disappeared, and I let them in the house to install the bugs when you were at a meeting."

Fahim screwed up his face as his father marched forward until the muzzle of his pistol was right between his eyes.

"Bugs," Hassam shouted. "How many?"

Fahim shrugged. "Loads; they're in every room."

Hassam cursed, then shoved Fahim against the shoe

cupboard. "Traitor," he screamed. "Tell me everything you know or I'll kill you right now."

But Asif glanced at his Rolex. "We need to leave now," he said. "Whatever Fahim knows, you can find out when we reach the safe house, and if there's more than one bug, someone will be coming for sure."

Fahim trembled as his father squeezed his arm and shoved him toward the front door.

"My apologies," Hassam said, smiling at the blood-drenched, shivering cleaner. "I guess you were telling the truth."

But Hassam didn't want her crawling out onto the patio and screaming for help, so he shot her in the thigh before striding out to the car.

CHAPTER 30

RUN

Lauren's phone vibrated as she ran with a small equipment pack slung over her shoulder; Rat was faster, but he didn't know the way. She slowed down and grabbed her cell out of her jeans.

"What's up, Jake?" she gasped.

"Mac needs to know where you are," he answered. "We've just driven out of Sainsbury's, and he's going nuts. We've both got voicemails from Fahim on our phones."

"Just spoke to him," Lauren said. "Me and Rat are running to the house. We're about to turn into Fahim's road."

"Mac's on the blower to MI5," Jake explained. "They're

getting an emergency team to review the surveillance recordings. Hopefully, they'll have a better idea of what occurred inside the house in a few minutes' time."

"Rat picked up our receiver, and he's monitoring the live signals," Lauren said. "The house is quiet. I think they left by car about five minutes ago. We're planning to go inside to see if we can work out where they've gone."

There was a pause while Jake explained this to Mac, who was finishing his call to the MI5 surveillance team.

"Have you got weapons?" Mac asked as he snatched Jake's phone.

"Stun guns and pepper spray," Lauren said.

"Okay," Mac said. "Only go inside the house if you're *certain* they've left."

"Got that," Lauren said. "I'll keep in touch."

She started running up a slight hill past gated homes. Rat used his extra speed to arrive first and began scaling the gate. Lauren was tense but couldn't resist smiling as she punched the entry code and opened the metal door alongside it.

"Bloody hell," Rat moaned as he balanced precariously on the spikes atop the gate.

"I've got a front door key too," Lauren said with a grin, "but you're welcome to try battering it down."

Rat made sure that his tracksuit bottoms weren't snagged on the spikes before dropping onto the gravel inside. His earpiece fell out as he landed, but he reattached it and had a quick listen to the iPod-size receiver.

"It's dead in there," he said.

"We can't be certain," Lauren warned. "Hassam found

the relay and busted it, so we're only getting signals from half the house."

Lauren held a stun gun in one hand as she unlocked the front door and stepped into the hallway. She looked down at the blood-spattered marble, but Rat was the first to see the cleaner's feet, sticking out of the toilet door.

"Jesus," Rat gasped. He looked away, but the image of the badly beaten woman with chunks of splintered thigh bone jutting through her skin still made him retch.

Lauren felt almost as bad, but she managed to stare for long enough to see the woman's chest move. "She's breathing."

"That's something," Rat said, still too squeamish to look.

Lauren stepped reluctantly through the congealed blood and grabbed Sylvia's wrist to take a pulse.

"It's *so* weak," she said urgently. "Call an ambulance."

Shocked by Sylvia's horrific injuries, the pair had neglected to make sure that the house was empty. As Rat called an ambulance, Lauren made bloody sneaker prints as she checked the upstairs and the basement, before finishing off with the kitchen and the office annex.

"All safe," Lauren shouted. "Hassam must have called Asif and decided to bolt as soon as he found the bug. There's no sign of any packing."

"Why didn't he just get in a car and drive?" Rat asked.

Lauren shrugged. "We put tracking devices in all his cars; maybe he suspected us."

As she came back through the high-tech kitchen, Lauren picked the rectangular relay box off the floor tiles. Hassam had tried breaking the box open with a screwdriver or knife, but the plastic hadn't split. To her astonishment, she could hear a distinct whistling sound as she moved it close to her face.

"Bastard's faulty," Lauren said furiously as she moved back toward Rat and held it to his ear. "He never should have found that relay, but listen."

Rat shook his head with disgust. "It might have cost a life. The ambulance is on its way; five to ten minutes."

Lauren glanced at Sylvia, something she found easier now the shock had worn off. "I know first aid, but there's not much I can do for her, and I don't want to have to explain myself when they turn up."

"Who'll let them in, though?"

Lauren thought for a second. "There're bar stools in the kitchen. We'll use one to wedge the front door, and we'll open the front gate so they can drive right up to the door."

Lauren's phone rang as she jogged toward the kitchen.

"Mac," she said, before explaining what had happened.

"Okay, listen," Mac said. "MI5 got an emergency team to skim through the last recordings before the gunshot. It sounds like Hassam and Fahim are moving to a temporary safe house, but we've no idea where that is. Asif was planning to go and collect some valuables and fake documents from a warehouse. They didn't mention an address, but I suspect it's a rented warehouse I saw mentioned in the Bin Hassams' accounts.

"I'm in my car now, but the traffic's solid. MI5 are trying to get someone out to the warehouse, but you two are nearest. Is there a vehicle there you can use? If we lose Asif now, there's a chance that we'll lose the whole family."

"Hassam's cars are all here," Lauren said as she opened a door into the garage.

She grabbed the door handle of a Bentley Azure, but it was locked. "Rat, go look for car keys," she shouted.

"I've got the address," Mac said. "Have you got a pen and paper?"

Lauren found a notepad and jotted the details while Rat searched.

"Took you long enough," Lauren moaned. "We've got to get out of here before the ambulance turns up."

"It's a big house," Rat said as he rushed into the triple garage, jangling a starter fob for the big Bentley. "Lucky Hassam left it in the jacket hanging on his bedroom door."

Lauren climbed into the sumptuous leather driving seat and pressed the engine start, followed by the button that activated the garage door and main gate, but Hassam was a big man, and she had to waste valuable seconds adjusting the electric seat so that she could reach the pedals.

Rat sat in the passenger seat. He tapped the address Lauren had written down into the satellite navigation as she rolled the big car onto the gravel drive.

"*Trip programming complete,*" the synthesized voice said as Lauren warily pulled the luxury car out of the front gates. "*Distance: three point two kilometers. Estimated arrival time: eight minutes.*"

"Think I can hear the ambulance," Rat said as he looked down into the footwell and saw the mess their bloody sneakers were making of the cream-colored carpet.

261

CHAPTER 31

FEAR

Hassam dragged Fahim out of Asif's BMW X5 and shoved him across the street toward a Volvo coupé usually driven by his sister-in-law.

"Call me when you leave the warehouse," Hassam said, looking back at his brother. "Is there anything I need to do at the house?"

Asif shrugged. "You can pray they're not following us, that's about all."

Fahim didn't dare look at his dad as his aunt's little Volvo crawled through Saturday morning traffic. He peered aimlessly out of the window, envying the normal lives of the people around him: kids being driven to football games and adults in weekend wear, heading for Ikea or the shopping center.

"Is Mum dead?" Fahim asked unexpectedly.

Hassam tapped his fingers on the steering wheel and pretended not to hear him. "I don't like driving automatics," he said, reaching for a gear lever that wasn't there as they pulled away at a junction, before turning right for the beginning of the M1 motorway.

Fahim had always been scared of his father, but in some ways, the revelation of his betrayal was liberating: whatever he said now could hardly make things any worse.

"If you don't answer, I'll take it as a yes," Fahim said. Then, as the car pulled off the curving slip road and accelerated to motorway speed, "Why did you kill her, Dad?"

Fahim turned to look at his father. His knuckles gripped the steering wheel so tight, they were white, and sweat streamed down his face.

"Don't stare at me, Fahim," Hassam growled. "I swear to god, I'll pull this car over and blow your head off."

"You gave the gun back to Asif," Fahim said. "Why did you kill Mum?"

"She left me no choice," Hassam said finally. "She took a vow to obey me. When she broke her vow, she became nothing to me."

Fahim had believed his mother was dead for days, but he'd always harbored faint hope, and the confirmation hit him hard. "What about me?" he asked, smudging a tear.

"I can't stay with you," Hassam said, smiling coldly. "Even in Abu Dhabi, I'll be a wanted man, but there are many places to hide. I'll see that your grandfather sends you off to school. Pakistan, perhaps, in the mountains. Five or six years of frost, bad food, reciting the Koran, and regular beatings should scour the Western mush from your head."

"Are we flying?" Fahim asked, trying his best not to sound upset.

"You'll know what you need to know when you need to know it," Hassam said sternly. "I might not have the appetite to kill my only son, but when we get to the safe house, you'll feel my belt like never before."

"We've got a trace on Asif's cell phone," Mac said. He'd phoned Lauren, but Rat took the call while Lauren concentrated on the road. "He's using an unregistered phone for his calls, but luckily, the idiot's left his normal phone switched on. He's at the warehouse now, or close to it. Jake and I are in the car and on our way, but we're way behind you."

Rat glanced at the Bentley's giant sat-nav screen. "We're less than a kilometer away," he told Mac. "But this is the worst possible car to be driving. Everyone stares, and you should see the looks we're getting when they spot Lauren behind the wheel. And it doesn't help that she can't drive to save her life."

"Hey," Lauren snapped. "I can drive, but it's all narrow streets, and this thing's bigger than the bloody *QE2*."

"Don't start fighting among yourselves," Mac said firmly. "When you arrive, remember that Asif almost certainly has a gun."

They were snarled up behind a bendy bus and a

queue of traffic as Rat ended the call and pocketed Lauren's phone.

"Screw this," Lauren said impatiently.

She turned the steering wheel to its fullest extent and blasted the horn. The big engine roared as they swerved into the oncoming traffic. The car accelerated quickly past the jam, and the traffic coming toward them had to brake sharply to avoid the imposing Bentley grille. The driver of a tiny Smart car pulling out of a turning lane wasn't so lucky, and the big Bentley crunched its front end.

"Careful," Rat yelled.

Lauren growled as she pulled back to the correct side of the road. "You moan when I'm too timid, you moan when I'm assertive."

"*Turn left in fifty meters,*" the sat-nav said.

With another horn blast to warn pedestrians, Lauren swung into a side road and hit the accelerator. The big car had soft suspension, but not soft enough to stop the front bumper scraping the ground as they hit a speed bump at fifty miles an hour.

"Jesus," Rat shouted.

"Did you hit your head?" Lauren grinned as she glanced at Rat. "Good."

The navigation screen told Lauren that they were less than four hundred meters from their destination. Not wanting to attract undue attention, she slowed to normal driving speed before taking a final turn into a cul-de-sac.

"*You have now reached your destination.*"

The wire-mesh gates in front of the dilapidated warehouse building were unlocked. Asif's X5 was the only car in the small lot, and Lauren parked the big Bentley across the gates, blocking his way out.

"Do we wait, or try inside, or what?" Rat asked as he grabbed Lauren's backpack.

Lauren thought for a second before answering. "Right now we've got the element of surprise, but the moment Asif steps out of the building and sees Hassam's Bentley, he's gonna know something's up. And if he's got a gun, it'll be too risky to chase him."

"Where's your body armor?"

"Back at the flat; there wasn't time to put it on."

They approached cautiously, Lauren's stun gun at the ready as they headed toward a door with flaking paint at the rear of the warehouse. Rat crouched low, then peeked inside through a filthy window.

"Light's on," he whispered. "There're a couple of bags and a backpack inside the door, but I can't see Asif."

Lauren had her lock pick gun ready, but the door came open when Rat turned the knob. It hadn't been oiled in years, and the rusty hinges squealed. They gave Asif a few seconds to respond to the noise before straddling the bags in the doorway. Rat peeked inside the smallest one, a FILA backpack containing fake passports and wads of pounds, UAE dirhams, and American dollars held together with elastic bands.

As grit on the floor crunched underfoot, the sound of a toilet flushing came from the opposite side of the echoing space. Using the rushing water to camouflage their noise, Lauren and Rat hurried between two racks of metal shelving toward a washroom door with a 2004 topless calendar pinned next to it.

The pair crouched on opposite sides of the door as the toilet cistern refilled and Asif Bin Hassam's hands splashed under a running tap. Lauren took deep breaths as she held the stun gun in her hand, her trigger finger ready to fire the electrified barbs at Asif before he could grab his pistol.

Asif had nothing to dry his hands on, and he shook them vigorously as he came through the doorway. He was startled to see Rat looking up at him, but before he could react, Lauren shot him in the chest. The four electrified barbs sprung upward and there were a dozen clicks, each one sending a fifty-thousand-volt pulse through the razor-sharp hooks.

Asif blacked out and hit the floor hard. Rat knelt across his chest and ripped the gun out of the holster under his blazer.

"Who are you?" Asif moaned.

"Friends of Fahim," Lauren said as she held the stun gun up so that Asif could see it. "If you don't tell me where we can find him, I'm gonna zap you again."

"I don't know what you're talking about," Asif said.

Both kids backed off as Lauren gave a quick squeeze on the trigger. Asif screamed and twitched as the air filled with the smell of burned skin.

"Tell me now," Lauren demanded.

Rat pulled the cap off the pepper spray. "I'm gonna count to ten, then I'm gonna hold your eyeball open and spray it right in. Tell me where Fahim is, dirtbag!"

Lauren accidentally nudged the trigger, giving Asif another fifty thousand volts and almost frying Rat in the process.

"Jesus," Rat screamed. "Careful with that thing."

The third shock made Asif bite his tongue, and blood began trickling out of his mouth.

Lauren and Rat had to sound confident, but cherubs weren't supposed to threaten captives unless someone was in immediate danger of death, and while Fahim *was* in danger, they had no grounds to believe that Hassam was going to kill him.

"I'd better ring Mac and get permission," Rat said nervously as he pulled out his phone. "We could get in deep shit if we overdo this."

Jake took the call. "What's going on?"

"I need Mac," Rat shouted. "We've got Asif, but he won't talk."

"Mac's on my phone talking to the Met police. He's trying to see if their license-plate cams have picked up any of the Bin Hassams' cars."

"We need permission to extract information from Asif," Rat explained. "We've given him a few stun-gun blasts, but I can't go any further unless Mac clears us."

Jake tutted. "I can't believe there were no incoming calls logged on his phone."

Jake's words hit Rat like a slap in the face. He looked up at Lauren. "His cell," Rat gasped. "If there're calls from whatever phone Hassam is using, we can take the number and track his cell signal."

"Oh crap," Lauren said.

Checking Asif's cell phone was the most obvious thing to do, but in their panic neither Rat nor Lauren had thought of it.

Jake overheard Lauren's cursing on the other end of

the phone, and laughed. "Good job I mentioned it before you started pulling out his fingernails."

Rat stared anxiously as Lauren pulled out Asif's cell. "Looks like a cheap pay-as-you-go," she said as she flipped to the incoming calls. "We're lucky the stun gun didn't fry the circuits."

Asif moaned and clutched his bleeding mouth as Lauren opened up the incoming-calls menu. She saw that all of Asif's calls that morning had been to a single number and hit the green button to dial it. It rang three times before Hassam's voice came on the line.

"Asif, where are you? Is everything okay?"

Lauren hung up without saying a word. "It's him," she said, looking at Rat. "I'll call the number through to campus. They'll be able to triangulate Hassam's position in less than a minute."

"Thanks for the tip, Jake," Rat said before ending the call.

"Outwitted by the little squirt," Lauren sighed as she dialed the campus control room. "I'll never hear the end of this."

CHAPTER 92
BELT

The Volvo stopped in front of a mock-Tudor detached, with a FOR SALE sign planted on the front lawn and a rear garden backing on to a golf course. Hassam and Asif part-owned an estate agency, which gave them access to a number of vacant properties.

Asif's wife, Muna, opened the front door as they stepped toward the house. Her seven-year-old daughter Jala was happy to see her older cousin and came running out to give him a hug.

"Everyone inside," Hassam said firmly, giving his niece a pat on the back of her long dress. "Best to keep out of sight."

While Fahim's mum had adopted Western dress and

lifestyle after leaving the Middle East, Muna was in every way a traditional Arab wife. Fahim found his aunt a mysterious figure, because his Arabic was far from perfect, and Muna's English was even worse.

The smell of unpainted plaster clung to the air inside the newly refurbished property.

"How's my Asif?" Muna asked anxiously.

"Okay, I think," Hassam said as they moved up the hallway. "He's fetching our documents and should be here soon."

"Have you spoken to him?"

"I had a dead call," Hassam said. "But he's not used to that phone, so he probably just nudged the redial or something."

Fahim hoped his father had forgotten the threatened beating and was happy to let his little cousin drag him through to the kitchen, where she had a card game set out on the table. But Hassam called him back.

"Upstairs," Hassam growled.

Fahim was slow turning around. Irritated, his father grabbed a handful of his tracksuit top and shoved him toward the staircase.

"Why are you going?" Jala asked.

"He's been a naughty boy," Hassam explained before making Fahim walk up the stairs and into an unfurnished room.

"Bare your back and lean forward," Hassam ordered, smiling nastily as he ripped his belt from his trousers. The only object to lean on was the fireplace, and Hassam placed his son's chubby hands on the slate shelf.

Fahim looked over his shoulder and saw that his father

was preparing to use the buckle end of the belt. The pain would be bad, but it was his father's coldness rather than outright fear that brought him out in goose bumps.

"Look at the wall," Hassam shouted before taking a few practice swings and lashing Fahim's bare back. "You'll suffer like this until the day you learn some respect."

The metal tore a huge gash in Fahim's flabby back. His legs buckled, and his knees hit the bare boards with a thud.

"Stand," Hassam ordered as he loomed over his son. "On top of everything else, you're a weakling. If I'd made that much fuss when your grandfather whipped me, he'd have started again from scratch."

"Please," Fahim sobbed, holding his hands over his eyes as Hassam crouched down and punched his son between the shoulder blades before spitting in his face.

"You'll have to be in a fit state to travel," Hassam grunted as he reluctantly threaded the belt back through his trousers. "But you wait and see what's in store when we get to the Emirates."

"Mac," Lauren gasped into her phone as she squatted on the dusty warehouse floor. Rat stood with the stun gun poised, while Asif bit down on a handkerchief to stop his tongue bleeding. "We've got a trace on Fahim's location. It's less than eight kilometers away, on a golf course off junction three of the M1."

Mac was at the wheel of his Peugeot. He'd finally made it out of the traffic around the supermarket and was speeding along a dual highway. He glanced at the sat-nav screen as Jake tapped in a zip code Lauren had texted him seconds earlier. The device took about twenty seconds to calculate a route.

"If there are no jams on the motorway, I can reach the safe house in under ten minutes from here," Mac said. "But we don't know what we're up against, and I came straight from the supermarket, so I've got nothing except my phone and a pen knife. We've still got no idea what Asif and Hassam are up to, but we can arrest them for what happened to the cleaning woman, so I'll get the local cops to come in as backup."

"Do you want us to head over?" Lauren asked.

"What's the situation with Asif?"

"He's in a daze, but he overheard more than we'd have liked, and I've got a nasty feeling the cops are on the lookout for our wheels. It's a dirty great Bentley. I had a bit of a prang and a couple of near misses, so someone must have called the cops."

"Right," Mac said before pausing as he negotiated a busy roundabout. "Call the control room on campus and get them to try swatting off the cops."

"Already did," Lauren said.

"The most important thing is that Asif doesn't get a chance to blab about you guys. Have you got any knock-out drops in your equipment pack?"

Lauren nodded. "I should have a couple of vials of ketamine. That should take him out for a few hours."

"That's the stuff," Mac said cheerily. "Give him the jab to knock him out. We'll send a medic across from MI5 headquarters; they can give him a psychotropic to scramble his short-term memory."

"Gotcha," Lauren said. "And while we're waiting for MI5, I'm gonna have a rummage through Asif's bags and see what I can find."

"No harm trying," Mac said. "I'm just pulling onto the motorway, so I'd better break off and call in the cops."

The house was bare and Fahim had no change of clothes. He sat on the lid of a newly installed toilet, bare-chested. His face was twisted with pain, and tears streaked down his face. He'd soaked his T-shirt in water and held it tight against his back to stem the bleeding. Downstairs, Hassam anxiously paced the living room, waiting to hear from Asif, while Jala and Muna continued their cheerful game of snap in the kitchen.

Fahim groaned as he stood up and peered out of the window above the toilet cistern. The back garden had a high fence, but there was a barred gate which opened directly on the golf course. Despite less-than-brilliant weather, pastel-clad golfers could be seen striding the fairways behind an impressive copse of willow trees.

He considered making a run for it, but Fahim was overweight and got out of breath quickly, even when his back wasn't in agony. His aunt Muna wouldn't catch him in her long dress and high heels, but he reckoned he'd have to incapacitate Hassam to stand any chance of getting away. A furnished house provides an array of potential weapons from kitchen knives to china vases, but this one had white walls and bare floorboards. There wasn't even a bar of soap to wash his hands.

Fahim checked out the three upstairs bedrooms. He opened the fitted wardrobes and gave the tie racks and clothes rails a tug, but they were all screwed in tight. The boiler cupboard also drew a blank, and he ended up going downstairs and walking into the kitchen. The bleeding had mostly stopped, but the red stuff always makes a mess and seven-year-old Jala shielded her eyes in horror.

His aunt rose silently and inspected the wound. "A boy must learn to respect his father," Muna said in her cautiously phrased English. "I have a first-aid kit in my car."

Hassam leaned suspiciously into the hallway as Muna walked toward the front door. "Where are you going?"

Muna turned and bowed to her brother-in-law. "For bandages and antiseptic."

Fahim didn't know whether to be sad or disgusted by the way his aunt fawned, just because Hassam was a man.

"Be quick," Hassam ordered as he glanced at his Rolex. "I'm giving Asif another five minutes. If he's not here by then, we've got to assume the worst and move on without him."

Muna looked shocked, but her tone didn't change. "Isn't he collecting the passports and money? Surely we need those."

"There's more than one way to skin a cat," Hassam said, although Muna didn't understand the phrase. "He'll catch up with us when he can, but we can't risk getting caught."

CHAPTER 33

GOLF

The sat-nav announced that they'd arrived as Mac's Peugeot turned into the street of detached houses. The signal from Hassam's phone could only be triangulated to within a hundred meters, meaning he could be inside any of a dozen residences.

"Any idea what we're looking out for?" Jake asked.

"Not sure," Mac said, driving as slowly as he could without it looking suspicious. "Car license plates might do it. Dial up the campus control room and tell them to stand by for some vehicle checks."

Mac's eyebrows shot up as Jake dialed. "See something?" the boy asked.

Mac slowed to a crawl as they passed a house with a

pristine driveway and rectangular FOR SALE board fastened to the front wall.

"Hart McFadden estate agents," Mac said excitably as he speeded up again. "I've seen that name in the accounts we ripped off Hassam's computer. Get control to check the Volvo, GK57 NNP."

By the time the campus control room ran the plate, Mac had pulled up three houses down, with two wheels up on the curb of the narrow road.

"Looks like you got it in one, boss." Jake grinned as he moved his cell away from his mouth. "It's a company car belonging to Bin Hassam Dubai Mercantile Limited, London N7."

"Excellent," Mac said, pulling the tailgate release lever as he placed his foot in the road. "Make sure the control room lets the cops know that it's house number sixteen."

Jake passed on the message before snapping his phone shut and following Mac around to the back of the Peugeot.

"We'd better take a look up there," Mac said.

"Shouldn't we wait for the cops?" Jake asked. "What if they've got guns in there? All our equipment's back at the apartment."

Mac shook his head. "I've asked for an armed response team, but they're not gonna be here for a while, and Hassam must be getting suspicious about his brother by now. He could move at any minute."

As Mac said this, he lifted up the tailgate, pushed half a dozen Sainsbury's shopping bags aside, and removed the piece of carpet covering the spare wheel. A tire-changing kit, including a jack, a pressure gauge, and a pair of large spanners shared the space with the new wheel.

"Not ideal, but better than nothing," Mac said as he took out a long metal bar with padded feet. It was designed to fit under the car to stop the paintwork getting scratched when you jacked it up, but it would also make a very effective weapon.

"Grab this," Mac said, handing Jake a spanner. "Just in case."

Jake slipped the brand-new spanner into the pocket of his tracksuit bottoms and pulled his sweatshirt over the bit sticking out as they strolled toward the house.

"Stop and do the lace on your sneaker when we get there," Mac said.

It took twenty seconds to reach the open gravel frontage of number sixteen. While Jake undid his lace and reknotted it, Mac studied the house.

"It's got a for sale sign," Mac said as he took the tire pressure gauge out of his coat pocket. "That's a perfect excuse for wandering up and taking a look through the windows. You take this and let as much air as you can out of the Volvo's front tire."

As Jake crouched down and scuttled across the gravel toward the Volvo, Mac took on the role of an elderly house hunter, strolling up to the front of the house and brazenly staring into the front windows.

Muna's little Volvo was only a few months old, but the plastic cap over the tire valve was crusted with dirt, and Jake had a real job getting it loose. By the time it dropped into the gravel, Mac had spotted the back of Hassam's head in the bare living room. After that, he strolled around the side of the house with the long metal bar swinging innocently at his side.

Jake glanced back to make sure that nobody was watching from the street before pushing the pressure gauge into the valve on the tire and squeezing the release button to let out a sharp hiss of air. Letting down a tire was a basic piece of espionage that every CHERUB agent was trained to carry out. The problem is that letting enough air out of a tire to make a car undriveable takes four or five nerve-racking minutes.

After less than two, the front door rattled. Jake bobbed his head up and peered through the car. He ducked down as an Arab woman stepped onto the gravel driveway and pressed the remote to unlock the car doors. Jake's heart thumped as he pocketed the tire gauge and tried to stay calm. He wasn't sure if Muna had a gun, but he'd heard how ruthlessly Hassam and Asif had dealt with Sylvia back at the house.

Mac also heard the front door open, and he stood at the corner of the house with the metal bar poised. It had been more than a decade since Mac last found himself active on a mission, and the tension gave him a peculiar feeling; as if he was an old man watching a younger version of himself from a distance.

He kept the metal bar poised as Muna walked around to the back of the car and raised the tailgate. Hopefully, Muna and Hassam were the only adults inside the house. Mac's strategy was to let Jake deal with Muna if she discovered him, while he'd run out and ambush Hassam if she raised the alarm.

Jake crept through the gravel and moved around to the front of the car, between the headlights, as Muna opened the tailgate and leaned inside. There was a rip of

Velcro, and she emerged a second later holding a green first-aid box. Jake and Mac both wondered why it was needed, but it was also a relief because you wouldn't carry it into the house if you were about to leave.

Mac ducked farther into the alleyway at the side of the house as Muna turned and headed back inside. The instant the front door clicked shut, Jake crawled back around to the side of the Volvo and slotted the pressure gauge back into the valve.

Muna had a piece of gravel from the driveway trapped inside her high-heeled sandal. Fahim watched from the kitchen as his aunt stood in the hallway, brushing the sole of her foot. He was getting more and more worried. The longer he waited, the less likely it seemed that anyone from CHERUB had tracked him to the safe house. He had to make his move before his father decided to leave.

"Here we are," Muna said sympathetically as she rested the first-aid box on the table and flipped the plastic catches holding it shut. Jala had overcome her distaste for blood and craned her neck, intrigued by the assortment of plasters, bandages, and ointments inside.

Muna's first step was to run a cloth under the cold tap and wipe as much blood from Fahim's skin as she could. Streaks of cool water trickled down his back, making the waistband of his tracksuit bottoms soggy. After this, Muna opened a bottle of antiseptic and swabbed the cold liquid onto the cut.

"Stings," Fahim gasped as the pain made him squeeze his eyes shut.

Muna gently rested a hand on Fahim's shoulder.

Although his aunt had a very different personality to his mum, Muna was of a similar age and physique, and her feminine touch evoked powerful memories.

"Better than a nasty infection," Muna said soothingly as Fahim found himself imagining the final desperate moments of his mother's life.

He studied the scissors as his aunt cut a square of bandage and stuck it on with surgical tape, but the snub-nosed blade made them useless as a weapon. His glance strayed toward the warning sticker on the side of the antiseptic bottle: *Severe irritant, do not swallow, do not use around eyes or mouth.*

"All done," Muna said brightly.

Fahim's T-shirt was wet and bloody, but the house was unheated, so he slid his tracksuit top over his bare chest.

Hassam was coming down the hallway with a chunky cell held to his face. "Asif's still not answering," he said anxiously as Fahim sneakily pulled the disinfectant bottle off the table and unscrewed the childproof cap. "Gather your things, we're leaving now."

Hassam wasn't great with technology. He usually got his son to sort out problems with his computers and program the memories and stuff whenever he got a new cell. Fahim hoped to use this to his advantage.

"Are you sure you're not trying to text or something instead of dialing Asif's number?" Fahim asked. "Give us a look; you know what you're like with cell phones."

Hassam didn't trust his son, but reluctantly passed over the unregistered phone.

"Why can't you get simple phones where you dial

a number and speak?" Hassam complained. "Instead, every phone has to be a camera, and an Internet, and buttons so small you always press three at once—"

As Fahim grabbed the phone with one hand, he thrust the disinfectant bottle forward, splashing the pale green liquid in his dad's face. His sneaker squealed on the tiled floor as he spun around and lunged toward the back door.

Mac snapped his phone shut and turned to Jake. After Jake finished letting the tire down, they'd retreated behind the front hedge of a neighboring house, but they still had a decent view over the gravel drive in front of number sixteen.

"That was the commander at the local police station," Mac explained. "Two armed response units should be here any second. Unmarked cars, two officers in each. The first unit is going to meet us here, the other pair is going to enter the golf club and cover the back gate. Plus, there're a couple of blue-and-whites filled with uniformed officers coming in as backup."

"Sounds good." Jake nodded as a faint clang sounded behind the houses. "Did you hear that, boss?"

"What?" Mac said, glancing around curiously.

"I think it came from behind number sixteen, the back gate maybe."

"My hearing isn't what it was twenty years ago," Mac admitted.

"Shall I check it out? I can cut through the neighbor's garden and peek through the fence."

Mac glanced at his watch. "Carefully." He nodded. "No

stupid risks. I'd better wait here for the cops to show."

There were no signs of life inside number eighteen as Jake walked swiftly up the gravel driveway, keeping low enough not to be seen over the dividing wall. A tall wooden gate blocked access to the rear garden, but it was no problem for Jake, who sprang deftly onto the wall before grabbing the top of the fence, hauling himself over and jumping down onto the crazy paving inside.

As he flew through the air, he saw Hassam running through the open back gate of the house next door.

CHAPTER 31

WILLOW

"Traitorous shit," Hassam shouted, spitting furiously and rubbing his burning eyes as he charged through the gate. Number sixteen had been redeveloped with the keen golfer in mind, and the gate opened directly on to a paved path which led toward the eighteenth green and an opulent clubhouse with colonial-style verandas.

Fahim was less than twenty meters ahead, fighting for breath as he brushed aside strands of the giant willow trees overhanging the path.

"Boy!" a golfer in the queue to tee off at the first hole shouted pompously as Fahim rushed past. "Boy, what do you think you're playing at?"

Fahim tried looking at his dad's phone as he ran. He wanted to dial Lauren or Mac, but he couldn't remember their numbers.

"Get back here," Hassam shouted as the gap closed to less than fifteen meters.

Not for the first time in his life, Fahim regretted his bulk. He'd never outrun his father, but he recognized salvation in the golf bag resting up against a portable toilet. He swiped the first driver he could, and while he was surprised by its lightness, it was good enough to send his dad sprawling when it whacked him in the face.

The owner of six hundred pounds' worth of titanium driver wasn't impressed as he emerged from the temporary toilet, doing up the fly of his cream-colored slacks.

"They're not members," a woman shouted ridiculously as the golfer snatched his club from Fahim's grasp before clamping an arm covered in a Pringle sweater around his chest.

"You've got to help me," Fahim screamed as Hassam staggered back to his feet. "He's killed my mum. Someone call the cops."

A trickle of bemused golfers emerged from the nearby clubhouse to watch Fahim spitting, kicking, and turning bright red. Sensing his desperation, the man holding Fahim let go and tried calming him down with a friendly hand on the shoulder.

"Come on, son," he said gently. "It can't be all that bad."

"He has emotional problems," Hassam explained politely, trying to sound like a decent parent despite stinging eyes and a huge welt where the club had struck his face. "I'm terribly sorry."

"You've got to believe me," Fahim shouted, looking at the golfers as his father found his feet. "Don't let him touch me. Someone call the cops."

"Fahim Bin Hassam?" a woman shouted.

All eyes turned toward a pair of policewomen sprinting out of the clubhouse. They carried assault rifles and wore full protective gear, including Kevlar helmets and visors over their faces.

"Over there," a lady golfer shouted, as the magnitude of what was occurring rippled through the crowd.

Fahim felt an instant of relief, but as the crowd focused on the approaching cops, Hassam pulled a knife from inside his jacket. He grabbed Fahim by his collar and put the serrated blade to his throat.

"Stay back," Hassam shouted. "Lower your weapons or I'll slit him open."

As Hassam trembled, the metal teeth nicked the skin around Fahim's throat. The golfers were all taking refuge inside the clubhouse, leaving a stand-off between Hassam and the two armed policewomen.

"Put the knife down," the taller of the two officers ordered, eyeing Hassam through her scope. "If you make me shoot, I guarantee I won't miss."

But Hassam knew the officers couldn't risk firing while the blade was so close to his son's throat and he started backing into the shadows beneath the willow trees.

"It's over, Dad," Fahim choked as his father dragged him backward. "Let me go."

"I won't rot in prison," Hassam whispered coldly, backing up to a gnarled trunk. "If they shoot me down, I'm taking you with me."

Muna leaned out of the back gate of number sixteen. A wave of panic hit her as she saw the standoff between her brother-in-law and the two armed officers less than fifty meters away.

"What's happening, Mummy?" Jala asked as the seven-year-old tried getting a look for herself.

"Back," Muna said firmly. She pulled the metal gate shut and gave her daughter a shove toward the house. "Run inside, pick up your things. We're leaving."

"But what about Daddy and Fahim and Uncle Hassam?" the little girl asked as her mother rested a hand against her back to make her hurry.

"We'll all meet up later," Muna said impatiently. Her mind was churning. She didn't know what to do or where to go, but she realized she had to clear out. Her main hope was that Asif would call back and arrange a place to meet.

As Muna scooped her keys and cell off the kitchen cabinet, Jala began shuffling her card game back into its cardboard packet.

"No time for that," Muna said, grabbing her daughter's wrist.

"But it's my favorite," Jala whined as her mother dragged her toward the front door.

"We'll buy another one, sweetie. It's not safe here now, we have to leave."

Muna unlocked her Volvo with the remote and walked

around to the driver's side as Jala opened the front passenger door and clambered through to her booster seat in the back. But Muna froze when she discovered the flattened front tire.

She cursed in Arabic before crouching down to try to see what had caused the wheel to deflate. Jala screamed as she saw the guns coming toward them through the bushes.

"Hands in the air," an armed cop shouted, straddling the low wall between the houses. His partner came out from behind a hedge on the other side. "Do you have any weapons?"

Muna didn't answer, but Jala screamed, "Don't kill my mummy," from inside the car.

"No weapons," Muna shouted, holding her hands out wide as the cops stopped walking a meter behind her.

"Who else is inside the house?"

"Nobody," Muna said. "They went out the back gate."

As the first cop frisked Muna, the second called in a backup unit parked fifty meters down the road.

Mac ran across the gravel as a pair of uniformed officers put Muna into handcuffs and coaxed a sobbing Jala from inside the car. He overheard news about the standoff from a police radio as one of the armed officers used Muna's key to enter the house.

The officers pointed their guns up the stairway, and one raced upstairs shouting, "Police, surrender," as his companion kicked open the doors of the living and dining rooms before checking the kitchen and the cupboard under the stairs.

Once they were sure the house was clear, Mac headed

out of the back door and jogged down to the bottom of the garden. He levered the gate open a few centimeters and poked his head through the gap to see what was going on.

Two minutes had passed since Hassam had backed into the shadows beneath the willow trees, and nothing seemed to have changed. The two female officers still had their guns pointing at Hassam while Fahim stood quaking with the knife at his throat. But Mac was stunned to see another outline crawling through the shadows toward them.

Unlike number sixteen, the neighboring house didn't have a rear gate. To make it on to the golf course, Jake had to drag a toddler's plastic playhouse across the lawn and then stand on it to scale a fence almost two meters tall. As he dropped onto the path leading toward the clubhouse, he saw Fahim whacking his dad with the golf club.

Jake pulled the tire spanner out of his pocket and set off toward Hassam, intending to come up from behind and finish him off. But Jake made it less than fifteen meters before the armed cops appeared, and as soon as he saw them, he assumed Fahim would be safe.

He didn't want to risk getting caught and having to explain himself, but there was no easy way back over the fence, so he cut under the willow trees, intending to phone Mac and let him know what was going on. But before he'd finished dialing, he saw Hassam backing up toward him with the blade at Fahim's throat.

By the time Hassam stopped moving, Jake was crouched behind a tree trunk less than five meters away. His first instinct was to run, but as he took his first step toward the fairway of the first hole, he heard Hassam's grim threat to take Fahim with him and realized that he was the only person who could do something.

Jake's head spun as he realized that it was the biggest moment of his life. He'd spent years in training, and if he saved the day, it would more than cancel out the mistakes he'd made earlier in the mission.

The trouble was, he didn't have a clue what to do. The magnitude of the situation overwhelmed him, and all he could think about was Lauren telling him that he was a cocky brat who was out of his depth and needed more training. But was Lauren really so perfect? She didn't even have the brains to check Asif's telephone and was lucky not to have fried the circuits when she gave him fifty thousand volts. . . .

Jake thought about the training chant: *This is tough, but cherubs are tougher.* He'd earned his gray shirt the same way everyone else had. He just needed to calm down, use what he'd learned and switch his brain into gear.

The first thing he'd been taught was to observe a situation carefully before acting. He leaned out cautiously and saw that he had a reasonable view of Hassam and Fahim standing with their backs to a tree trunk. He thought about using the big spanner, but he faced the same problem as the armed police officers: Hassam only needed a fraction of a second to cut Fahim's throat with the knife, and with the blade so close, even a stumble or sudden movement might lead to Fahim's death.

Jake couldn't leave things to chance. He had to move

in and take control of the blade before Hassam even knew he was there. But this was easier said than done, especially as Jake was a smallish eleven-year-old while Hassam was a heavily built man.

The spanner was too clumsy, but as Jake turned back for another glance at Hassam, he remembered the tire pressure gauge and pulled it out of his pocket. The chromed gauge was shaped like a fat pen, and while the ends were hopelessly blunt, the shaft had an arrow-shaped metal clasp that enabled it to clip over the edge of a pocket. It wasn't sharp, but the point would puncture flesh if he used enough force.

Jake bent the clip outward, then experimentally gripped the shaft of the gauge inside his fist with the clip protruding between his fingers. It made a pretty feeble weapon, but Jake was confident that it would do the job he had in mind.

After switching off his phone in case it rang and taking two deep breaths to calm his nerves, Jake dropped onto his belly and began crawling the five meters toward the tree where Hassam held Fahim captive.

"He's your son," one of the armed policewomen shouted, more in hope than expectation as Jake closed in. "Do you really want him to die?"

"He's no son of mine," Hassam shouted back. "He works for you lot."

Jake checked the ground carefully when he reached the base of the tree. He leaned cautiously around the trunk, ending up with his head just centimeters from the heel of Hassam's shoe. His attack would rely upon basic knowledge of human reflexes, which he'd learned in combat training. When you're surprised, everyone's nervous system reacts identically. Jake knew that Hassam's arms would fly outward if he got stabbed below his rib cage, but he had to be certain that the knife wasn't being held in such a way that the reaction would draw the blade along Fahim's throat.

"Dad," Fahim sobbed as a bead of Hassam's sweat hit the mulch just centimeters from Jake's face. "I'm sorry."

Fortunately for Fahim, you need to dig a knife deep behind the windpipe to cut someone's throat effectively. As the standoff dragged on, Hassam moved the blade a few centimeters from his son's skin to stop his trembling hand from causing more accidental damage.

From such close range, Jake's position would be given away by a breath or a downward glance. He acted the instant he knew that the blade was in a safe position. His training kicked in, and he felt strangely confident as he fixed his eyes on the serrated blade.

"Don't shoot," Jake shouted as he thrust up from the ground and jammed the point of the tire gauge beneath Hassam's ribs. As the arm holding the knife flexed outward, Jake smashed the spanner against the back of Hassam's hand.

Fahim ducked out of his father's grasp, and the cops closed in as Hassam's fingers sprang open and the knife clattered to the ground. Hassam looked down and gave Jake a brutal kick in the ribs as the eleven-year-old scooped the knife off the ground. Fahim made it onto the fairway of the first hole as Jake caught his breath and stumbled away with the knife. The cops stopped when they got within three meters of Hassam and kept the guns trained as the two male officers closed from behind.

"Hands in the air," one of the women shouted.

"I've got a gun." Hassam smiled as he plunged his hand into the pocket of his blazer.

With hindsight, it might have seemed obvious that if Hassam had a gun, he would have already used it, but the four armed officers each had to make an instant decision, and the woman closest to him didn't hesitate to pull the trigger. The bullet carved into Hassam's chest, passed straight through his heart, and caused a shower of razor-sharp splinters as the bullet exited and slammed the tree trunk.

As Hassam slumped to the ground, dead, Mac dived out of the back gate of number sixteen and raced toward the two boys, who'd collapsed onto the fairway of the first hole less than a meter away from each other.

"Took you two long enough to get here, didn't it?" Fahim gasped, smiling with relief as he fingered the spots of blood on the front of his neck.

CHAPTER 35

NICK

"Hello?"

Lauren and Rat turned to see a slim woman leaning into the warehouse door. She carried a leather bag and wore a tight black coat that gave her a slightly sinister air.

"Can I help you?" Lauren asked.

"I'm Dr. Turpin, I had a call from Mac. My team has worked with CHERUB agents before, so we know the score."

Lauren pointed her hand at Asif, who was now dead to the world with a block of foam Rat had found on one of the shelves under his head.

"Nice work!" The doctor smiled as two more MI5 agents came into the warehouse, wheeling a metal trolley between them.

"How will you work it?" Rat asked.

Dr. Turpin shrugged. "We'll give him the once-over with a rubber weapon, so that he ends up with a few cuts and bruises. Then I'll inject a cocktail of LSD and other hallucinogens, so that he'll spend the rest of the weekend in a daze. He'll come around in a secure hospital bed, and we'll tell him that he got into a fight with police trying to arrest him, took a nasty bump on the head, and suffered a minor stress-related heart attack.

"Hopefully, his short-term memory will be so shot that he won't remember getting taken down by a pair of kids, but even if he does, his brain will be so fried that he won't know what's real and what isn't."

"Isn't treating a suspect like that illegal?" Rat asked as he held Asif around the middle and helped the two men lift his dead weight onto the trolley.

The three MI5 agents all laughed, and the taller of the two men spoke. "Are you trying to tell me that knocking a suspect unconscious, beating him with rubber weapons, and giving him drugs that scramble his brain is illegal?"

"Nah." His colleague smiled. "It *can't* be."

Lauren tutted. "For god's sake, Rat, practically *everything* we do is illegal. Every piece of evidence we uncover has to be doctored so that it can be presented in court. If the civil liberties mob ever found out what CHERUB and the rest of the intelligence service gets up to, they'd spontaneously combust."

Rat hummed uncertainly.

"Look at it this way," Dr. Turpin said as the two MI5 men wheeled Asif into an unmarked ambulance. "Is what we're doing to Asif better or worse than blowing up three hundred and fifty people over the middle of the Atlantic?"

"Speaking of which," Lauren said, "I've been rummaging around while we were waiting for you guys to turn up. Do any of you know anything about the crash investigation?"

"We're just a response team," Dr. Turpin said. "Our job is to clean up messes like this one, but I can get someone from the crash-investigation team to come up here if you like."

Lauren shook her head. "Mac knows as much about the investigation as anyone. He'll be here any minute."

"What do you think you've found?" Turpin asked.

Lauren shrugged. "Just some junk, but it might mean something."

The doctor looked at her watch. "We'd better scoot, but tell Mac that I said hi. Oh . . . and pass on my condolences about his wife and grandchildren."

The unmarked ambulance left discreetly, and one of Dr. Turpin's assistants drove off in Hassam's Bentley. Jake and Mac pulled into the parking lot a quarter of an hour later, by which time Rat had visited a nearby diner to buy KitKats and tea in polystyrene cups to ward off the cold.

"Where's Asif?" Jake grinned as he swaggered into the warehouse, back to his cocky self for the first time in days. "You didn't give him too many volts and finish him off, did you?"

"MI5 have been and gone," Lauren said, glowering at him.

"Does Mac know that we forgot to look at the phone and started zapping him?" Rat asked warily.

"My lips are sealed," Jake teased. "At least as long as you make it worth my while."

"Just as *my* lips are sealed about you breaking down in tears on the first night of the mission," Lauren said. "Me and Rat might get a reprimand from Zara, but you'll get ripped to shreds by Bethany and all your mates if that story leaks out."

Jake looked worried.

"Did he really cry?" Rat smirked.

"Well, he's only a little baby cherub." Lauren grinned. "He was all better after a big hug and a good night kissy."

"Screw you both," Jake growled. "And I *didn't* cry. . . . Well, barely . . . and only because I was in a lot of pain. And Mac says the way I saved Fahim was straight out of the textbook and one of the bravest things he'd ever seen."

Mac came through the door and gave the agents a suspicious look. "What are you three whispering about?"

"Nothing," the trio said in unison before Lauren asked about Fahim.

"The cops have taken him to the ER to get the wound on his back stitched."

"Will he really be coming back to campus?" Rat asked.

"Of course." Mac nodded. "I'm not convinced that he'll pass the recruitment tests, but we made a promise, and we'll stick to it."

"I can imagine his big arse on the assault course," Jake snickered.

Lauren poked him in the back. "I thought you liked him."

"He's okay," Jake said defensively. "I was just saying . . .

Like, when he takes his shirt off, he's got all rolls of flab. He looks like a little Buddha or something."

"Jake Parker, you're seriously out of order," Mac snapped. "He's lost both parents in the space of a month. You're probably the closest thing he's got to a real friend."

"*All right*," Jake said indignantly. "Didn't I just save the dude's life, for god's sake?"

Rat laughed. "Don't start crying again, Jakey-poos."

Jake made a zapping noise like a stun gun firing, which shut Rat and Lauren up. Mac was mystified by this, but he'd spent enough years working among kids to know that you never get anywhere when you probe into their private jokes.

"Lauren, you said you had something to show me," Mac said.

"Yeah, over here." She nodded. "After we gave Asif his injection, I put on some plastic gloves and took a rummage through the bags he'd placed by the door. The first one had money and passports like you'd expect; the second had all this weird junk inside, and it kind of looks like bits out of an aeroplane."

"Really?" Mac said, raising an eyebrow.

Lauren gave Mac a set of polythene gloves from her equipment pack. Unfortunately, they were her size, so it was a squeeze getting them on.

"Most of it's in this one," Lauren said, pointing out a wheeled Delsey case with a broken strap. "The weird thing is the boxes look new, but the stuff inside them is ancient."

Mac's gloved fingers rustled as he picked out a small

box that had been opened by Lauren. Inside was a dusty contraption, with a battered-looking circuit board which had a tiny electric pump attached to it. The outer casing had been daubed with thick yellow paint and a red hologram sticker with the initials FCX on it.

"Wow," Mac said, breaking into a relieved smile.

Jake curled up his nose as he peered inside the bag. "Looks like a load of junk to me."

"FCX," Mac said, sounding increasingly excited as he opened a couple more cardboard boxes.

"It's painted on all of them." Lauren nodded. "What does it mean?"

"It means I'm guilty of the same crime as the kids in Fahim's class who called him a towel head and a suicide bomber," Mac said.

Lauren was baffled. "Eh?"

"Someone gives you an Arab name like Hassam Bin Hassam and tells you that they're linked to the destruction of an airliner. What does it make you think they've done?"

"Terrorism, obviously," Lauren said.

"And that's why we've been pissing into the wind for the past two weeks," Mac said, pounding a jubilant fist into his palm. "If Fahim's family had been Dave and Bert Spratt from Bognor Regis, would we have thought that they were terrorists? No. All the evidence about Hassam and Asif was that they were traders, not terrorists. Tax evaders and rule breakers, but no links to terrorism apart from an Arab surname."

"Mac," Lauren said firmly, "I don't mean to be rude, but you're ranting on and on, and I haven't got a clue what you're talking about. What does this random junk have to do with the plane blowing up?"

"FCX stands for Flight Certification Expired," Mac explained. "The Anglo-Irish airliner that crashed over the Atlantic was twenty-one years old. It was no spring chicken, but airliners cost tens of millions of pounds, and they're built to last a good thirty years.

"However, many components inside a plane have a significantly shorter lifespan. They might only be certified for three years, five years, ten years, or whatever. When aircraft are brought in for scheduled maintenance, the components are replaced. As the pieces are removed, they're sprayed and given an FCX sticker so that they can't accidentally be reinstalled. They're then supposed to be taken away and destroyed, but this lot clearly haven't been."

Jake finished the story. "So Hassam and Asif buy the parts from someone inside the maintenance hangar, or from a local scrapyard. Then they clean off the paint and the stickers, give them a spruce up, and they end up doing another ten-year stint inside another aircraft on the opposite side of the world."

"Got it," Mac said. "Although this haul only indicates that Hassam and Asif were using their container business to move the illegal parts. They could just be part of a much larger smuggling operation."

Lauren nodded. "That would explain why we couldn't find any evidence in the accounts."

"That's right," Mac said, realizing that he hadn't thought of this. "It would just show up as a container of goods being shipped on behalf of one of BHDM's customers, and if it was a routine shipment, there'd be no particular reason for Hassam and Asif to have discussed it—which is why a week of surveillance picked nothing up."

"So you reckon ancient parts like these were fitted to the plane that crashed when it was overhauled?" Jake said. "And these bits of junk are actually worth enough money to make all this worthwhile?"

"I'd guess they're worth a few hundred pounds each," Mac said. "Maybe even thousands to the right buyer once they've had a clean and the serial number's been doctored. Aerospace companies sell their planes for less than it costs to build them, *but* once a plane is delivered, they're guaranteed thirty years of revenue selling spare parts. You can't just set yourself up making widgets for a four-hundred-seat jet in some back alley. Airlines have to buy components from the original manufacturer, and they can set prices sky high."

"So who's behind it?" Rat asked. "I mean, is it the airlines wanting cheaper parts, or the owner of the maintenance hangar?"

Mac shrugged. "It's too early to say. This is a breakthrough, but it's only the first step in a major investigation."

Rat looked at the rows of boxes in the bag, then pointed up at the sky. "So, how many planes are up there right now, relying on bits of scrap metal to keep flying?"

CHAPTER 96

SENSATION

AIRPORT GRIDLOCK!

- CHAOS WORSENS AS HALF-TERM FAMILIES MAROONED
- 185 PLANES NOW GROUNDED WORLDWIDE; MORE EXPECTED
- AIRLINES CRIPPLED, 35 HEATHROW FLIGHTS CANCELED TODAY
- SIX MONTHS BEFORE ALL JETS ARE CLEARED TO FLY

Airports worldwide are facing a second day of chaos as America's Federal Aviation Administration grounded another sixty-five airliners suspected of being fitted with dangerously worn-out parts.

In a further shocking revelation, arrests made in Dubai and India over the weekend have led investigators to believe that British-based brothers Hassam and Asif Bin Hassam were just a small part of a global network trading in uncertified and fake aircraft components.

At Heathrow more than five thousand passengers faced canceled flights this morning. Airlines have warned that the huge number of grounded aircraft means it could be months before all of them are inspected and suspect parts replaced.

Long-distance rail routes across Europe are fully booked, while an estimated five thousand Brits are stranded in the United States and other long-haul destinations. Some face waits of up to a week for a flight home.

While some airlines with younger aircraft fleets are unaffected, most major airlines have canceled some flights. Anglo-Irish has been worst affected. Its entire fleet underwent maintenance and cabin upgrades at the DNM works near Madras over the last two years, and only one of its eighteen jets remains in service—a plane leased to replace the airliner that crashed over the Atlantic on 9 September.

Anglo-Irish shares plunged by more than 70 percent on the London Stock Exchange and were suspended within ten minutes of trade opening. Industry experts say that Anglo-Irish is unlikely to survive the massive disruption to its services. The airline's collapse would result in the loss of over eight hundred jobs. Other airline shares also fell steeply.

While authorities in the EU, North America, and most of Asia have grounded suspect planes with immediate effect, controversy surrounds more sluggish action in developing nations and the former Soviet Union, where it is thought that dozens of potentially dangerous airliners are still flying.

London News—Tuesday 9 October 2007

Lauren, Bethany, and Rat all had just-washed hair and red faces as they headed outside after an exhausting combat session in the dojo. There was a twenty-minute break before third period and they were heading for a mid-morning snack in the dining room, but Lauren darted off the path as she spotted a white-coated man heading into the medical unit.

"What's up with you?" Bethany shouted.

"I'll only be a sec," Lauren said. "Get me a hot chocolate and an almond croissant while you're in the queue."

"What did your last slave die of?" Rat yelled, but Lauren ignored him and kept running.

After cutting across a muddy lawn, she passed through a pair of automatic doors and entered the oppressive heat of the medical unit. She'd caught up with the slender doctor who supervised the medical examinations of every CHERUB recruit.

"'Scuse me, doc," Lauren yelled.

"Yes," the doctor snapped, with a German accent. He clearly didn't appreciate being called *doc*.

"Sorry, I mean Dr. Kessler. Sir, I think you're doing a physical on Fahim Bin Hassam this morning, and I wondered if he was doing okay?"

"Look behind you," Kessler said, frowning so hard his eyebrows practically switched sides.

Lauren turned and saw a line of muddy sneaker prints on the immaculate white floor.

"Oh god, I'm really sorry. Is there a mop or something?"

"Nurse Halstead will do it. Just take those filthy things off your feet before you make another step."

Lauren removed her sneakers, revealing novelty socks with eyeballs on top and a grubby yellow bit around the toes that was meant to resemble a duck's beak.

Kessler cracked a smile. "Very fetching."

Lauren flushed with embarrassment. "I've been away, and I'm behind with my laundry. It was these or a pair of bright yellow football socks I picked up in Australia."

"I heard about your latest mission," Kessler said, his voice becoming friendlier. "My wife is marooned in Hamburg thanks to your investigation."

"Sorry," Lauren said. "Better safe than sorry, though, isn't it?"

"Two extra days without my wife is a blessing." Kessler grinned. "Her miserable face saps my will to live."

Lauren laughed. "So am I allowed to know how Fahim's doing?"

"I have a sprain from the training course that needs attention, but if you go through the third door on the right, you'll find the observation room and you'll be able to see for yourself. He's unfit, but I've seen worse."

"Thanks," Lauren said.

"And remember you mustn't speak to—"

"Can't talk to orange." Lauren nodded.

The rule that you can't talk to guests wearing an orange shirt on campus was strictly enforced, although it seemed pointless under the present circumstances.

Third on the right took Lauren into a space two meters wide and four long, with broad rubber strips hanging across the doorway at the far end. The wall contained a slit of one-way glass, and Lauren crept up to it and shielded her eyes to block out reflections.

She'd never been in this viewing area before, but the two identical stations in the fitness testing area triggered grim memories. All new recruits go through a grueling medical exam and fitness assessment when they're first recruited. Once they're accepted, cherubs have a six-monthly checkup, plus an extra one after any mission lasting more than six weeks.

While a few push-ups and a short run could determine Fahim's current fitness level, CHERUB needed to know not how fit Fahim was, but how fit he had the potential to become. X-rays determined bone density, ultrasound had been used to examine the composition of his muscles, then urine and blood samples were taken.

After monitoring equipment had been attached to Fahim's body, the fitness test proper began. Eighteen tests measured everything from muscle strength and body fat, to how fast Fahim could run and how long he could hold his breath. These tests pushed young bodies to the limit, and while Lauren herself had never thrown up during a test, the smell of puke and disinfectant always hung in the air.

Lauren watched as Fahim took one of the easiest tests. He was walking briskly on one of the two treadmills, with an oxygen mask over his face and electrode patches stuck to his chest. Nurse Beckett kept one eye on him as his blood sample spun in a centrifuge. Beckett's role administering fitness exams had earned her the nickname Miss Sickbucket, but she was actually a gentle-mannered lady with permed gray hair.

Fahim wore a mask and his breath passed down a fat tube, similar to a vacuum-cleaner pipe. A machine measured the oxygen level in the air and compared it with the amount of oxygen he breathed into the pipe. The less oxygen Fahim exhaled, the more efficient his lungs were and the greater his chances of passing basic training.

Lauren had only intended to ask Dr. Kessler how Fahim was doing and run back to catch up with Bethany and Rat, but she became engrossed as Fahim wobbled and perspired through a test that didn't even involve breaking into a run. It didn't look good.

When Nurse Beckett stopped the treadmill, Fahim ripped off the mask and wiped his sweaty face on his orange CHERUB T-shirt. Lauren could tell that he'd already been through most of the recruitment tests. A bloodshot eye suggested a painful encounter with an experienced opponent in the dojo, there was chicken blood on his shorts, and he had a seriously grazed knee, most likely from mistiming the zip-wire jump at the end of the height obstacle.

"Hello, Lauren," Nurse Beckett said as she pushed her way through the rubber strips and looked at her clipboard. "You're not due for a test, are you? I've only got one orange shirt scheduled for this morning."

"Not until December," Lauren said, shuddering at the thought. "I came to see how Fahim was doing. Dr. Kessler was busy, so he told me to take a look for myself."

Nurse Beckett stepped out of the doorway and showed

Lauren the clipboard with the assessment data from all Fahim's tests. The document ran to a dozen pages, each with boxes on which the person making the assessment had stuck colored dots.

"Just like traffic lights," Beckett explained. "Green for a pass, amber for borderline, red for a failure."

"Oh," Lauren gasped as she saw that more than a quarter of the dots were red. "Is it even worth carrying on?"

The nurse nodded. "It's nowhere near as bad as it looks. Nobody ever gets all amber and green. His academic scores are up to snuff, and he has good Arabic and some Urdu. Both are very desirable skills for a cherub in the present political climate."

"So how many more red dots can Fahim get away with?"

"You're only disqualified if you get a double red dot."

"How would he get that?"

The nurse paused for a second, thinking of a way to explain. "You can see here that I gave Fahim a red because of poor endurance, but his potential fitness is good, so he'll get amber in most other categories. There's no fixed pass/fail score. Zara Asker will make the ultimate decision as to whether his score is high enough to be accepted. I'd only give him a double red if I discovered something like a heart problem, or a postural or skeletal defect that would lead to serious difficulty during basic training."

"And so far he hasn't got any?" Lauren asked.

Nurse Beckett shook her head and smiled. "We don't torture you kids for the fun of it, you know. If someone gets a double red, that's the end of the recruitment process."

Lauren crossed her fingers on both hands and held them in the air. "I'd better get going or I won't get anything to eat before my next lesson. I'm not allowed to talk to Fahim while he's wearing the orange shirt, so can you tell him that I wished him luck?"

"Of course." Beckett smiled. "He's under a lot of pressure, so I'm sure it will cheer him up."

As the nurse headed back between the rubber strips, Lauren thought of something. "Just a sec," she yelped.

"What?"

"You know you said that if Fahim doesn't fail anything, the ultimate judgment comes down to Zara? Do you reckon it might help his case if I tried to corner her and put in a good word?"

The nurse looked uncertain. "You're a black shirt, so I guess your opinion counts for something. I certainly couldn't see it doing any harm."

"Right," Lauren said as she picked her muddy sneakers off the floor. "I'll give it a go."

"Love the socks by the way," Nurse Beckett said as she disappeared back into the examination room.

CHAPTER 37

PAINT

James and Kerry still faced their punishments for the unnecessarily violent assault on Danny. By Tuesday, James had run his fifty laps and done six out of twenty hours' decorating duty. Kerry's punishment of three hundred laps and a hundred hours' decorating was more daunting and would eat up all her spare time for five or six weeks.

The junior block was a converted Victorian school that had been CHERUB's headquarters until the main building was constructed in the early 1970s. James and Kerry had both been over the campus height obstacle enough times for the three-story scaffold to present no problems.

All the building's rotting sash windows had recently been replaced with double-glazed plastic units. These didn't need painting, but knocking out and replacing the windows had left a mess inside and out. The bare plaster outside had to be sanded, sealed, and painted, while the area around the windows on the inside needed new wallpaper and fresh paint.

The new interior paint wouldn't match older faded paint, so Zara had decided that it was the ideal opportunity to redecorate the entire building. Rather than the security risk of bringing decorators on to campus, the work was being done by cherubs on punishment duty under supervision of the three-man building maintenance team. Older kids like James and Kerry worked outside and did trickier indoor tasks like wallpapering. Younger miscreants were given emulsion paint and rollers to do the more straightforward painting indoors.

When classes ended in the afternoon, more than a dozen kids who were on punishment donned blue overalls and put in two or three hours before they washed up and went for a late dinner.

"Missed a bit," James said to Kerry as he walked along the scaffold two floors up. She sat on the edge of a wooden board, sneakers dangling as she painted a window ledge.

"Do I give a damn?" Kerry growled. "Two months of this crap, just for busting up a head case . . . Why aren't you working, anyway? Every time I look, you're wandering up and down while everyone else is working."

James pointed inside. "I did some papering, then one of the red shirts knocked her roller tray off the ladder. Fortunately, it landed on a plastic sheet, but she got all upset, and I had to help her clean up."

"The red shirts are a waste of space," Kerry tutted. "We

spend more time cleaning up their messes than they do useful work."

"Must admit I kind of like it up here," James said as he grabbed a metal pole above his head and swung from side to side. "Painting's really mellow. It's just you and the brush, and at the end of the job, you feel like you've achieved something."

"Hippy," Kerry tutted. "You only got twenty hours; you're practically half done already."

"With my record, I'll probably be back."

"Shakeel starts tomorrow." Kerry grinned. "He lost his temper and head-butted someone in the dojo after Miss Takada blew the whistle."

"Tea up," a woman shouted from inside.

Kerry opened the window she was working on and checked that she didn't have paint on the bottom of her Nikes before swinging on a pole and squeezing through onto the carpet inside. It was a typical red-shirt room, shared by a pair of young girls.

"This is *very* pink," James said, shielding his eyes in mock disgust as he stepped around ballet tights, a dolls' house, and Barbie's Volkswagen convertible.

They stepped out into the hallway as the tea lady—who was really one of the junior-block carers—came through with a metal trolley laid out with mugs of tea and individual Twix bars.

"Cheers, Chloe." James grinned as he heaped sugar into his mug. "You're looking beautiful today."

The carer furrowed her brow. "Why is it if you stick a man in a set of overalls, he immediately thinks he's god's gift to women?"

"Beats me." Kerry smiled. "Although in James's case, you don't actually need the overalls for him to think that."

As Chloe moved down the corridor to serve tea to the rest of the decorators, James and Kerry went back into the pink paradise to eat their Twixes and warm cold hands on their mugs. They both had painty hands and filthy overalls, so they couldn't sit down.

"I hear Bruce is on his way home," James said.

Kerry bit the end off her Twix and nodded. "He touches down at Heathrow early tomorrow."

"You don't exactly sound overjoyed."

"I dunno." Kerry shrugged. "He's a nice guy, but . . ."

"But what?"

"No sparkle," Kerry said.

"How do you mean?"

"With you and me it was exciting. I mean, you treated me like crap, you cheated on me every chance you got, you dumped me and completely broke my heart, but if someone said you've won a free meal at a nice restaurant and you can go with anyone you like, no strings attached, I'd still pick you over Bruce."

James was flattered and ran the calculation for himself. "Maybe I'd pick you over Dana." He grinned.

Before James knew it, Kerry had placed her mug in the turret of a fairy castle, and their overalls were almost touching. They started kissing, and James could taste chocolate and biscuit crumbs all around Kerry's mouth, which was gross and sexy at the same time.

The shape of Kerry's face and taste of her spit were like visiting an old friend, and before he knew it, James had unzipped Kerry's overalls and gotten his hand around her boob. She grabbed his bum as he shoved her up against the wall.

"God, you're sexy," Kerry moaned.

James was turned on like crazy, but Dana's face kept popping into his head.

"Shit," James said as he pulled away, crushing a toy pony under his boot as he stepped back. "This is insane."

Kerry looked at James longingly. "It's still there, James. I pretended that I hated your guts, but I could never manage it."

"I don't know," James said, running his hand through his hair and realizing that this gesture is a bad idea when you've got paint all over your fingers. "This is screwed up."

"I've seen the way you look at me, James. I *know* you still fancy me, and I'm more mature now. If you wanted to go all the way, like you do with Dana. . . ."

"Everyone thinks we're at it, but we're not," James protested. "I didn't break up with you because you didn't put out. We're just too different, and what I have with Dana is really special."

Kerry realized she'd made herself sound cheap, and turned bitter. "So what just happened? Was that nothing?"

"Kerry, I'll always fancy you." James squirmed. "But our relationship was the romantic equivalent of fitting the *Titanic* with jet engines and steering it toward Hurricane Katrina."

"We had fights," Kerry said, nodding, "but there was a lot of great stuff, too. Maybe some of the best times of my whole life."

"For me too," James sighed. "Remember the heatwave,

when we sneaked out of bed and swam in the lake?"

Kerry smiled. "The KMG mission, when we had our first proper snog."

Memory lane felt like a trap, and James didn't want to fall in. "Those days are gone," he said firmly. "When we started chatting on the bus to work two weeks back, I kept thinking about you. But we've broken up twice, and to be honest, I don't want to go through all that stress again. Just because two people fancy each other, it doesn't mean that they make a good couple. And I'm sorry if I hurt your feelings when we broke up, but it really works between me and Dana."

"Shit!" Kerry screamed, lashing out at a turret and sending a tide of Playmobil men and plastic fairies over the castle walls. "Why's it got to be like this?"

James choked as he saw the tears welling in Kerry's eyes. "You said it yourself: I treated you like shit. One day you're gonna find the bloke you deserve, and I hope I'm there to see it as one of your best friends."

"I tried so hard to hate you when you dumped me." Kerry sniffed. "But I never hated you inside. I guess you *are* better off with Dana. I'm a complete basket case."

"No, you're not," James said soothingly, feeling sorry for Kerry but also getting a rush out of the fact she still wanted him. "You're the sanest person I know. But it's hormones and stuff, you know? Once the chemicals kick in, our brains turn to mush."

"Gemma called me earlier," Kerry said, changing the subject as she took a tissue from a box beside one of the little girls' beds. She dabbed her eyes, but was careful because of the paint on her fingers.

"Is she doing okay?"

"Not bad," Kerry said, smiling doubtfully. "Danny's out of hospital. Gemma's looking after him, but apparently he's been laying down the law and making snide remarks about what he's gonna do when he gets better. And she's still ticked off about the way Danny used her as bait."

"You think she might be considering dumping him?" James asked hopefully.

"Fingers crossed." Kerry nodded. "Gemma wants us to go out for a beer on Friday; you, me, and Dana. I told her that Bruce was due back, so I guess he'll come too."

James twisted his boot against the carpet pile. "Are you gonna dump Bruce? Because he doesn't have much experience with girls, so go easy on him."

"I'll see how it goes." Kerry shrugged. "I've not even seen the guy for two months."

"I always thought you two had fun together."

"Sometimes . . ." Kerry smiled. "Quite a lot of times, actually."

James jumped as a girl rapped on the window. "Okay, lovebirds, tea break's over, get your arses out here."

The girl had no authority, and James flicked her off, but they were also being supervised by one of the campus maintenance workers and their time wouldn't be counted against their punishment if they took more than a ten-minute break.

"They want me to put some filler in a crack over the other side," James said as he swung out onto the scaffolding.

"James," Kerry called after him.

He peered back through the window. "What?"

"I didn't freak you out, did I? We can still stay friends, and apart from the whole poaching-her-man thing, I'm getting on really well with Dana these days."

"Of course we're friends." James smiled. "Nothing should ever get in the way of that."

It was only as he walked along the scaffold, ducking around the aluminum poles with the warped planks rattling underfoot, that his conversation with Kerry really sank in: She'd offered him her body, and he'd turned it down because he loved Dana. He was so shocked at himself that he walked into an open can of paint.

The tin toppled off the edge of the scaffold and rotated as it fell, streaking the brickwork and a gray shirt who was working directly below before hitting the ground with a metallic clank.

"Watch where you're going, Adams," the kid shouted as he reached up and banged furiously on the wooden boards above his head. "Have you got shit in your eyes, or what?"

CHAPTER 38

SLEEPWALKER

Lauren didn't sleep too well and woke up at six on Wednesday morning. She turned on her laptop to check on a movie she'd set to download overnight and saw there was an e-mail from Mac in her inbox.

```
From: terence.mcafferty@cherubcampus.com
To: lauren.adams@cherubcampus.com,
jake.parker@cherubcampus.com
Subject: FAA preliminary finding
(do not discuss openly at this stage!)

    Hi both,

    I've been on the phone with Geoff
Glisch from the Federal Aviation
```

Administration and I thought you'd be interested to hear that on Friday, they're planning to announce a preliminary finding on what caused the Anglo-Irish jet to crash.

Having been unable to find any traces of explosives in the wreckage recovered from the Atlantic, Geoff said that the investigation team already felt that a bomb was an increasingly unlikely cause for the crash.

Our discovery of the uncertified parts led the team to concentrate their investigation upon components that were replaced during the overhaul at the DNM maintenance hangar in Madras.

Their preliminary finding is that some of the tubing in the fuel system was not replaced according to the maintenance schedule. At the same time, four valves within the fuel system were improperly replaced with elderly components that have now been traced back to an aircraft burned deliberately in a fire-fighting exercise at Gatwick Airport in mid-2005.

Not only were the components from this burned-out aircraft old, they had been exposed to extreme heat and this is believed to have made the plastics brittle. When a section of the badly maintained tubing ruptured, valves which should have shut down the leak failed to operate and fuel began leaking into the cargo hold. This fuel then ran into electrical

systems within the aircraft. These
systems short-circuited and the
resulting sparks caused an explosion.

This led to the first bang heard
by passengers aboard the aircraft.
It also damaged the control flaps in
the right wing, causing the aircraft
to roll. The pilots were able to
stabilize the plane, and automatic
fire control systems extinguished
the blaze. However, the part of
the aircraft between the wing and
fuselage—known as the wing box—was
torn open by the explosion, and the
force of air entering the hole at
more than 600kph eventually caused
the wing to separate completely. Once
this happened, the pilots had no
option but to ditch into the sea.

The crash investigation team
are confident that this will be
their final conclusion, but they
won't make the announcement until
a team of engineers from the
aircraft manufacturer have concurred
with their findings. Until the
announcement is made, please keep
this under your hats.

Speak soon,
Dr. McAfferty

Lauren smiled halfheartedly. She was glad that her mission had helped solve the mystery, but the businesslike

tone of Mac's e-mail belied the fact that he'd lost four members of his family. She knew he was hurting more than he let on.

After taking a shower and making sure that she had all the right books and equipment for morning classes, Lauren headed downstairs to the reception area on the ground floor. She knew Zara started work early on mornings when her husband got the kids ready for nursery, and wanted to catch up with the chairwoman before she got snowed under with meetings and phone calls.

"Enter," Zara said after Lauren knocked.

You weren't supposed to barge in on the chairwoman unless it was extremely important, so Lauren craned her head in the door sheepishly. "I couldn't make an appointment; your secretary isn't here yet."

"Come in," Zara said warmly.

As Lauren stepped in, she was surprised to see Mac sitting in one of the armchairs by the fireplace.

"Did you get my e-mail?" he asked.

"Very good news." Lauren nodded. "If Fahim hadn't made that phone call, another dodgy plane might have gone down before they worked it out."

Zara smiled. "Nurse Beckett mentioned that you wanted to give a character reference for Fahim."

Lauren nodded again. "I know he'll need a lot of work on his fitness, but I genuinely think he'll be great."

"Unfortunately . . . ," Zara began.

Lauren knew it wasn't good news just from the tone. "Why not?" she gasped. "He'll be really good if he can shift some of that weight."

"Calm down and take a seat," Zara said as she picked up a remote control and used it to rewind a VHS tape. "I was about to show the footage to Mac, anyway."

Lauren felt cold as she sat in a leather office chair and turned it around to face the TV.

"My biggest concern with Fahim was the psychological reports on his temperament," Zara explained. "I've read a lot of guff written by educational psychologists about kids with behavior problems. Usually, they're nothing more than symptoms of boredom and a bad home life, but the stories about Fahim's panic attacks and sleep-walking concerned me."

Zara pressed the play button, and the LCD screen switched from static to greenish night-vision footage of Fahim under a duvet. He was tossing and turning, while muttering about blood and chickens. Then he kept asking for his mum and saying *must do well*, over and over.

"Dr. Rose has watched the whole video," she said. "Apparently, Fahim talks like this for up to a third of the time he's asleep."

Lauren's mouth dropped open. "He's talking about everything he's done."

"Most people mutter the odd word or three in their sleep," Mac explained. "But you can't risk sending someone like that on an undercover mission."

"Fahim, you stupid boy," Lauren groaned. "What did you have to go and do that for?"

"It's totally subconscious," Zara said. "You can't blame him for having an overactive imagination. Now, if I just fast forward a quarter of an hour, there's another interesting bit."

It was Mac's turn to look aghast as the screen showed Fahim climb out of bed and slide his feet into a pair of pool sandals. "Am I nuts or is he still fast asleep?" Mac asked.

Lauren watched in disbelief as Fahim stood up and walked toward the door. He took three paces. They weren't little zombie steps like sleepwalkers in the movies, but normal paces. On the fourth step, Fahim hit the wall and woke up with a start.

After looking around guiltily and taking a few seconds to work out where he was, Fahim rubbed his face before turning around and clambering back under the duvet.

"I'm as sorry as you are," Zara said as she stopped the tape and looked at Lauren. "At best, he'll do himself an injury while sleeping in unfamiliar surroundings, at worst talking in his sleep could blow a mission and put lives in danger. We can't take that risk."

"Isn't there any kind of treatment?" Lauren asked.

"Dr. Rose says there is, but it's only partly effective, and apparently this kind of behavior is worse when you're under a lot of stress, like when you're on a mission."

"He's gonna be so gutted," Lauren said sadly. "Hell, *I'm* gutted. He's such a nice guy. What's gonna happen to him?"

"That's why I called Mac in," Zara said. "There's a possibility that Fahim will have to be a witness if his aunt and uncle are put on trial. I suspect that the aircraft parts scandal will go to the top of some serious criminal gangs, which means Fahim will need protection."

Mac took over the story. "And down the road there's

a big house, with an old man who now lives all on his own."

Lauren smiled. "That's cool; if he lives with you, we'll still be able to see him sometimes."

Mac nodded. "He won't be allowed on campus, but you'd be more than welcome to visit him; and Jake too."

"Fahim's sleeping up on the seventh floor," Zara said. "This isn't my favorite part of the job, so if either of you fancies going up there and breaking his heart, feel free to volunteer."

Mac stood up nobly and smiled at Lauren. "Are you feeling brave, young lady? Do you fancy a ride to the seventh floor with me?"

"Someone's got to," Lauren said as she followed Mac out into a corridor. "At least he knows us."

Lauren and Mac didn't relish their task, and they smiled uneasily at each other as they waited for the elevator.

"I got something else from the crash investigators yesterday," Mac said solemnly as he reached into the inside pocket of his jacket. "It's from my grandson. It's a photocopy, but they found the original in a seat pocket, tied in a plastic bag."

Lauren took the piece of paper and saw the Anglo-Irish Airlines logo at the top and a boy's messy handwriting. She read the message as the elevator cruised up to the seventh floor.

Dear Dad,

It looks like the end. I wanted to write to say that I love you and everyone else.

The plane is going to crash. Megan is upset, but Mum is cuddling her. Grandma has her eyes closed, and she keeps kissing her cross.

I really wish I'd got to be older than eleven, but I hope we meet someday in heaven.

At least I won't get in trouble with Mr. Williams on Tuesday because I forgot to do my history project (ha-ha!).

Love u lots,
Angus McAfferty
9 September 2007

Anglo-Irish Airlines was declared bankrupt in January 2008. Its assets and fleet were purchased by a rival airline, but more than two hundred staff still lost their jobs.

Despite initial newspaper claims that it would take six months to identify and remove all the suspect components from grounded airliners, most airlines were able to get all of their planes back in the air within five weeks. Over eight hundred suspect components were removed from two hundred and sixty-five airliners. Eighteen more aircraft nearing the end of their useful lives were declared beyond economic repair and scrapped.

A global investigation into the scandal is ongoing and has so far led to more than fifty people being arrested and charged. New measures have been brought in to ensure that parts removed from airliners are destroyed on site.

Aircraft manufacturers are also looking at ways to make the manufacture of fake parts more difficult, but it is still believed that fake parts are a growing problem, especially in poorer countries and places such as Iran, where genuine parts are unobtainable due to trade embargoes.

FAHIM BIN HASSAM has settled into living with CHERUB's retired chairman. He attends a local school and occasionally meets up with Jake and his friends on the weekend.

Regular jogging with his new guardian has enabled him to shed most of his excess weight. He also attends regular counseling sessions with Dr. Rose, and his emotional problems and sleep disturbances are under control.

Fahim's grandfather made legal moves to adopt him and take control of his late father HASSAM BIN HASSAM's assets. British authorities turned down the application and placed Fahim under secure custody as a potential witness in the trial of his uncle Asif.

Hassam's assets have been frozen and placed in a trust fund. Any money left after paying compensation claims from Anglo-Irish Airlines and crash victims will pass to Fahim on his eighteenth birthday.

Despite an exhaustive murder inquiry, the body of YASMIN HASSAM has not been found.

Cleaning lady SYLVIA UPDIKE spent nine weeks in intensive care. She came close to death on several occasions and spent eleven days in a coma. After more than a dozen operations to repair her fractured thigh bone she is now able to move a few steps with the aid of a walker.

ASIF BIN HASSAM was charged with the attempted murder of Sylvia Updike. Both Sylvia and Asif's nephew Fahim were witnesses at his trial. The judge sentenced him to fifteen years' imprisonment.

Asif and his wife, MUNA, may also face charges relating to the shipment of suspect aircraft parts. However, the evidence against them is complex, and the chain of responsibility linking them to the airliner crash is difficult to prove and spans several countries with different laws. Police in the UK and USA remain hopeful that they will one day be brought to justice.

Following the death of his wife, DR. TERENCE McAFFERTY has recommenced working on CHERUB campus on a voluntary basis. So far, his experience has been put to use helping out some of the younger mission-control staff on a variety of missions.

Mac's report into the Anglo-Irish plane crash mission complimented LAUREN ADAMS's performance. JAKE PARKER was praised for his brave actions at the end of the operation, and Mac commented that he might have received a navy shirt had he not made several elementary mistakes earlier on. Mac recommended that Jake undergo refresher training in several key areas before being sent on further missions.

The faulty relay unit that led Hassam Bin Hassam to discover that he was under surveillance was dismantled and analyzed by CHERUB technical director TERRY CAMPBELL. He identified a weakness in the design, and the unit has been withdrawn from use by all British intelligence services until the manufacturers implement and test a revised version.

While DANNY BACH's fractured limbs healed, two of his bouncer colleagues took control of the increasingly profitable Wednesday night gig at the Outrage Club. When Danny recovered, his former colleagues refused to pay him any share of their profits.

A violent altercation followed, during which Danny stabbed and seriously wounded both men. After three weeks on the run, Danny was arrested while staying with relatives in the northeast. Police initially charged Danny with attempted murder, but the charge was later dropped when he pleaded guilty to a lesser offense. Because of his lengthy criminal record, the judge sentenced Danny to seven years.

GEMMA WALKER was promoted to assistant manager at Deluxe Chicken. She dumped Danny shortly before he went into prison, and their flat was later repossessed by the mortgage company. Gemma spent several months living in a bed-and-breakfast accommodation with her two children. She gradually lost touch with James and Kerry, but when they last heard, she'd moved into a terraced house with her sister MEL and was expecting a baby by a new boyfriend.

BRUCE NORRIS returned from Australia and resumed his relationship with KERRY CHANG.

JAMES ADAMS celebrated his sixteenth birthday in wild style on CHERUB campus. The climax of the celebrations was a drunken paintball match, followed by impromptu fireworks around the campus lake. James, DANA SMITH, and several of his friends received fifty hours' decorating duty for damage to paintballing equipment, setting off fireworks without permission, and hurling fruit from an eighth-floor balcony.